"Men don't know the meaning of trust,"

Erin exclaimed bitterly to Simon Grayson. "They use the word when it's convenient for them and drop it when it's not. And then they wonder why one gets upset!"

All Erin's pent-up anger at being deceived by her ex-fiancé burst forth. She would have been surprised at how revealing her outburst was to this dark stranger who had just saved her life.

"So you've been crossed in love," Simon said, quietly, matter-of-factly. "You'll get over it, my dear. It's a necessary part of growing up, painful but transitory."

Erin was grateful that he'd rescued her from drowning—but his calm, philosophical attitude to her heartbreaking experience infuriated her. What did he know about it anyway—unless he, too, was unhappy and unloved....

Early Summer

by

JAN MacLEAN

Harlequin Books

TORONTO・LONDON・NEW YORK・AMSTERDAM
SYDNEY・HAMBURG・PARIS・STOCKHOLM

Original hardcover edition published 1979
by Mills & Boon Limited

ISBN 0-373-02295-6

Harlequin edition published in November 1979

CHAPTER ONE

THE landlord, handing her the key, explained again, 'I wish I could come with you, but I'm expecting a long-distance phone call, so I'd better not leave.' Doubtfully he added, 'The house is quite isolated, Miss McCourt, you may not like it. There's a summer cottage on one side, but that's empty now, and your nearest neighbour to the south is about three-quarters of a mile away—and a bit of a stickler for privacy at that.'

Erin clutched the key firmly, inwardly rather pleased that she should see the place alone for the first time; choosing where she should live for the next year seemed a momentous decision to her, and one she would be better able to make without the company of the garrulous Mr Stone, pleasant though he was with his portly frame and kindly eyes under bushy white brows. 'Well,' she temporised, 'I'll have a look at it, and let you know what I decide within a couple of hours. Is that all right?'

He nodded, again surveying her slender frame in its youthful jeans and open-necked shirt. 'There's a phone in the house, of course. But you may not care to be so far away from other people, a little bit of a thing like you. If you decide not to take it, I know my sister-in-law in town can fix you up in a boarding house. That would be much more suitable.'

Annoyed that he should consider her totally helpless simply because she was a woman, Erin smiled goodbye and left quickly before he could change his mind. Little did he know how much she longed to be away from other people, she thought wryly, as she turned her car back on the main road that led into Abbotsford. She was on the crest of a hill, the little Maritime town spread beneath her, its multi-hued clapboard houses scattered to the very edge of the cliffs along the shoreline, a cluster of them surrounding the shipbuilding industry, a conglomeration of sheds and warehouses and wharves. She could see the main street with its

5

neat row of shops and business establishments, its red brick
post office flying the Canadian flag. The streets were lined
with trees, a white-painted church steeple piercing the
crowns of the stately elms. A hill sloped gradually up from
the town, and on it sprawled the grey stone buildings of
Abbotsford College, where, in two days' time, Erin would
start work in the Fine Arts department. Her stomach
cramping with nervousness, she turned her attention beyond the town, where the rocks gave way to a pale crescent
of sand and a forest of spruce. The house she was to in-
spect lay in that direction, she knew; she would go there
first, before further exploring the town.

Within ten minutes she turned off the main road and
steered her car down a narrow dirt track. When the house
came into sight, she put on the brakes and with growing
pleasure surveyed the scene before her. It was evening and
the sky was tinted with the rose and gold of sunset, the
same hues colouring the mirror-like surface of the ocean.
A solitary seagull flew past, mewing plaintively. The house,
small and white-shingled, was nestled in a grove of dark,
spiky spruce trees; its lawn sloped steeply to the rocks, beyond which lay the beach.

Erin turned off the engine and got out of the car. It was
so quiet that she could hear the flutter of some small bird
in the shrubs and the chirping of a cricket in the grass; the
steady rhythm of the waves fell upon her ears, infinitely
soothing. This was what she needed, this peace and solitude. Maybe here she could forget Peter, their broken engagement, her desperate, omnipresent loneliness...

As though mesmerised, she walked past the house to the
cliff's edge and knelt down, her fingers absently rubbing the
weather-smoothed bark of a long-dead tree, as her blue eyes
drank in the sweep of sand and sea. There was no one in
sight, the beach stretching far into the distance in an unbroken curve except for a single wharf and jetty, with a
sailboat moored offshore, curtseying gently on the swell. On
impulse she clambered down the rocks and jumped to the
sand. Slipping off her sandals, she rolled up the legs of her
jeans and wandered down the shore, letting the waves lap
at her bare feet. Deliberately she emptied her mind of both

the unhappy past and the uncertain future, concentrating instead on the ocean's chill, the air's salt tang, the seagull's cry. Because she was so sure she was alone, and hence unobserved, she began searching for flat rocks and childishly skipping them across the top of the water, grinning to herself when one hit the surface a dozen times before finally sinking. And then, like a thunderbolt, a great black creature leaped out from behind a nearby clump of rocks and rushed at her.

She cried out in fright, realising too late to smother her fear that it was only a dog, a giant Newfoundland dog, plumed tail now wagging a friendly greeting as he loudly and thoroughly sniffed at her ankles.

'You don't have to be afraid,' a bored voice said, with an edge of contempt, 'he's perfectly friendly and very well-mannered. Sit, Robbie.'

The dog collapsed on its haunches, its huge tongue lolling across white teeth in a canine grin. Erin looked up, meeting the stranger's eyes. Stung by his tone, she said sharply, 'He startled me. I'm not normally frightened of dogs.' His look of disbelief caused her to add, 'In fact, I love them.'

'Ah, so you're one of those sentimental females who loves dogs,' he said sardonically.

'You needn't worry, I won't embarrass you—or him—by getting down on my knees and flinging my arms around him,' she retorted crisply, annoyed by his air of lazy disdain.

'I scarcely think that would embarrass me,' he replied softly, allowing his rock-hard grey eyes to survey her from head to foot in a leisurely fashion that was subtly insulting. Erin felt a blush warm her cheeks, and opened her mouth to speak ... anything to distract him from his cool appraisal. It was almost as though he were mentally undressing her, she thought, a shiver rippling across her nerves. She fumbled to do up the top button on her blouse, knowing that the neckline was gaping open to expose her skin; for the first time she wished her jeans were not quite so tight, did not outline quite so faithfully the curve of her hips and slender length of her legs. Again the painful colour mounted in her cheeks.

'Here,' he said coolly, 'let me.' He stepped closer and before she could guess his intention, his fingers were brushing her throat as he did up the offending button.

'How dare you!' she gasped, wanting to move away, yet paralysed by his nearness.

'It's all right, I'm quite harmless,' he answered drily. 'But a kid like you shouldn't be wandering on the beach alone at dusk, you know. Unless you're looking for trouble, that is?'

'I seem to have found it, whether I'm looking for it or not!'

To her chagrin he merely smiled, a smile that did not reach his eyes. 'No one's ever been able to accuse me of robbing the cradle.' He glanced at her heaving breast. 'Not yet, that is.' Abruptly he added, with a resumption of an air of boredom so palpable that she felt as though she had been slapped, 'I came here to be alone, so if you'll excuse me ... come along, Robbie.' With a brief inclination of his head, he turned on his heel and strode away from her, not once looking back.

Trembling with reaction, Erin sank awkwardly down on a sharp-edged boulder, her emotions in a turmoil. Her heart was thudding in her breast while her treacherous flesh persisted in re-living the cool touch of his hands on her neck, the forced intimacy of his gaze on her body. Even though she closed her eyes, she could not banish the vision of his mocking grey eyes piercing her fragile defences, nor forget how his big body had towered over hers. Yet as her anger and fright slowly subsided, and as the gathering darkness swallowed up his distant figure along the shore, she was left with one overriding impression: whoever the stranger was, and whatever had been his motive in so disturbing her, he was not a happy man—of that she was sure. Happiness had not carved those lines in his tanned face, nor sprinkled his thick, dark hair with grey. And because she had, during the past month, for the first time in her twenty-two years, experienced disillusion and pain and betrayal, she felt a rush of fellow feeling for the unkind stranger.

She gave herself a little shake, compressing her soft lips. This was nonsense! The man was nothing to her—a

stranger who would remain a stranger. She thrust him out
of her thoughts, got to her feet and hurried back along the
beach to the house, reaching for the key in her jeans' pocket.
It didn't take her long to look through the house: one
bedroom, a cramped kitchen, a fairly spacious living-room
with a picture window overlooking the ocean, tiny bathroom, and a den which would function admirably as a
studio and work area; the whole place was clean and adequately furnished. It would do, she decided. She would
complete the formalities with the landlord, spend tonight
at a motel and tomorrow move in with her belongings.

And that was what she did. All the next morning she
scrubbed and polished, letting the late summer breezes waft
through the open windows to banish the slight mustiness.
She put up curtains, placed her books on the shelves and
made a quick trip to town for groceries. Then last of all
she hung her pictures—oil paintings and watercolours
given to her by friends, and her own exquisitely crafted
photographs. But although she knew in her bones that this
house by the sea was what she craved, and that the job at
the college would suit her very well, yet she could not enjoy
the first day in her new surroundings, and more than once
abandoned what she was doing to go and stand by the window, staring sightlessly at the distant horizon, her slim
body tense and still.

Her Irish ancestry was betrayed by the true blue-black
of her hair, smooth as silk, by the clear sapphire blue of her
eyes, and by the creamy perfection of her complexion. And
even more she owed her present unhappiness to the intensity of her Celtic nature. She had never been a creature to
do anything by half measures, and so to Peter she had given
all the love and laughter and tenderness of which she was
capable, accepting with perfect trust that he returned her
love, for he had asked her to marry him and his ring had
sparkled on her finger. But then one weekend just over a
month ago, her fairy castle had toppled in ruins at her feet.
Erin could recall every detail of that dreadful day . . .

Peter had been required to attend a conference in Quebec
City, or so he had said; so, on the spur of the moment, she
had decided to spend a couple of days at his cottage on the

shores of the St Lawrence. But the cottage had not been empty as she had expected. Peter was there, and he was not alone. Erin had recognised the woman immediately— Vicki Travers, a wealthy young divorcee who was filling in her time between husbands by taking two courses at the university, one from Peter.

Sheer horror had rooted Erin to the spot. Peter's garbled explanation had fallen on deaf ears; pierced by a pain that was actually physical, she had realised that he had lied to her and deceived her with another woman, and thereby in one blow had destroyed her joy—and her innocence.

Within a week she had resigned from her job at the university in Montreal and had been fortunate enough to find a similar position as lecturer in photography at Abbotsford College. Which was where she now found herself ...

Her reverie was interrupted by the shrill peal of the doorbell. She started nervously, remembering all the landlord's warnings about the isolation of the house. Who on earth could it be? Perhaps one of her new associates from the college ... ruefully conscious of her far from clean shirt and faded jeans, she pushed a strand of black hair from her face; she was not in any state to entertain visitors. The bell jangled again. 'Coming!' she called, and ran to open the door. But before she could reach it, the visitor opened it himself and stepped from the sunshine into the hall.

Erin stopped dead, grabbing at the wall for support. 'Peter!' she whispered, the colour draining from her face. 'Oh, Peter ...'

'Hello, darling Erin,' he said softly, his eyes shrewdly assessing the extent of her shock.

'But—how did you know where to find me?' she asked, seeking an explanation for the near miracle of his appearance.

'Does that matter? All that matters is that I've found you —God, I was a fool to lose you, Erin!' Before she could say anything else, he moved swiftly towards her and pulled her to him.

She buried her face in his chest, shy of meeting his eyes; so unhappy had been the past month that it seemed an age since he had held her. But now she was in his arms at last, she thought incoherently. How often in the last few weeks she had longed for this! She felt his hand raise her chin and then he kissed her, slowly, lingeringly, confidently. She tried to respond—for after all, she loved him, didn't she?—but she felt suddenly suffocated and pushed him away, her blue eyes panic-stricken. He's not as tall as the man on the beach, she found herself thinking irrelevantly, and with horrifying clarity remembered how her flesh had burned at the stranger's touch.

'What's wrong?' Peter demanded. 'Aren't you glad to see me? Oh Erin, honey, I love you. I can't wait to take you back with me.' He stroked her cheek, smiling down at her.

Searchingly she gazed at him, almost as though she was seeing him for the first time—smooth blond hair, neatly trimmed sideburns and moustache, eyes of an indeterminate shade of blue-grey. As usual his clothes were immaculate, his grooming faultless; he spent a great deal of time and money on his appearance, she knew, and why not? He was a startlingly handsome man ... and again she was disturbed by a lightning-swift vision of untidy dark hair, ruffled by the sea wind, and of broad shoulders in a worn fisherman's knit sweater; the stranger had been wearing old corduroy trousers and hiking boots, she recalled, briefly surprised that she had noticed such details ... whereas Peter had on light beige dress slacks with a knife-like crease, and highly polished loafers...

Distractedly she rubbed her forehead. 'Back with you?' she murmured in confusion.

'Well, of course. Why do you think I've come all this way? I've driven seven hundred miles since yesterday afternoon. And we do belong together, Erin, you know we do.'

'But what about Vicki? Do you and she belong together too?' Erin asked pointedly.

'Honey, that was a dreadful mistake, I don't know what came over me. But it's over now, I promise you that.'

'And how long before it happens again, with someone else?'

'It won't happen again,' he said a shade petulantly. 'Don't make so much of it, darling, it was only a passing thing.

You're making a mountain out of a molehill.' He recovered
his poise and smiled at her with supreme confidence. 'Can
I help you pack? Let's get out of this one-horse town, we
can reach Halifax in time for dinner. I want to wine you
and dine you, and dance with you again, honey.' With
practised ease he gathered her again into his arms. 'We
can be back in Montreal by tomorrow evening. I spoke to
Dr Lavery and your old job's still open for you. We can
just forget that all this happened.'

Erin closed her eyes ... to enjoy a candlelit dinner with
Peter, to sway on the dance floor with him, to drift back
into the familiarity of their old relationship, how wonderful
it sounded! She opened her mouth to acquiesce and to her
consternation heard herself say, 'But I haven't agreed to go
back with you.'

He drew back, a frown marring his perfect features.
'What do you mean? Of course you'll come back with me!'

'Peter, you seem to be behaving as though nothing's happened, as though Vicki never existed!'

'Look, I've said I'm sorry——'

'Have you? I don't think I heard you.'

'I'm sorry about Vicki,' he repeated sullenly. 'What do
you want me to do—go down on my knees?'

'Of course not,' said Erin, her eyes pleading for understanding. 'But, Peter, it will take time to rebuild my trust
in you. When I saw you and Vicki together and knew you'd
lied to me, it hurt me terribly.' Her voice trembled. 'You
say it won't happen again—I want to believe you, God,
how I want to believe you! But it isn't easy. One can't
pretend the past didn't occur, convenient though it would
be.' She stared at his shirt button, abstractedly twisting it
in her fingers. 'There's another side to it, too. I just can't
pick up and leave here now, I'm supposed to start work tomorrow and I'm committed to staying for at least the first
semester. Surely you can see that?'

'So the job's more important than me!'

'No! But I do have to be practical.' Coaxingly she added,
'January is not that far away, Peter. And anyway, to be
apart for a while might be the best thing in the world for
us. Love—true love—can stand a short separation. By then

we'll both be sure we want each other. After all, marriage is such a serious step, and I'm old-fashioned enough to want mine to be for ever.' She smiled at him persuasively, certain she had made the right decision.

Sharply Peter answered, 'I'm not talking about January, Erin, I'm talking about now. As far as I can see, you just want to make me suffer. Is that how you're getting your revenge?'

'Peter, it's not that!' she cried, distressed that he could not grasp something that seemed very simple to her. 'Do you think I don't want to come back with you?'

'I'm beginning to wonder.'

'Of course I do, but——'

'Well then, come.'

Visibly she wavered and he pressed his advantage. 'I love you, Erin. I want to be with you now. We could get married right away if you like—go back as Mr and Mrs Peter Hall. How does that sound?'

'It sounds lovely,' she said honestly. 'But truly, Peter, it will sound just as lovely in January, you'll see. I really can't come now, I've signed a contract at the college and I have to keep it. I can't go back on my word.'

Peter dropped his hands from her shoulders to his sides. 'You've made your mind up, haven't you?' he said venomously. 'I hope you know what you're doing, honey, because January's a long time away, and I may not wait around for you. Had you thought of that?'

The strain of the scene was beginning to tell on Erin. Her voice shaking a little, she begged, 'Please, Peter, don't be cruel to me.' Trying to lessen the tension, she went on, 'Look, I bought a couple of steaks this morning and I can make a salad. Let's forget all this for a while, my head's going around in circles. We can talk about it again after supper.'

His mouth creased in an ugly smile. 'Now it's my turn to say "no". I'm leaving, Erin.'

'But you haven't eaten,' she stammered, aware even as she spoke of how foolish she sounded.

'You should have thought of that sooner.' Seeing her stricken face, he changed tactics, briefly relenting. 'Oh, I'm

sure I'll see you in January, Erin. In the meantime, take care
of yourself.' He tipped her chin with one finger and kissed
her quickly. 'In spite of the way you're behaving, I love you
—remember that. I'll give you a phone call in the next few
days.'

'I—I love you too,' she faltered, bereft of further speech
as he walked out of the door and up the slope to his car. The
engine roared into life, and with a wave of his hand he was
gone.

Erin wandered back into the living-room and sat down,
gazing out over the sea, scarcely able to comprehend what
had happened. He had gone, she thought incredulously,
and she was responsible for sending him away ... she must
have been crazy! It had seemed the right decision at the
time, but now, with the silence of the empty house pressing on her ears, her behaviour took on a new light. She
had been incredibly foolish ... unable to sit still, she went
into the kitchen to start cooking her supper, but the mere
sight of food repelled her. Then she thought she heard a
sound outdoors and hope flared in her breast—he had come
back! She ran to the door, only to see a huge porcupine
plod away under the trees, the dry grass rustling as he went.
Her disappointment was so acute that she knew she could
not bear to remain in the empty house for another minute.

Even though it was late afternoon, the sun was still warm
on her face; impulsively she decided to go for a swim,
feeling the need for some violent physical exercise. If she
could tire herself out, perhaps later she would be able to
sleep ... anything to end this ghastly day. In the bedroom
she hastily pulled on her flowered bikini and grabbed a
towel, then padded on bare feet across the lawn to the
beach, relieved to find it empty. Just to make sure, she went
as far as the boulders, but there was no black dog, no dark-
haired stranger. Throwing her towel on the rocks, where it
made a patch of vivid scarlet, she ran into the water, diving
into a wave. Surfacing on the other side, her black hair
sleek against her head, she began to swim with a smooth
overarm crawl, straight out to sea.

She was a strong and competent swimmer, who under
normal circumstances would never have swum alone on an

unknown stretch of shore. But today her usual caution and good sense were blunted by distress. As she stroked through the waves, her actions purely automatic, she began to replay the scene with Peter, wishing she could have the chance to do it over again, but knowing only too well that life rarely gave one a second chance. How badly she had mishandled him! She had not even thanked him for driving so far just to see her. Why had she not simply relaxed in his embrace, accepted his dinner invitation, and gone back to Quebec with him? She could have returned to her old job and resumed her normal life, an existence that now nostalgically took on an air of perfection.

But deep within her heart she sensed a bitter ache of disappointment that Peter had not even acknowledged her dilemma, her shattered trust because of Vicki, let alone attempting to understand it. To have become involved with him again would only have been laying herself open to more hurt. Were all men like Peter, she wondered, and did love always bring with it pain and disillusion? She had so blithely given Peter her heart, and with frightening casualness he had trampled on it, apparently not even realising what he had done.

Erin paused to get her breath, treading water as she sombrely viewed the vast expanse of sky and sea. The only sign of life was a pair of terns a short distance away, circling an outcrop of rocks; milk-white foam, like a border of lace, surged about its jagged edges. She felt diminished by the ocean's desolate grandeur, so that a sense of absolute loneliness struck her to the core ... never had she felt so totally isolated from all humanity as she did now ... when she returned to her house, too briefly inhabited to feel like home yet, there was no one to whom she could turn for comfort and companionship ... she was a stranger in town, and Peter, her only contact with love and friendship, had left.

Tears began to mingle with the salt water on her face. In a frantic attempt to break free of her misery she struck out again, but the desperate urgency of her strokes soon slowed and became laboured, for she was tired. Within a few minutes she stopped swimming, her breathing harsh in her throat. Gulping in great mouthfuls of air, she looked back to shore, and with icy swiftness was overcome by her own foolhardiness. While she had been swimming, a brisk wind had sprung up, ruffling the water's surface into waves that slapped angrily at her face, the spray temporarily blinding her, so that although she craned her neck she could scarcely distinguish the faraway beach. From the other direction came a deeper roar—the surge and backward fall of the sea against the reef; it was much closer than it had been a few brief minutes ago, close enough that she could see the encrustation of white barnacles and the golden-brown strands of kelp flung and tattered by the water's force.

All thoughts of Peter dropped from her mind; with a distinct effort of will, she smothered the panic that threatened to overwhelm her and deliberately trod water, taking long, slow breaths in an attempt to relax. She had been unbelievably foolish to have come so far, but if she could swim out here, she could swim back. She would take her time, and have frequent rests, and all would be well.

Turning her back on the jagged rocks, Erin began to swim, a slow steady breast-stroke that she knew from past experience could take her for long distances. But the sea seemed to be actively fighting her, mocking her puny efforts. Twice it flooded her mouth and nostrils, rasping her throat so that she choked. Her limbs felt like lead, while the frantic tattoo of her heart against her ribs almost deafened her. Almost, but not quite . . . the pounding of the surf was louder now. She looked back over her shoulder with an inarticulate cry of fright. The reef was barely ten feet away, and with sickening suddenness she knew the reason for her lack of progress; she was caught in the grip of a current, a current that was inexorably carrying her helpless body nearer and nearer to the cruelly sharp rocks—and with every passing second, farther away from the safety of the shore.

Mindless with terror, Erin thrashed her arms and legs, animal-like sounds of fear bursting from her lips. Then a wave crested against the reef and fell back, totally submerging her in its backwash of foam. She was sucked still deeper as the undertow seized her, whirling her body so that she lost all sense of direction. Terrified and disorientated, she opened her eyes, seeing through the sea's grey curtain a perpendicular wall of granite. Frantically she tried to break free of the water's greedy embrace, but she was too late. Her leg struck a hidden outcrop, and the searing pain slammed the remaining air from her lungs. Beyond fear now, she knew with a cold, sharp clarity that she was going to die—here, alone in the clutch of the hungry ocean. It was useless to struggle any more. Her oxygen-starved lungs stabbed her with agony. Cartwheels of fiery light exploded behind her eyes and her limbs went limp. Her last dazed recollection was of Peter, whom she would never see again ... perhaps this was the best way for it to end ...

She did not see the half-naked body that surged through the water towards her, nor did she feel the strong fingers that grabbed her unresisting wrist and hauled her upwards, away from the murderous rocks. Only when two sharp blows stung her cheeks did she by reflex begin to fight for air, her tortured throat burning like fire. Dimly she felt someone force her chin back. Water gurgled and sucked at her ears and flowed out of her mouth, and feebly she strove to free herself, in terror that the sea would again close over her face and strangle her with its cold, wet grip.

'Hold still—stop fighting me!'

Her blue eyes, rinsed of everything but fear, fastened on the face of her rescuer. His dark hair was soaked now, plastered to his forehead, and his eyes were grim, intent —and as angry as the grey sea behind him. His face came closer, his arm strong about her waist, and then his lips met hers as he breathed life-giving air into her mouth. Four times, five times, he repeated this action until a trace of colour appeared in the paper-whiteness of her cheeks, and her lips lost some of their bluish tinge. He said, speaking in harsh gulps. 'That's better. You look a little less like a drowned rat. You might even survive—if we can make it back to shore, that is.'

Incapable of speech, Erin leaned against him limply, her hair spread over his shoulder like an ebony fan, her breast rising and falling in slow, deep breaths. Her legs entangled with his, as his body sheltered from the breakers; never had she felt anything so comforting, so utterly safe, as the haven of his embrace. As her head drooped against the hardness of his collarbone, reality receded into a dream-like world of a man's taut body, a man who would look after her and keep her safe . . .

'For God's sake, don't pass out now!'

By an immense effort she looked up at him. He held her gaze with an almost hypnotic power and spoke with brutal frankness. 'If we want to live to tell this tale, my little mermaid, you'll have to help me. We must get free of the current, to start with, and if you're going to be nothing but a dead weight, I won't be able to do it. Do you hear me? We'll both drown.'

'I'll help.' The words were little more than a hoarse whisper, but they seemed to satisfy him. 'Good. Turn over on your back, and I'll hold you by the chin. If you can kick at all, do so. In this situation every little bit helps.'

Because there was a kind of grim humour in his voice, Erin was emboldened to meet his eyes again, a look of such mute gratitude and trust in hers that he gave a muffled explanation of comical dismay. 'Don't look at me like that, girl, I'm not Sir Galahad and we're not home safe yet.'

Unbelievably she smiled; a rather wobbly smile, but nevertheless a smile. He had not seen her smile before, and she was quite unaware of how enchantingly her lips tilted, her eyes darkening to a pansy-purple. A wave buffeted them, driving her against his chest. 'We'll be all right,' she said huskily, her slim fingers gripping his shoulder.

Her own confidence infecting him, he threw back his head and laughed, the sound torn away by the wind. 'Sure we will!'

And so began a journey that despite their initial optimism rapidly became a nightmare. Erin kicked her legs and stroked with her arms as much as she was able, but she was close to total exhaustion and inevitably it was her rescuer who bore the brunt of their struggle against the ocean's wrath. By sheer brute strength he battered his way through the waves, and it was not until he paused to tread water that Erin realised how great the toll had been on him. 'We're clear of the current,' he gasped. 'Thank God for that!'

Frightened for him, no longer even thinking of herself, she noticed the lines of fatigue furrowing his features, the greyness of the skin about his tightly held mouth. Then, because she was paying scant attention to her surroundings, a breaker drove water into her mouth and she sputtered and coughed. Immediately his eyes flew open, his concern all for her. 'Are you okay?'

She nodded, and even through her desperate weariness was able to inject encouragement into her gamine grin. 'I should have kept my chin up—literally as well as metaphorically!'

A flash of amusement relieved his face of its normal sombreness, and across the foot of water that separated them Erin could feel the powerful attraction of a charm she had not suspected. Breathless from more than her exertions, and oddly frightened by the total transformation he had undergone, she panted, 'At least the tide's with us now.'

'Yeah.' Again his hands encircled her chin, his fingers cold on her wet skin. Trustingly she gave herself up to his hold, and they battled on. The slow minutes merged into one another, and Erin's consciousness blurred into a maelstrom of wind and water, of a numbing cold and an all-consuming tiredness. She was barely conscious when the breakers finally threw them both up on the shore, spewing their two unwanted bodies on the wet sand.

Again it was the man's voice that roused her. She was being pulled to her knees and shaken as a terrier shakes a rat. 'Get up, girl!'

'I'm okay—I can manage,' she muttered. Dazedly she staggered to her feet, his hands steadying her. For one brief instant her eyes, stinging from the salt water, took in the scene before her: a line of pale sand spread beneath the gaunt cliffs; a forest of spruce inching to the very edge of the bank; massed purple clouds in the late afternoon sky. Never had the earth felt so comfortingly solid beneath her feet. Her voice shaky with reaction, she said in tones of deep thankfulness, 'We're safe.'

'Yes. We're safe.' There was an undertone of menace in his voice. Alarmed, she looked up. His face was bleak, his eyes blank of all expression. 'My house is about a ten-minute walk from here. Let's go.'

'I—I don't need to come with you,' she stammered. 'I only live a little further up the beach.' But as she spoke a gust of wind whipped her slender body, making her shudder with cold, and she probably would have fallen had his arm not tightened around her.

'Don't be silly,' he said brusquely. 'You know perfectly well you're incapable of going home on your own.'

He was right, of course. Humiliatingly right. But even so, she was unprepared for his next action. One arm slid down her body and in a single smooth movement he picked her up. Feebly she tried to free herself, mortified that he should carry her like a child. 'Please—put me down!'

'Just keep still. You know damn well you're worn out.'

Rigid with suppressed chagrin, her eyes downcast, she allowed herself to be carried from the beach up a wooden stairway that scaled the cliff, and then along a trail through the densely growing evergreens. But as his house came into sight through the trees, she could not forbear staring at it from under her lashes.

She had never seen a dwelling so perfectly attuned to its environment, with contours fitting the land so subtly. The walls were of weathered cedar, grey as fog; the angles and peaks of the roof were as natural as the V-shaped sheltering spruces and as sharply defined as the cliffs themselves. A vast beachstone chimney dominated the northern façade of the house, while a smooth expanse of glass doors opened into a sundeck overlooking the ocean.

Taken aback by the understated luxury of the stranger's home, Erin again tried to struggle free of his hold, knowing that she did not want to go through the varnished doorway to meet a wife, children ... or anyone lucky enough to live daily in such magnificent surroundings.

'What's wrong now?' he demanded.

'N-nothing. But your wife——'

'I'm not married.'

There was something in his clipped tone that forbade further questioning. Dumbly Erin submitted to being carried through the back door, where the great black dog greeted them sedately. He traversed a hallway, then went up a long flight of carpeted stairs. He pushed open the door of a bedroom and with scant ceremony deposited her on the wide bed. For a moment, in spite of herself, her weary muscles relaxed against the pillows, cushioned by their softness. He switched on a bedside lamp that threw a soft golden glow over the room, and drew the heavy green silk curtains, shutting out a view of the omnipresent sea, of manicured green lawns, and of white-trunked birch trees, their leaves tossed by the wind. Then he knelt by the granite fireplace and touched a match to the carefully piled kindlings and logs. They burst into cheerful flame, lending a spurious intimacy to the scene; no greater contrast could be imagined to the bitter struggle they had waged against the sea.

Erin bit her lip, wishing she could control the violent tremors that shook her frame, she was chilled to the bone. Almost subconsciously her ears were straining for the sounds of any other occupants of the house—surely he did not live totally alone? But no one came. As he rose to his feet, she asked, 'Do you live by yourself?'

He raised one eyebrow, showing that he thought the question impertinent. 'Yes.'

Abruptly she became aware of the brevity of her wet bikini clinging to her figure, and of the white sprawl of her legs on the dark green bedspread. He moved towards her, and childishly she cowered against the heaped-up pillows, her teeth chattering ignominiously, her eyes huge in her pale face. Ignoring her, he walked past the bed to an adjoining bathroom, coming back with a softly textured bathtowel, which he flung at her. 'Dry yourself off,' he said callously. Opening a handcrafted pine wardrobe, its wood honey-coloured, he extracted a deep red velvet dressing gown.

Hurt by his seeming indifference, Erin fumbled with the fleecy white folds of the towel, trying to rub a little warmth into her cold body, only her pride preventing her from burrowing her head into the bed and crying her eyes out. With an impatient exclamation he pulled the towel away from her and, wrapping her in its softness, began vigorously massaging her. Although he was being far from gentle, she at first submitted to his ministrations, limp as a rag doll. But finally she protested weakly, 'You're hurting me!'

He paused, looking straight at her for the first time since they had entered the house. With a sinking sensation in the pit of her stomach, she realised he was blazing with pent-up anger, and that from this anger had stemmed his suppressed violence with her. 'It's no more than you deserve,' he said vehemently. 'You little idiot! I've seen some foolish things done in my lifetime, but what you did today beats them all. What the hell were you trying to prove?'

'I wasn't thinking of——'

'You sure weren't. Don't you know that one of the cardinal rules is not to swim alone—and certainly not straight out to sea?'

She drooped her head, knowing only too well how right he was. But he jerked up her chin, forcing her again to meet his gaze. 'You can just thank your lucky stars I happened to go down to the beach this afternoon, that's all. And now, get that wet swimsuit off and put this on.' He held out the rich velvet garment.

She pulled the towel around her protectively, shrinking away from him.

'For God's sake,' he exclaimed, 'I wouldn't have thought this was the time for modesty. But I'll turn my back, if it'll make you feel better.'

He suited action to his words. The firelight flickered over his body, casting shadows on the muscles of his long back, for he was naked to the waist. Her vision was obscured by a sheen of tears as she stripped off her bikini, dropping it on the pearl-grey carpet. The dressing gown was luxuriously soft, and she pulled it about her, belting it snugly around her waist. It was far too big, the sleeves falling over her wrists. From its fabric came a tantalising masculine odour of shaving lotion and expensive tobacco. That she should have to wear a garment belonging to the arrogant stranger was the final straw. The tears were raining down her cheeks now, beyond her control, for all the accumulated stresses and tensions of the day had finally conquered her. She caught her breath in a sob of utter misery.

He pivoted sharply. At the sight of the forlorn little figure on the bed an indefinable emotion flickered across his features and was gone. But the harsh lines of his face softened, and the anger fled from his eyes. He knelt in front of her, holding her shoulders, his face on a level with hers. 'I'm sorry I was angry, little mermaid,' he apologised. 'You've had about all you can take, haven't you?'

Speechless, she gazed at him through drowned blue eyes. With an incoherent exclamation he gathered her to him, pressing her cheek against his chest, stroking her wet hair with gentle fingers until finally her sobs ceased. He reached into the pocket of the velvet robe for a handkerchief, and as he did so the garment fell back from her leg, revealing an ugly scrape on her thigh. 'You're hurt!' he exclaimed, a note in his voice that she had not heard before, and which she was unable to place.

'It's nothing,' she disclaimed weakly. 'I banged it on the rocks.' And involuntarily she shivered as she remembered that dreadful instant out of time when she had been so sure she was going to die.

'Stay there,' he ordered. As though she had any intention —or the capability—of moving, Erin thought with a touch of wry humour. In a moment he was back with a business-like first aid kit and proceeded to clean and bandage the wound, his long, lean fingers exquisitely gentle, his brow furrowed with concern. When he had finished, he said calmly, 'I'm going to dry your hair now—you shouldn't be sitting there with it wet—and then I'll get you something hot to eat.'

'What about you?' she protested. 'You shouldn't be waiting on me, you must be tired too.'

He flicked her a quick glance, almost as though gauging whether or not she was sincere. Her puzzlement at this reaction must have shown. Briefly he grinned, and intuitively she knew he was grateful for her concern. 'I'm okay. Why don't you come by the fire and I'll get a dry towel for your hair.'

Erin could not have disobeyed had she had the strength to do so; there was something in his tone of voice, in his intent grey eyes, that she was powerless to resist. Wordlessly she nodded. As she pushed herself up from the bed, his hand was at her elbow, supporting her. She subsided with instinctive grace onto the carpet, holding her slim, ringless fingers out to the warmth of the flames. When he returned with the towel she obediently bent her head, the strands of wet hair falling away from the delicate nape of her neck. She felt suspended in a world far removed from reality, yet so much more real than anything she had as yet experienced. From a great distance came the crackle of the burning wood in the grate, the pressure of his hands rubbing her scalp, and finally the sensuous tug of a brush through her hair. And then his voice, quiet, prosaic. 'There . . . I think it's dry now.'

She straightened, throwing back the fall of silken blackness, her dark eyes regarding him gravely. She had never been a vain girl, and was now quite unaware of her startling beauty. The firelight gleamed along the raven hair, touching her cheekbones with gold and shadowing the hollows of her slender throat; she looked fragile and totally feminine in the heavy wine-red folds of his gown, like a figure in a medieval portrait. As though he could not help himself, he stretched out one hand and traced the curve of her cheek to the corner of her mouth.

Her lips parted and trembled at his touch. Unbidden, her imagination allowed his hand to follow the line of her neck to her breast, where it would lie, incandescent as fire, against her flesh. And simultaneously his image was burned indelibly into her brain: dark hair that had dried into loose, clustered curls; sensually curved mouth, eyes that penetrated her very soul. He had broad shoulders and a deep chest, covered with a tangled mat of dark hair; her cheek had lain against it, she thought in wonderment, and her tears had trickled down his lean belly. Every nerve end in her body quivered at the memory.

The silence between them extended from moments into minutes. Then a log crashed to the hearth, flinging a shower of sparks up the chimney. His eyes shifted from hers and the spell was broken. Lithely he got to his feet. When he spoke his voice was so completely matter-of-fact that Erin felt a stab of disappointment—had she dreamed that strange little interlude? 'I'm going downstairs to heat up some food for you,' he said. 'Stay by the fire and keep warm, won't you?' Not waiting for any response he left the room, closing the door quietly behind him.

Robbed of his presence, Erin huddled by the fire, gazing into the flames as she thought over the past few minutes. Now that he was gone, her own behaviour seemed both incomprehensible and wanton; she blushed with shame as she remembered how she had longed for his hand to caress her. The first time they had met, on the beach, what was it he had said? '... unless you're looking for trouble, that is?' He must be convinced now that she was, so blatantly had she betrayed her feelings ... feelings she had never experienced before.

She found she did not want to follow this train of thought, for inevitably it would lead to Peter. Her eyelids heavy with tiredness, she got to her feet. The bed with its heaped up cushions looked so inviting that she lay down on it, pulling the velvet gown around her. She would hear him coming back, she thought muzzily, and almost instantly was asleep.

CHAPTER TWO

SHE was dreaming.

Her feet thudding in the sand, she was running down a beach peopled with vague dark shadows that watched her flight with indifference, neither helping nor hindering her. Behind her was an undefined menace, an accumulation of all her childhood fears, that, despite her desperate burst of speed, was gaining on her. It would catch her unless ... she plunged into the sea to escape, but its cold grey waters mounted into a monstrous wave, sucking her towards its crest to suffocate her in its deadly fall. Horror-stricken, she began to scream for help ... 'Peter! Peter ...'

Someone was shaking her by the shoulders. 'Wake up!' a voice grated.

Her eyes, dilated from the terror of the nightmare, flew

open. For an instant of blank incomprehension she saw a stranger's face, dark and forbidding, and an unfamiliar room. Then the events of the past few hours rushed back into her consciousness, and with a heartfelt sigh of relief she relaxed in his grasp, a tiny part of her brain noticing how attractive he looked in a pair of brown suede trousers and an open-necked cream silk shirt. 'Thank goodness you woke me,' she murmured, giving him a brilliant smile of gratitude. 'I dreamed I was drowning ... it was horrible!'

But there appeared no answering smile on his face. For an instant he glanced downwards and to her consternation she noticed that the folds of the gown had gaped open, exposing the full curves of her breasts. Blushing hotly, she pulled the garment about her; but there was no lessening of the stranger's inimical stare. 'What's wrong?' she faltered, only to be completely taken aback by his reply.

'Who's Peter?'

'Peter? How do you know his name?'

'You were calling for him in your dream.'

'Oh.' Again she blushed. It seemed a lifetime since Peter had visited her earlier in the day and had so precipitately driven away, leaving her alone. Did he really love her? Or was he just using her? And how could she ever trust him again?

She did not realise how her unhappiness and indecision were mirrored in her telltale features. 'I asked you a question,' the man repeated with heavy patience. 'Who's Peter?'

Summoning a vestige of her normal spirit, she retorted, 'I can't really see that it's any of your business.'

'I think you're forgetting I saved your life, little mermaid,' he answered with an unpleasant smile. 'In consequence, you're very much my business.'

'I haven't really thanked you for that, have I?' she said apologetically, appalled by the oversight. Involuntarily she leaned towards him, resting one hand on his wrist, her fingertips drawing warmth from his skin. 'Thank you,' she said simply. 'There's really nothing I can say but that.'

He acknowledged her gratitude with a sardonic bow of his head. 'Oh yes, there is something else you can say. You can tell me who Peter is.'

pressed upon her ears in the little house down the beach: no greater contrast could be imagined with the whirlwind days of her courtship with Peter ... 'We fell in love,' she continued softly, 'and then he asked me to marry him. I could hardly believe it was happening to me, I didn't feel I deserved such happiness.'

'Why ever not?'

He sounded dangerously angry. Surprised, she said, 'Well, I was just an ordinary girl with a fairly ordinary job, while he was a very well known figure in artistic circles in Montreal.'

'It sounds to me as though you have one hell of an inferiority complex.'

'I don't! I'm just being realistic about the difference between us.'

'Nonsense! To start with, have you looked in a mirror lately?'

'What's that got to do with it?' she asked, puzzled.

'Has no one ever told you you're a very beautiful woman?'

Erin blinked, a rush of warm colour flooding her cheeks so that she did indeed look very beautiful. 'Oh—thank you,' she stammered, adding with a thread of genuine amusement, 'Conversations with you certainly aren't dull!'

'And talking about conversations, that's another thing—what the devil did the two of you have in common?'

'Lots of things!'

'Name a couple,' he challenged cynically.

'We're both involved in the arts,' she said hotly. 'I'm a photographer and he's a university lecturer in art history. So that gives us a whole common background.'

'I grant you that one. What else?'

'Well, we had a lot of friends and——'

'Friends—or rather acquaintances—can be a great cover-up. What did you talk about when you were alone?'

'I guess we weren't alone that much. Peter is a very busy man,' she said defensively, wishing she could give him a different answer but unable to be anything but honest. 'But we were in love, I told you that.'

'If you were both in love, why the broken engagement?'

Avoiding his penetrating grey eyes, that seemed to pierce her fragile layers of self-defence, she said flatly, 'I found out he'd been regularly seeing another woman and had even gone away with her for a weekend when I thought he was at a conference.' Unconsciously her fingers were tugging at the fringe on her belt and it was with visible effort that she maintained self-control. Only wanting to end her narrative, she said, 'I gave him back his ring, resigned from my job, and got a job here at the college. So here I am.' She tilted her chin defiantly, dreading that Simon Grayson should extend the same facile sympathy with which her acquaintances had greeted the news. She should have known better.

'Good for you! It was time you showed a bit of spirit.'

Erin gasped in outrage. Her voice shaking with fury, she said, 'You have no right to say something like that! You're talking to me as though I'm a dewy-eyed teenager. You're not my father, you know.'

His eyes had narrowed to slits, his body still as a mountain lion's before the pounce. 'I have no desire whatsoever to be your father, Erin McCourt,' he said silkily. 'And I can only think of one way to make that perfectly clear to you.'

She had no way of anticipating his intention; he moved, cat-swift. His hands at her shoulders pushed her back against the pillows and the weight of his body pinioned her there, a taut and helpless victim. With deliberate sensuality he lowered his head to hers, one hand stroking her heavy hair back from her face as his lips moved from her high cheekbones down the curve of her cheek to finally find her mouth and claim it for his own.

Erin had been kissed before, but never like this. It was as though she were a musical instrument from which he was eliciting all the response and warmth and richness of which she was capable. At first powerless to resist, and then no longer wanting to, she parted her lips under his as an ache of desire smouldered within her and burst into flame. Her hands moved to encircle his neck, her fingers buried in his thick hair as she drew him closer, their legs entwined on the bed as they had been earlier in the sea. His hands left her shoulders to caress the smooth skin of her throat, and then his lean fingers sought and found the soft swell of her breast. Erin gave a tiny moan of pleasure, her truant body completely within his power to do with as he wished.

As though he sensed this, he freed his mouth from hers and for a moment rested his face in the hollow of her throat, where a pulse was frantically beating against her skin. Then he raised his head, so close that she could see the tiny flecks of rust in the probing grey of his eyes; his lashes were long and almost black, as thick as a woman's. When he spoke, his words came like a dash of cold water. 'Have I proved to your satisfaction that I cherish no fatherly feelings towards you?' he drawled, his voice totally self-controlled.

Aghast, she felt the sweetness and passion he had evoked in her turn to ice. Trying to twist free of his hold, she panted, 'So it was all a game to you! A cheap trick to show how clever you are.'

'You must admit I proved my point.'

'The end justifies the means,' she said bitterly. 'That's a typically male point of view. You and Peter are the same. You use women as though they were objects, pieces of furniture.' Hysterically she swept on, 'You don't care about us at all—you're so wrapped up in your own egos, you're incapable of understanding genuine emotion!'

'Be quiet, Erin,' he ordered. 'Because you've been let down by your precious Peter, you can't go around making sweeping generalisations about all men.'

'I can if I want to,' she retorted, aware of how childish she sounded. 'Anyway, Mr Simon Grayson, you're not doing much to improve my image of the opposite sex.'

'Your arguments are totally illogical,' he murmured, a wicked glint of humour in his expression. 'Just like a woman ...'

She hardened her heart against the appeal of his smile, having no desire that he should know how much it affected her, and with undignified haste scrambled off the bed. 'I'm going home,' she announced. The solitude of the little house now appeared like a welcome haven after the twin assaults he had launched on her body and mind.

'How?' he asked blandly.

She stared at him, refusing to be put out of countenance. 'I'll walk.'

'In my dressing gown?'

'I'll wear my swimsuit.'

'My dear girl, it's pitch dark and far from warm.'

Feeling as though he was playing with her, like a cat with a mouse, she demanded, 'Then what do you suggest?' Before the words were out of her mouth, she found herself wondering if he intended that she should stay all night. And what would she do if he did? Only too well did she know his physical strength and his personal ruthlessness. Involuntarily she moved back a pace towards the door.

'Relax, I'm not planning to abduct you.'

Goaded beyond endurance she cried, 'Stop it!' Humiliatingly her voice wavered, tears misting her vision. 'Please . . . just stop teasing me.'

'You're tired out, aren't you? Sorry,' he said with one of his swift changes of mood. 'I'll drive you home, Erin. While you were sleeping, I brought these clothes up. They'll be a bit too large for you, but they're the best I can do.'

For the first time she noticed a heap of clothing on a brocade-covered armchair in the corner; jeans, a pale pink blouse and a lambswool sweater—undeniably female attire.

With a shudder she did not recognise as jealousy, she wondered whose they were. That he should have deceived her seemed more than she could bear. 'I—I thought you said you lived alone.'

'I do.'

'Don't lie to me,' she said harshly.

'Erin, I'm not lying. I am not married and I live alone.'

'Sure—that's why you have a wardrobe full of women's clothes.'

'Those few things hardly qualify as a wardrobe,' he retorted, becoming angry himself. 'Anyway, they belong to——' he broke off and regarded her soberly, his head on one side—'but no, I won't tell you. Try trusting me, instead, Erin.'

'No!' she cried. 'I'm never going to trust a man again.'

'For heaven's sake, don't be so melodramatic,' he said

coldly, and she had the oddest sensation that he was disappointed in her. 'Get changed. I'll wait for you downstairs.' He left the room, pulling the door shut behind him with exaggerated patience.

Doggedly Erin got dressed, her one desire to be back in her own house, alone. The blouse and sweater fitted fairly well, but the jeans were far too long; so she was tall and slim, this woman who knew Simon Grayson well enough to leave her clothes at his house. Not stopping to analyse the jumble of feelings this thought aroused in her, she gave his bedroom one last glance. Understated luxury would describe it best, she thought, knowing her entire yearly salary could not have furnished it. That painting over the bed, for instance—an exquisitely crafted tempera of children playing in the snow, their bright jackets vivid patches of colour in an otherwise bleak landscape, the artist's name that of an increasingly well known young Canadian—that alone would have cost a small fortune. Why, she wondered, had that particular painting appealed to the childless Simon Grayson? Well, it was no business of hers, and the sooner she got out of here the better. Withstanding the temptation to peep into the other bedrooms, she walked down the carved oak stairwell, the wide legs of the jeans flapping around her ankles. He was waiting for her in the hall, the black dog sprawled on the floor at his feet. 'Ready?' he asked.

'Yes.'

Wasting no time, he ushered her out of the house to his car, parked under the spreading branches of a white pine; she was not surprised to see that it was a sleek Mercedes sports model. Going straight to the driver's seat, he left her to let herself in, and in total silence drove her up a winding, leaf-shadowed lane to the main road. Erin's house was in darkness, and uneasily she remembered that she had not bothered to lock the doors before going for her swim; she had not expected to be gone long. Simon Grayson pulled the car to a halt near the front door but made no move to get out. In the faint glow of light from the dashboard she could see his expression, harsh and forbidding, and it became obvious he had no intention of speaking first.

'Thank you for the drive,' she said coldly, mutinously refusing to thank him again for saving her life. He stared at her sardonically and she shifted uncomfortably in the seat, certain that he had read her mind. 'I hope I won't have to trouble you again,' she added.

'I'd like to think I could depend on that.'

There seemed no adequate reply she could make to this. Trying to sound far more composed than she felt, she murmured, 'Goodnight,' and without looking at him again got out of the car and ran to the door. It took her a minute to find the unfamiliar light switch; by the time she had, his car had purred smoothly out of sight. She was alone, as she had wanted to be ... more tired than she had ever been in her life, Erin stumbled up the stairs to her room. Stripping off her borrowed clothes, she folded them carefully and with a strong sense of relief put on her own nightgown and slid between her own sheets. Scarcely had her head touched the pillow than she had fallen into an exhausted slumber.

It was nearly ten the next morning by the time Erin parked her little car in the Fine Arts parking lot, noting with a certain satisfaction that she already had her own space, with a neatly lettered sign, 'E. McCourt.' She supposed she should be nervous the first day of a new job, but now that the time had come she felt quite confident of her ability to handle it and was looking forward to meeting her new colleagues. For a moment she stood by the car, drinking in the crisp September air. Most of the students had not yet arrived, so the campus was quiet, basking in the sun. The grey colonnaded façade of the Fine Arts building, generously festooned with Virginia creeper, faced the oval lily pond with its fountain and pair of stately white swans; further down the sloping lawn was a modernistic chapel of stone and then the Gothic bulk of the business and administration building, its mullioned windows reflecting the sun. Decorative shrubs, scarlet geraniums and frilled orange marigolds flanked a statue of the founder of the university, while late roses bloomed in the crescent-shaped garden by the art gallery, and chestnuts and drooping lindens shaded the gravelled pathways connecting the various buildings. Through the trees could be glimpsed the distant blue of the sea.

Erin gave a small sigh of satisfaction, professionally pleased by the artistry of the landscape; for some indefinable reason she felt at home here, welcomed by the vista of so much beauty. How glorious it would look in the winter, with the diamond sparkle of snow carpeting the ground! But of course, she might not be here by then ... she might be married to Peter.

Not wanting to follow this line of thought, she walked briskly towards the varnished oak doors, her footsteps crunching in the gravel. As she entered the building a robust, grey-haired man smoking an evil-smelling pipe came bouncing out of the nearest office, accompanied by a tall girl in an artist's smock. He advanced on Erin, who couldn't help responding to his infectious grin. 'You must be Erin,' he said, pumping her hand up and down in a crushing grip. 'I'm Dave Holden, the head of the department.' He looked her up and down in frank appraisal, noting the silken swing of her black hair, her chic blue tweed skirt worn with a navy blazer and tailored white shirt, and slim black leather boots. A minimum of make-up enhanced the delicate precision of her features, the intelligence of her clear blue eyes. 'Very nice too,' he said with such unabashed approval that Erin could not possibly have taken offence.

Instead she said laughingly, 'Do I pass?'

'Most assuredly,' he grinned, and then indicated the girl by his side. 'By the way, this is Nadine, who's to be your assistant.'

Erin said hello, wondering whom it was that Nadine reminded her of. Dark brown hair worn in two girlish pigtails, pleasant regular features with friendly grey eyes and a vivacious smile ... Unable to pin down any relationship, she listened to what Dr Holden was saying.

'... she's a whiz in the darkroom, knows where everything's kept and generally keeps the place running like clockwork. Nadine, why don't you show Erin her office? I left several files for you to look at, Erin, just ask me if there's anything you don't understand. Staff meeting tomorrow morning, nine sharp. I guess you'd better check in at the Dean's office this afternoon, Nadine will show you where to go. Have a good day!' And with a breezy wave of his hand and another eruption of dense blue smoke, he disappeared up the stairs, taking them two at a time.

Feeling a bit breathless, Erin said to Nadine, 'Is he always like that?'

The other girl chuckled. 'Sometimes worse! But underneath all that bonhomie is a very shrewd brain and a very kind heart—he's a super boss. Come on, and I'll show you your office, it's on the third floor. The darkroom and all the photography equipment are just down the hall from it.'

The office was a fair size, and Erin was delighted to see that it overlooked the sea. The campus was elevated enough that far down the shore she could even discern her house ... and beyond it Simon Grayson's stone chimneys. 'What an incredible view,' she murmured, for something to say.

'Isn't it?' Nadine agreed. 'Every now and then I get the itch for city life, but then I look out of the windows here and I'm caught for another term. Of course, you've just come from the city, haven't you?'

'Yes,' Erin said shortly. 'Is the Dean's office in the administration building?'

Although Nadine looked a little taken aback by the quick change of subject, she said agreeably enough, 'Yes, it is. Why don't we meet at the faculty club for lunch—if you don't have other plans, that is—and then I can show you where to go afterwards.'

Warmed by the other girl's friendliness, Erin said, 'That would be lovely. What time?'

'Around one? That should give you time to become suitably confused by all the paperwork. See you later.' A quick smile, a sparkle of grey eyes and she was gone, again leaving Erin with the teasing impression of someone she had met before. But then the files Dr Holden had left claimed her attention. There were lists of prospective students and of equipment that had been ordered; outlines of the two courses in which Erin would be involved; correspondence concerning a proposed photograph exhibit in November ... she was still immersed in all this welter of information when Nadine came to get her at lunchtime.

The faculty dining-room was panelled in dark oak with ornate crystal chandeliers hanging from the vaulted ceiling.

A subdued buzz of conversation came from the discreetly separated tables. The two girls ordered their meal, and while they waited Nadine began telling Erin about the town and its early history, her account enlivened by more than one spicy anecdote about some of the supposedly respectable citizens of days gone by. Highly entertained by all this, and already knowing she had made a new friend, it was some time before Erin noticed in a corner diagonally opposite her an only too familiar profile. With a jolt of her heart she recognised Simon Grayson, deeply engrossed in conversation with his companion, a petite, and even from this distance, very beautiful blonde woman.

Noticing Erin's abstraction, Nadine said bluntly, 'Someone you know?'

'Simon Grayson. I—met him yesterday.' Which was the understatement of the year, she thought wryly.

Nadine's eyes widened in inexplicable amusement. 'Did you indeed? What did you think of him?'

Erin made an expressive face. 'Well, a bit of a dictator with a wicked edge to his tongue. I wouldn't want to be on the wrong side of him for too long.' She paused, her brow puckering as she strove to be fair. 'And yet I sensed a basic —integrity, I guess is the word. I think if he was on your side, you could depend on him absolutely.'

'For someone you only met yesterday, you seem to have studied him pretty closely.'

Erin blushed. 'He's not exactly what you'd call unobtrusive.'

'Far from it!'

'Is he on the faculty here?'

'Yes, English department. One of the best professors on campus too. Some of his teaching methods are quite unorthodox, which adds to his popularity with the students! Besides his teaching he's also a damn fine writer and he has that rare ability to make learning exciting, to bring literature to life.'

'It sounds as though you've studied him pretty closely too,' Erin rejoined.

Nadine's eyes twinkled. 'You could say so.'

'Who's the woman with him?'

'Oh, her—that's Francine Haley, daughter of the President of the university. He's all right, in fact he's a very effective president, but I can't stand her. She's out to get her man; Simon's going places and she wants to go too.'

'How does he feel about that?' Erin asked, impelled by a kind of insatiable curiosity to find out more about the controversial Simon Grayson.

'Ask him!' Nadine laughed.

'Don't be ridiculous!'

'I was only kidding,' Nadine replied, privately amused by Erin's vehemence. 'To be honest, I don't know. He doesn't seem to stick with anyone for very long ... he's a loner. And yet, you know, he can't be blind to the practical advantages of an alliance with Francine. She is the President's daughter, when all's said and done. There are those who say Simon will be the next President and Francine will graduate from president's daughter to president's wife. I suppose they could be right.

'Why don't you like her?' Erin asked, wondering if Nadine herself was attracted by the man.

'She's a crashing snob. And she leads such a useless life, flitting from one party to another, always making the society pages. I think he deserves better than that. But she's very beautiful, there's no denying it, and he's only human after all. Heavens, here they come. We'd better talk about something else!'

With a quickened heartbeat, Erin watched the couple approach; they would pass right by her table on the way out. Unwillingly she admitted to herself what a startlingly attractive couple they made; Francine Haley, a doll-like figure beside her handsome escort, looked entrancingly frail and feminine in a frilled chiffon blouse and pale suede jumper; her long blonde hair was arranged with elaborate casualness into a cluster of curls on the crown of her head. As for Simon, a dark business suit teamed with a figured tie and grey silk shirt set off his rugged good looks, subtly emphasising his breadth of shoulder and lean build. His head was bent to listen to Francine, but just then he looked up and squarely met Erin's watching eyes. Her lashes flickered downwards in confusion.

'Hello, Nadine,' he said imperturbably. 'And Miss McCourt, we meet again. In somewhat less dampening circumstances, wouldn't you say?'

Erin's midnight blue eyes glared at him, but before she could think of a suitable retort, he continued, 'May I present Francine Haley . . . Erin McCourt. My new neighbour, Francine.'

Francine Haley did not look particularly pleased by this piece of information. 'I never did understand why you have to live outside town, Simon darling,' she said, tucking her hand in his sleeve in a proprietorial manner. 'Have you just moved here, Miss McCourt?'

'Yes, two days ago.'

Francine's eyes widened in an exaggerated fashion. 'Goodness, however did you meet Simon so quickly? He's a regular hermit.'

'We met on the beach,' Simon interposed smoothly, not missing Erin's discomfiture. 'Which department are you in, Erin?'

'She's the new photography lecturer,' Nadine put in. 'You should have heard Dave Holden rave on about her references.'

'So you have Nadine as your assistant,' Simon observed quizzically. 'Make sure you keep her in line, she needs a firm hand.'

'Pooh!' said Nadine rudely, displaying an easy familiarity with Simon Grayson that Erin found surprising.

Francine tugged at his sleeve. 'We're playing tennis at two, darling, and I have to change. We'd better go.'

'I suppose we had,' Simon said equably, without moving. He ruffled Nadine's hair. 'When are you coming to visit me? I haven't seen you for ages. Why don't you bring Erin with you when you come?'

'I might just take you up on that,' Nadine said lightly, and Erin was instantly aware of the little shaft of pure dislike that Francine Haley's pale blue eyes projected at the other girl.

'Do come along, Simon,' she said petulantly. 'You know I hate having to rush.'

'Okay. I'll see you, Nadine. Goodbye, Erin—until we

meet again.' And with a mocking salutation in Erin's direction, he left.

As soon as they were out of earshot, Nadine asked quizzically, 'Just what did happen when you met him? I think you must have made quite an impression. Or is it none of my business?'

The friendship with Nadine was too new to share all the events of yesterday. 'Oh,' said Erin evasively, 'he helped me out of a difficult situation, that's all.' Wanting to divert Nadine's interest, she went on, 'You seem to know him well?'

'I should—I've known him ever since I was born!'

'What do you mean?'

'He's my brother.'

'Your brother?' Erin repeated in consternation.

'Why yes, didn't you know?' She thought back. 'But I guess Dave did just introduce me as Nadine, didn't he? Not as Nadine Grayson.'

So that accounted for the mysterious likeness she had sensed in Nadine for someone else: the dark hair, the grey eyes with the same rusty flecks. But Nadine's open friendliness and bubbly personality had blinded her, so different were they from her brother's reserve. He was a man of hidden depths, of buried passions, whereas Nadine's heart would always be worn on her sleeve. And abruptly Erin recalled how she had described Simon as a dictator to his sister. Shamefaced, she said, 'I think I owe you an apology.'

'What for?' Nadine teased, knowing perfectly well what was coming. 'He can be an absolute bear sometimes, and dictator is as good a word as any. I've called him that myself! But what you said about integrity is equally true, Erin.' She fiddled with the cutlery for a moment, her mind far away. 'He's always been such a good brother to me.' Nadine smiled at Erin, who sensed things unsaid beyond these simple words. 'I owe him a debt of gratitude I'll never be able to repay. So you can see why I get upset when I see him with someone like Francine ... she's not good enough for him.'

Erin nodded her understanding. Then, propelled by a need she scarcely understood, she asked, 'Do you own a grey lambswool sweater and a pale pink blouse?'

Nadine looked understandably puzzled. 'Why, yes, I do. I believe they're at Simon's though.'

'Oh dear!' Erin gave a sigh of dismay. So the clothes she had worn last night had been Nadine's, Simon's sister's; he had asked Erin to trust his word and she had been unable to.

'You'll have to explain, you know!' Nadine said with a laugh. 'You can't leave me up in the air like this.'

'I had to change at your brother's yesterday, and when he loaned me your clothes, I practically accused him of having a mistress hidden away in some dark corner,' Erin confessed with mingled misery and incoherence.

Nadine's eyes widened delightfully. 'What on earth did he say?'

'I won't repeat it,' Erin said ruefully. 'Needless to say, we didn't part the best of friends.'

'But why did you have to get changed?' Nadine asked, obviously intrigued by the whole episode.

Deciding she had better give Nadine an expurgated account of the afternoon before Simon did, Erin said, 'Promise you won't tell anyone? It's not exactly a story that reflects to my credit.'

Nadine nodded. 'I promise.'

'I went for a swim at the beach yesterday afternoon and got caught in the current and carried out to the rocks.' Her eyes darkened reminiscently. 'I nearly drowned.'

'You wouldn't have been the first one,' Nadine said soberly. 'That stretch of beach has a bad reputation. The locals call the rocks the Devil's Reef, and with good reason. I can never understand why nobody's posted a warning sign for swimmers.'

'It was my own fault,' Erin said honestly. 'I should have known better. Anyway, luckily for me your brother came to the rescue. He got me to shore and took me to his house——'

'——and proceeded to read the riot act to you about people who go swimming alone on an unknown beach!'

'Exactly.' The two girls smiled at each other in mutual understanding. 'I'm afraid I was really rude to him,' Erin confessed. 'Especially when he produced your clothes.'

'I expect that was good for him,' Nadine said briskly.

'Far too many women—including Francine—fall all over him and agree with every word he says. That's very bad for a man's ego. And you know, he did say today that he'd like me to bring you over for a visit. So you can't have made too bad an impression.'

'I suppose not,' Erin agreed half-heartedly, wishing she could share with Nadine the scorching memory of Simon's kisses, and knowing it was impossible.

'Don't look so worried,' Nadine said kindly. 'I'm sure you must have given him quite a scare yesterday and that's why he got so angry afterwards.' She sought for the right words, her head tilted to one side. 'He's a very complex man, my brother. So much of the real Simon is hidden, buried. Part of it is that he was married once, but his wife and tiny daughter were both killed in a car accident, and I don't think he's ever recovered from that double tragedy. He loved them both so much ...'

Erin made a tiny sound of distress. How unintentionally cruel she had been to ask him if he lived alone!

'Well, that's eight years ago now. But Simon's never been the same since. It's as though parts of him have become frozen in a kind of perpetual winter. I would so like to see summer come for him, with warmth and love and happiness.'

Deeply affected, Erin blinked away a sheen of tears. 'I hope it will,' she said huskily. 'But it's September now, and another long winter ahead.'

'Then we must hope for an early summer.' Nadine looked at her watch, trying to shake off her unusual seriousness. 'Goodness, we'll both be fired if we don't get back! I'll show you where the Dean's office is.'

Knowing there was work to be done, Erin also got up, but deliberately she tucked the conversation to the back of her mind, knowing that later, when she was alone, she would take it out and re-examine it. So much had been added to her image of Simon Grayson that she needed the opportunity to absorb it all. Why his personality should be so engrossing to her, she did not stop to consider. She only knew that she longed for the chance to see him again and somehow right the situation between them.

CHAPTER THREE

DESPERATE in her desire to try to forget Peter and make a new life for herself, Erin threw herself into her work over the span of the next few weeks. Subconsciously, she also knew that the disturbing stranger, Simon Grayson, was somehow pushing his way into her life, not perhaps because he was trying to or because he wanted to, but because in the short time since their fateful meeting on the beach, she had somehow let him. She could not comprehend why she should be so affected by him, this cynical and cold man who obviously preferred the company of the wind in sails on a choppy sea and his own solitude to that of other people. Each morning she would see him sailing at the mouth of the harbour in his sloop *Early Summer*, returning home, always alone, just as she would be leaving for work. That she could feel even the slightest attraction for a man who could be so harsh and bitter, one who had such little use for people, led her to conclude that it was her bruised feelings for Peter, her vulnerability that made her susceptible. She decided that work was the cure, for such feeling could only germinate and grow when one was idle and Erin resolved that she was not going to be a slave to her emotions; she was done with that and from now on she firmly intended to be in control of her own life.

And so Erin worked long days with students and long nights in her studio at the college. Hours and hours of printing and developing. Sometimes she omitted lunch from her schedule altogether and often she would be too tired at night to think of supper and so she would buy a sandwich at the faculty club before going home, or else she would stop off at the small café in town. Regardless of her choice, Erin soon began to feel the burden of her enforced long hours and poor eating habits. She was not sleeping well and was lonely, for she had always been one who enjoyed being with people; people were her landscape, but now somehow she had come to feel that her very survival depended on keeping herself detached and aloof, despite the fact that she seemed to be choking something within herself by doing this.

It was a tired and tense Erin who returned to her bungalow one evening after a long day at work. She had had no formal classes but had spent long hours with students in the studio and again had taken no time for lunch, despite the scolding she had received from Nadine. In the evening she had not even stopped off for a bite to eat at the faculty club but had come straight home. All she wanted now was to relax within the privacy of her own home.

It was a chilly night. Strange how quickly autumn came here in Nova Scotia, she thought pensively. One day, a single day, seemed to mark the end of summer. A strong, cool wind would come from the sea and although the day would probably be bright and sunny, it nevertheless spoke the end of the warmth of summer, and after that day, the mornings and evenings were always cold.

Erin turned on the light. Heavens, she thought, what a tiny house this is! She was noticing the smallness more and more each day, feeling cramped and bound in this place that was becoming more like a cocoon as she spent more time here. She threw her sweater on to the chair and went into her bedroom and looked into the mirror. God, I look awful! Already I look as though I need a vacation, she considered with more than a little chagrin. But right now I'll settle for a hot shower.

The hot water soothed and relaxed her, her tiredness melting away and leaving her feeling a little more human. She had lost weight over the past few weeks, she realised, her slender hands feeling the slightness of her frame as she towelled herself dry. She knew fully well what was troubling her, but she refused to stop and deal with it, fearful that the old restlessness and loneliness would become unbearable and she would be lost. She had long ago decided to fight it by ignoring it, even now refusing to recognise that it could not be done. She didn't need Peter, she could make it on her own, she told herself adamantly. He had been faithless and she demanded more in a relationship. But try as she might, she knew that she had loved him and she could not forget him as quickly as that. No, she was not the kind who could love and then forget it, and a part of her still yearned for Peter to come to her and tell her that he had changed, that he loved her and only her.

She finished drying herself and slipped easily into a terry robe, warm and soft against her skin, looking around her at her house; it might be small and sometimes feel as if it was closing in on her, but it was her place, home for now. She went into the kitchen and put the kettle on for coffee, then walked slowly into the living room and drew the drapes over the picture window that looked out to the sea. She didn't like looking into the blackness that stared back from the ocean at night. Sometimes she couldn't see past the reflection of her own face in the glass and she felt that out there someone watched her; so she always felt more comfortable closing it out.

She put a record on the stereo and lay down on the couch to wait for the kettle to boil. Thinking of nothing in particular, she leafed through a magazine and then drifted off into a light sleep. She was awakened by the whistling of the kettle, which was boiling furiously, and by a loud and very decisive knocking at the door. Confused and disorientated, she went to the kitchen and took the kettle from the burner. The knock repeated itself. It was then that she realised the time—nearly midnight. Who could it be at this hour? Remembering how isolated she was here at the beach she thought at first that she shouldn't answer the door at all, although she knew that if anyone wanted to break in it would be a simple task indeed. Finally she was struck by the thought that perhaps ... perhaps it was Peter, coming to her as she had hoped and dreamed he would. Again the knock sounded.

'Just a minute, I'm coming!' She moved quickly to the door, for a moment fully expecting to be greeted by Peter's smiling and smooth face. But it wasn't Peter, and for a brief moment her disappointment must have shown on her face and in her voice. 'Oh, it's ... I mean ... hello, Dr Grayson, I wasn't expecting ...'

His arm, raised above his head, supported his tall body

as he leaned against the door frame. He had obviously been running, for he wore sweat pants and shirt, his hair was windblown, and his shirt was sweat-stained. His grey eyes were filled with a smoky darkness as deep as the black of the night and they gave no indication that he felt such a visit was in any way strange, even at this hour of the night. His voice was mocking and perhaps even a little harsh. 'Whom were you expecting, Erin McCourt, your faithful Peter?'

'No, I ...' She held tightly to the door, disconcerted and embarrassed that he should have guessed that she had indeed hoped to find Peter Hall standing where he was at this moment. 'No, I was just surprised that anyone should come by at this hour, regardless of who it is.' She made no move to admit him or invite him in. 'I was just going to have a cup of coffee and go to bed. It's quite late and I'm very tired. I ...'

'Are you trying to tell me to go away, or what?' he asked bluntly as he continued to stand there, giving no indication that he would depart.

Erin hesitated, then offered him entrance. 'Well, come in and have a cup of coffee. It's quite cold out tonight.'

He moved with smoothness and ease, unusual in so large a man, for he was well over six feet tall. Erin remembered being awed by his height and strength at their last meeting and seeing him again brought this back. She felt awkward and at a loss for words.

'How do you like your coffee?' she asked.

'In a cup,' he said flippantly, a smile curving at the edge of his mouth. 'Black,' he added quickly. 'Sorry for such a poor joke so late at night.'

She didn't respond to his attempt at levity but said self-consciously, 'Sit down and I'll get you some coffee.' As she walked stiffly into the kitchen that now seemed more than ever like a closet, she was all of a sudden unnerved by the smallness and closeness of the house. She poured the coffee, put some biscuits on a plate and returned to the living room.

'And the name is Simon, please, not Dr Grayson. No one but those who seem to dislike me a great deal call me that. Perhaps that's why you insist on calling me by so formal a label.' He leaned forward. 'Is that the reason, Erin?'

She blushed and fumbled with the napkins. 'Don't be ridiculous—I hardly know you. I couldn't possibly dislike someone I don't know.' She quickly changed the subject. 'Do you run a lot?'

'Depends on what you mean by running,' he replied, again with the same flippant tone he had used earlier. 'I'm what you call a "runner".' The word, as he used it, seemed to imply more than she had intended. 'I run early every morning and late at night, winter and summer. Sometimes, with weather as severe as we seem to have it here in the winters, that's not always possible, but I try to keep it a habit. Besides, when you can't sleep, you might as well run. So I run.'

Erin had the feeling he was telling her more than she had asked with her simple question that had been merely designed to fill the gap of silence. Perhaps more than even he realised. All of a sudden she saw him as a man alone, who had built a barrier between himself and others; what he was showing her now was a glimpse of the reasons for that barrier's existence, however vague and unintentional. There was so much about this giant of a man that she did not know, this enigmatic dark man who was really a stranger to her, and probably to most people who were acquainted with him, and would likely remain so.

Her musings were interrupted by a question that he was evidently asking for the second time. 'I'm sorry, I wasn't listening,' she stammered. 'What did you ask?'

His eyes were level with hers and he had the disturbing habit of looking unblinkingly straight at the person to whom he was speaking. Grey eyes searched hers. 'I asked you if you didn't find this place a bit cramped. It seems pretty small to me.'

'Yes, I do,' she nodded. 'It is confining sometimes, but then there's only me. I mean, how much room does one person really need? It's small but it's sufficient ... It's ...'

He leaned over and placed a firm, warm hand on hers. 'Calm down, wee Erin, I'm not going to bite you. I only dropped by to see how you're faring. Why are you so nervous?'

'Of course I'm not nervous! I'm fine ...'

He didn't let her finish, but stood up, and towering above her said, 'Show me the rest of this place, or is this all there is?'

'No, there's a bit more. My bedroom and a small work area, hardly large enough to call a studio, but it's good for some of my work. I use the equipment at the college mostly, but sometimes I use the kitchen here as a darkroom, and do finishing work in the so-called studio.'

He walked across the room and into the studio. Her pictures were piled on a drafting table; some had been recently mounted and some hung on the walls, while others were arranged in a portfolio on another table. He stood looking silently at them, his face expressionless, giving no visible reaction to any of the things he was seeing. Then he turned and looked at her intently, eyes deep and searching, as if seeking the answer to some question unknown, perhaps, even to himself. Finally he said in a low voice, 'Well, Erin McCourt, there certainly seems to be more to you than meets the eye, if you'll pardon me the use of the old cliché.'

'I don't know what you mean,' she said shyly.

'I mean that your work says a lot about you that you seem to take great pains and precautions to hide. Anyone who could have taken these pictures has a great deal of depth, sensitivity, and insight into what people are all about.' He turned away from her, staring once again at the pictures, and continued almost viciously, 'Tell me, how do you manage to appear so naïve and innocent, so untouched and pure, knowing what these pictures say you do? Do you just look at these things and see them only on the surface, untouched by any of it?'

She felt shaken to the core by his accusing words and the unexpected sharp thrust of an unleashed anger that had surfaced so suddenly. 'I don't know ... what you mean,' she said as she backed away from him.

But just as quickly he reached out and touched her face with strong lean fingers, tracing the fine lines of her cheek bones and slowly following the curve of her throat. 'You're a very beautiful woman, Erin. A competent and capable one as well, I believe,' he said huskily. She shivered at his touch, but did not draw away. Again she felt the power and magnetism of this Simon Grayson, this man she had met a bare three weeks ago and who strangely had the power to infuriate her in one breath and melt her to his will in another. 'Do I frighten you?' he asked. She shook her head and looked away from his searching eyes. 'Do I? What is it that you feel when I touch you, Erin, when I speak to you like this? Why do you shiver beneath my touch?'

She looked at him, fearing the feeling he was arousing in her. 'I'm not afraid of you, Simon Grayson, I'm not afraid of any man,' she blurted bitterly. She pulled herself away from him, walked quickly to the window, and stood staring out into the darkness.

'Those pictures on the wall—are they of your precious Peter?'

'Yes, that's Peter, but not *my* Peter, Dr Grayson.' Her voice was cold and biting.

'No? And probably a good thing, if you'd only realise it. You have nothing in common, you and this Peter, if your pictures tell the truth,' he said flatly.

She whirled angrily on him. 'What can you know about him? About me? You don't know either of us, so how can you be so quick to judge?' Her anger caught hold of her tongue and she rushed on, 'You know, now that I think about it, that's the thing I dislike most about you—you always seem so sure that you have the answer to any question, to any situation. Don't you ever get tired of thinking that you're right all the time? Men like you make me sick!'

'Whatever you say or think about me, Erin, I'd wager that if you'd married this Peter fellow, you would have been sick, but of a very different illness. I wonder how long it would have taken you before you tired of being a mother to the man you married.'

Her anger spilled over like molten lava. 'How dare you! How dare you come to my home and talk to me in this way! I think it's time you left, Dr Grayson.'

He showed no signs of leaving but continued to stare at her and puzzle over something that he apparently saw in her. 'What did he do to you, this Peter, that makes you act as if all men were your enemies? That makes you shut yourself away from the world and bury yourself in work?'

For a moment Erin was smothered by the desperation that welled inside her. Why was he asking these questions? It was none of his business—she was nothing to him. 'Look, Dr Grayson, I want you to leave—I want you out of my house now. You have no right to come here and talk to me like this. What I feel and what I've done with my life is none of your business, and it astounds me that you think that you can act as if it is. Now please go.'

He drew a heavy breath and when he spoke again his voice was quiet and apologetic. 'I'm sorry, Erin. I didn't mean to upset you. Look, we're going to be working at the same college and we're already neighbours, I don't think there's any value in continuing to be angry with each other. I'm sorry for what I said.'

She hesitated, unnerved by this sudden peaceful overture. She would never figure this man out; one moment he was on the offensive with her and the next he was offering peace and friendship. She sighed, her tiredness becoming an almost unbearable burden. 'You're right, of course. Truce, then?'

He smiled down at her. 'Truce, then, Erin.'

'Come on, finish your coffee,' she said, 'it's probably getting cold.'

In the living room he sat down on the couch again, picked up the coffee mug and looked at her over the rim.

'God, but we do seem to spark a fire in each other, don't we?'

'So it would seem. Maybe it's because I'm so tired lately. I think I've been working too hard and too long—I haven't done anything for the past few weeks but work at the college and then come back here to sleep.'

Simon put down his coffee and turned to her. 'But why, Erin? Why are you trying to bury yourself in work? You're too young for that.'

At first she reacted to this line of questioning by again feeling threatened, but he seemed to be honestly interested and not about to deliver one of his didactic sermons on how she should live her life. So she replied quietly and steadily, 'I don't know.' She shook her head. 'No, that's not true—I do know. It's Peter, really.' She looked up into his inimical grey eyes, sensing the strength and kindness that lingered there, even if he did at times take great pains to hide them behind a mask of harshness and coldness. 'I miss Peter—we were to be married this month.' She found herself listening to her own voice, calmly speaking of the feelings that had tortured her since she had left Peter in Montreal almost two months ago. 'I ... I loved him and I did want to marry him. But ...' She fought for control, the loneliness of the past months sweeping over her. 'I keep ... thinking he'll come for me. That he'll come to the door and stand there, a ... changed man ... and tonight I thought you were he.'

'Come to you a changed man, Erin?' Simon lit a cigarette, his hand steady and his voice soft and smooth as velvet. 'Why did you want him to change?'

She looked quickly into the smoky darkness of his eyes, but saw no censure. 'I wanted him to be honest with me. He was seeing someone else nearly the entire time we were engaged.' She paused, her hands tightened into a ball in her lap. 'I don't know why I'm telling you all this. You don't know me at all, surely you can't be interested in any of it.' She moved as if to end the conversation, but Simon placed a hand on her shoulder and she sank back into the soft cushions.

'Do you want him to give up this other woman and come to you, then? Is that what you're saying?' he asked quietly.

'I don't know ... exactly what I'm saying. I think I still love Peter, but it changed everything for me. I just don't feel the same way. I want more from a relationship than that. I want to share honesty with the man I marry, not deceit. I ... I just don't know what to do or what I feel half the time, but I do know that I need time and maybe Peter does too. Maybe there's something in me that made him do it—I have to sort the thing out, that's all.' She attempted a wry grin. 'So this is my sorting time, this year in Abbotsford.'

Simon got up and walked across the room and stood for a long time without speaking. 'Put on something warm and come for a walk with me, Erin. Please.' He didn't look at her but opened the door and walked out on to the veranda. She didn't make the excuse of it being too late, because for the first time in these long months she felt some relief. She had finally spoken the feelings she had so carefully buried deep inside her. She did as he had asked and followed him outside. 'It's cold, but it's sharp and clean and clear and you can get close to yourself here,' he said with conviction and a passion that revealed his love of the sea. 'Listen to the silence and the rhythm of the water playing its sea music.'

She was at once aware of the strength and smoothness of his touch as he took her small hand in his and they walked slowly down the beach. 'How long have you lived in Nova Scotia, Simon?'

He laughed gently. 'Since before I was born, it sometimes seems. I was born and bred here, can't you tell? A native son all the way. I was away at university in Ontario for a few years, but I had to come back in the end. I had almost no choice about it, the sea holds me fast, Erin.'

'Yes, I can see that. You sail a lot, don't you? When I first came here, I noticed your boat out there, just off the mouth of the harbour. You must go out nearly every day.'

'If I possibly can, I do. Lately it's a matter of things at the department getting bogged down, but if they don't interfere, I go early in the morning before my run.'

Astonished, she asked, 'But when do you sleep? Surely you need more rest than that?'

'I sleep, but not a lot. Sometimes it's not because I don't want to but because I can't.' His words were spoken with the same harsh bitterness that had been present during their argument of moments before. Erin shivered, feeling that there was definitely something driving this man to be alone, to live the life of one who sought isolation as a way of life. But that was foolish: he was a strong man and needed no one. He must live this way because he had chosen to do so.

They stopped walking and stood facing the sea. Simon's voice again broke the silence. 'Do you see what I mean? It's the edge of everything real. And when you're out there, on it, you're sometimes even farther than the edge ... you're a hair's breadth away from no longer existing.'

She pulled away from him, frightened by this note of fatalism in his voice. 'Now you sound ... you sound ...'

'Sound like what, Erin?' He laughed, a harsh, grating and yet somehow inexplicably sad laugh of one who had been to the very brink he described. 'Yes, you're right, Erin, I have been to the edge, and more than once. And fool that I sometimes—no, most of the time—think I am, I always manage to convince myself that there must be something in this life for me.' He kicked at the sand. 'You see, I'm an optimist. I always come back from the edge, I always come back to the hope of an early summer.'

They stood for a long time and then began to walk slowly back to Erin's house, not breaking the silence they shared. When they were nearly there, Simon pulled her gently to a standstill in front of him. She could see the sharp lines of his face in the light from her living room. 'Come sailing with me, Erin,' he said quietly. Strange that she should feel that somehow he was challenging her, but his words seemed to be a mixture of request and challenge.

'I don't think so, Simon. I've never sailed before, I wouldn't know what to do. I'd only hinder you.'

'No, you wouldn't. It's something you should experience, you know, if you want to understand the souls of the people of this place. We breathe to the rhythm of the sea, Erin.'

She knew he was daring her to come with him and discover a part of the essence of himself, but the idea frightened her. She didn't want to get close to him or anyone, not ever again.

'No, I can't come with you,' she said bluntly, and turned to walk up the steps to her house. But his voice stayed her retreat.

'Who's running now? Stop and look at yourself and what you're doing, Erin, for God's sake. You're running, running so fast that you'll never be able to really see the landscape through which you pass. What do you think, that if you run fast enough you'll never have to face what's in you? You think you're not going to have to stop and have a good look at Erin McCourt and say goodbye to her Peter Hall?' His voice rose in anger. 'Well, don't kid yourself, it can't be done. You'll run until you drop and then you'll shut yourself up in your darkroom until people think you've joined a convent and taken the vows of silence. And you can refuse to look at any person, any man, and see him for what and who he is—you can try all that, Erin, but it won't work, believe me, it just won't work. The day will come when you can't run and you can't hide any longer, and you'll grieve because you didn't have the nerve or the courage to face it all at the beginning.'

She whirled on him, her anger matching his own. 'How dare you! You think you know everything, don't you? Always it comes round to this, the mighty Simon Grayson making his weighty pronouncements on how other people should live their lives. Well, tell me what's so hot about yours, tell me that? What's so great about the way you live? You're all alone, aren't you? Maybe I should start making wise pronouncements about you and your way of life.'

His face darkened visibly and his voice held a tone that was at once threatening and yet almost a plea. 'You're right, I'm a runner too and I've run for quite a few years longer than you, child Erin.'

'Don't call me "child"! I'm not a child, I'm a woman, and I'm sick of your condescending attitude towards me!'

'I can hear you, and so can half of Abbotsford, I'm sure.' He paused and then repeated, 'Come sailing with me, Erin. I dare you to come with me.'

She laughed mockingly, throwing her arms in the air in a gesture of exasperation. 'You're incredible, do you know that? You're absolutely incredible! I've already said I don't want to go sailing with you. As a matter of fact, I don't think I want to do anything with you. I don't even want to stand here and continue this ridiculous conversation or argument or whatever it is. I . . .'

Simon moved dangerously close and muttered impatiently, 'I hear what you're saying, Erin, and so do you, if you'd only admit it. You're saying that you're afraid to come with me, you're afraid of people and you're especially afraid of men. You don't want to take the chance of anyone getting close enough to hurt you again. Now I'm saying to you—face it—face it and come with me. I dare you to start living again.' He reached out and took her hand in his again, holding it fast when she would have shaken it off.

'I ... I ... all right. All right, I'll come, I'll come with you on that damn boat of yours.'

In that moment, without any warning, he leaned down and kissed her firmly on the lips, then turned and walked down the beach.

For the next few days Erin found herself watching for his lone figure running along the beach in the mornings or for the sight of *Early Summer*'s sails off the harbour's mouth. But she caught no sight of Simon for nearly three days. Then finally on Friday night, the phone rang and she heard Simon's deep and resonant voice from the other end. 'Hi, how's Erin?' The very sound of his voice sent shivers up her spine. She was behaving like a foolish schoolgirl, but she had to admit she was glad to hear from him.

'Hi, Simon. How are you?'

'Fine, thanks, a little tired but otherwise fine. Glad to be home, that's for sure.'

'Oh, you were away?' she enquired coolly, trying to regain control over her rapidly beating heart.

'Yes, a conference of English professors. Dull stuff for a photographer, I'm sure.'

'Oh, no such thing, I'd like to know more about your work and your writing. I don't know how you can do both, but that must be one good thing to come out of your late nights and early mornings.'

'Probably, yes. Sorry I didn't call sooner, but things were piled up at work when I got back this morning, so I've spent the day digging out. What I called about was our sailing venture. Are you ready? Tomorrow's the day.'

'I guess so.' She paused and then added, 'Are you sure you want to take me? Really, I know I shall be quite useless.'

'Silly woman! The weather's going to be great this weekend. It could be the last really good weekend we'll get this year and there's a fine forecast for both days. A good trip up and a good trip back, what more could you ask for? My grandparents live in Halifax, Albert and Mary Grayson, so we can stay over there on Saturday night and start for home early on Sunday morning.'

The idea of an overnight trip with Simon startled her.

'Oh, but I didn't know it would be for an entire weekend. I thought maybe a few hours, but not an entire weekend. I don't know if . . .'

'Relax! I've got it planned and there's no backing out of it now, Erin McCourt. We leave tomorrow morning at dawn and sail up the coast to Halifax. We'll have lunch and you can do some shopping if you like. I'll even take you out on the town in the evening, if you feel so inclined. After all, how many times do you get a chance to go thirty miles to Halifax?'

'Are you sure your grandparents won't mind? I mean, they don't even know me.'

'Look, stop worrying. The house in Halifax is large enough to hold twenty people besides us. Really, it's okay and we'll be back on Sunday. Any other questions or excuses from the crew?'

Erin fell in with his lightened mood. 'No, sir. No questions.'

'Good girl,' he responded lightly, then added in a more serious tone, 'Trust me, Erin. I know you'll love it, unless I'm totally mistaken about you and the kind of woman you are.' His voice softened. 'Wear something warm and pack something pretty for tomorrow night in case you do decide you want to go out. See you at first light, sailor.'

Erin rose at dawn. Actually, before dawn. She had set the alarm the night before thinking she would never get up that early, but found herself awake before the alarm had gone off and before the faint threads of grey light touched the eastern sky. She was nervous and apprehensive about the trip ahead, but she also admitted to herself that she was excited and basically glad to be going. To her surprise, Simon obviously had been up long hours before her. *Early Summer* was rigged and ready for the journey. Tall and lean, Simon stood watching her as she made her way down the beach towards the wharf. He wore a heavy cable knit sweater, much like Erin's, and brown cords. At least, she thought to herself, she had worn the appropriate thing. That was the first thing right, anyway. He did not come to meet her but stood watching her closely as she approached the wharf. It bothered her to feel herself blush under his scrutiny.

'Morning, sailor.' His greeting was friendly and relaxed. She saw none of his old tightness and harshness. A smile played on his lips as he took her gear and stowed it in the sloop. He held out a hand for her and helped her aboard, seeming genuinely pleased that she had come.

They moved, under engine, away from the wharf. 'Well, Erin McCourt, do ye wish to remain a landlocked land-lubber all yer life or will ye be listening to some of the basics about the art of sailing as we head up to the port of Halifax? What say ye, matey?'

She laughed at his strange use of sailor's dialect, waived her timidity and wholeheartedly accepted his invitation. The world she entered was an entirely new one to her, a world more invigorating and exciting than any she had ever known. And Simon was a good teacher. Listening to him and watching his involvement in what he was saying, she had a new vision of what this man was like. Here was a man who could give himself totally to something, a man who came alive with the giving. Intrigued, she found herself watching him intently, struggling at times to keep her mind off the magnetic energy that flowed from him and to keep her attention on the words he spoke.

Simon finished explaining the rigging and some of the basic principles of the craft of sailing. 'You know, gal, I have the strangest feeling that you've been listening to only half of what I've been saying and hearing only a quarter of that. Now why might that be?' he asked with mock serious-ness.

Erin blushed visibly and quickly stammered her denial. 'Oh, no—I've heard every word, so help me.'

Simon broke into laughter. 'We'll soon see, Erin. You'll soon have to put into practice what you've supposedly heard.'

She gave him a playful shove. 'And what will you do if I fail, Captain?'

'Why, it'll be walking the gangplank for you, of course.' He became serious again and gently squeezed her hand. 'By the way, I'm really very glad you decided to come with me. I haven't sailed with anyone in a long time. Well now, let's go.'

Simon hoisted the mainsail and released the boom.

'Okay, gal,' he called out to her, 'clear the main halyard on the starboard side of the mast!' For a moment, Erin stuggled to remember if starboard was right or left and was pleased with herself when she chose the correct side. When Simon raised the jib, both sails were up, but they weren't moving with any speed. Disappointed, Erin asked, 'What's wrong? Why aren't we moving? Everything's ready, isn't it?'

'Wind, woman, we need wind!' Simon pushed the tiller to head *Early Summer*'s bow towards the wind. As the bow turned, the sails began to luff and as she came about, he pulled on the sheets until the luffing stopped. 'We're sailing across the wind now and that's called *reaching*. It's usually the fastest as well as the safest kind of sailing, as you can stop quickly by heading right into the wind or turning safely in either direction. On the other hand,' he continued, 'when a boat's sailing in more or less the same direction as the wind's blowing, it's called *running*. Running may seem like the easiest kind of sailing and in some ways it is, but it's hard to judge how strong the wind is when you're running, and it's also important to keep the wind coming over one side of the stern or the other, rather than from directly behind you. If the wind is exactly astern, a small change in its direction may cause the sail and the boom to swing violently across to the other side of the boat —it could hit one of us or break the boom.'

Erin carefully considered all that he was saying and shook her head. 'I'll never be able to remember all this— it's even a whole new language.'

'Relax, we're on our way to Halifax, at the probable speed of four to five knots. We should be there in six or seven hours. Sit back and enjoy yourself.' He pointed to the mouth of the harbour. 'We're going to take a long reach out of the harbour, then jib over and run before the wind as far as Sambro Head. Ready?'

'Ready,' she responded bravely.

He smiled down at her and placed an arm around her shoulders. Erin struggled against her desire to pull away from him and the opposing desire to push closer. She did neither but remained rigid under the weight of his arm.

'Loosen up, Erin, there's nothing to be afraid of. You'll see, Grayson's students are successful.'

During the next hours she watched Simon as he moved and worked as an integral part of the boat and the sea upon which he sailed. He was good and he loved it, that was obvious. She had never seen him so relaxed and at home and she knew now why he sailed alone each morning before going to his work at the college. She saw him respond to the wind which filled the white canvas with the breath of the heavens. She sat with him in the cockpit and watched his strong, sturdy body move with the rhythm of this beautiful machine and this gigantic expanse of blue ocean, which glistened gold in the yellow light of the warm September sun and swelled and rolled with the rhythm of the eternal ages. A lone gull floated effortlessly in the sky above, then dived sharply and skimmed bare inches above the surface of the water before climbing once again into the heavens.

'You're right, Simon,' Erin called to him. 'It is wonderful!'

He smiled, pleasure evident in his face. 'I knew you'd like it, if you'd give it half a chance.'

'I don't like it—I love it!' she exclaimed excitedly. 'It's the most fantastic thing I've ever done. It's . . . oh, what can I say? There just aren't any words for it!'

He laughed heartily. 'Things like this, experiences like this, don't need words, Erin. They really do speak for themselves.'

It was nearly two o'clock when they sailed up Halifax Harbour. Simon, stimulated by Erin's excited enjoyment, seemed pleased to talk about McNab's Island, George's Island, the race for cover of the *Chesapeake* from the *Shannon*, and the historic waterfront area.

'The place has really changed since I was a boy growing up here,' he said finally.

'I didn't know you lived in Halifax.'

He nodded and pointed to a huge apartment house on a hill overlooking the railyards and the Container Pier. 'That used to be Greenbank, I played there many a day for a good

many years. We lived in a mammoth house on Young
Avenue, Nadine and I.'

Erin realised how little she knew of this man, listening
to him talk about his days as a youth in the historic city.

'Your parents have moved from Halifax, have they?' she
asked.

He did not look at her, but his voice roughened notice-
ably, and she wished immediately that she had not asked
the question. 'Yes, they left Halifax quite a few years ago.
They left when I was fourteen, just after Nadine was born.
It would appear that Halifax was too small for them and
the kind of social life they apparently needed and two
children would only have held them back. And so, one fine
morning, Selma and Richard Grayson left for bigger and
better things, and left their children in the care of their
grandparents.'

The bitterness in Simon's voice made Erin uncomfortable and she was sorry that she had mentioned his parents
at all. Aware of her discomfort, Simon turned to gaze
steadily at her. 'Don't let it bother you, Erin. We didn't
lack for love, only parents. My Albert and Mary had more
than an adequate supply of affection for us. I thought
Nadine would have mentioned it to you, you both seem to
be so close lately.'

'No, she didn't,' Erin replied. 'And I'm sorry I did, it was
none of my business. I didn't mean to bother you with it.'

Simon's harsh laugh was a stark contrast to the bright
hours they had just spent together. There was a darker side
to this man, a darkness that filled Erin with an ominous
foreboding and fear.

'What's the matter, Erin, have you been so sheltered in
your life that you've never before met a son who despises
his parents and all they stand for?'

She did not answer, neither did he give her time. 'Well,
you've met one now. They're still alive, you know, and
we've never seen them, not once since that day when they
left. They live the good life they wanted so much, in
Europe—a fine, rich social life, I'm told. They put me
through my first year of university, but when I found out
where the money came from, I worked night and day to

pay it all back. After that anything I got or did, I paid for myself.' He continued bitterly, 'Nadine was only about eight months old when they left, so she doesn't remember them enough to miss them. I'm thirty-eight years old and I haven't seen them since that morning and I never want to. As far as I'm concerned, they no longer exist.'

Embarrassed by his angry outburst, Erin stammered, 'I'm sorry, it must have been very hard for you, knowing that ...'

He interrupted her, '... Knowing that my own mother and father didn't give a damn about their own children— their own flesh and blood? Yes, damn them, it was hard, but it's over now, finished.'

Erin didn't know why she said what she did, but she blurted out, 'Well, despite what you say, your anger doesn't indicate to me that it's finished. It seems to be still very much alive in you.'

His eyes narrowed as he looked sharply at her. 'Perhaps it's because, since then, I've met so many men and women like them—people who have children and couldn't care less for them. People who see children as a curtailment or an inhibiting nuisance.'

They didn't speak any more until they had moored at a pier by what Simon called Historic Properties. Unexpectedly, Simon gently and briefly touched the side of her face with the back of his hand. 'I'm sorry, Erin, I seem to have a habit of running people's good times aground. And we were having a good time. Maybe I'm allergic to happiness, it seems every time it gets near me, the runner in me starts moving. Maybe we're carved with the same knife. Forgive me?'

Erin smiled a little uncomfortably. 'Of course. You don't have to account to me or anyone for your feelings. It's really none of my business.'

He looked intently at her for a while, then spoke abruptly. 'Go below and change into something comfortable and made for walking. You, wee Erin, are about to be given a guided walking tour of old Halifax by one of its native sons.'

And walk they did. For hours. They lunched in a small

seafood restaurant on a wharf overlooking the harbour, then walked along the waterfront, wandering through antique stores and boutiques, surrounded by buildings dating back to the 1800's. Simon pointed out the Halifax–Dartmouth ferry. 'When I was a kid, it was a great treat to ride over and back. I'd offer you a ride on her, but for a sailor of your experience it would definitely be old hat.'

She stopped in the middle of the sidewalk. 'You're teasing me, Simon, and you'd better stop it. One of these days I shall be able to sail circles around you. And you'd better believe it.'

'Oh, I do—I do,' he laughed. 'I believe that if I put you in *Early Summer* right this moment you'd sail in circles, without having to try very hard at all.'

She pretended anger. 'You're impossible, do you know that?'

'Why, of course I know that. It's hard work being impossible, but I'm equal to the task. Or haven't you noticed?' They continued their teasing banter and laughter, totally enjoying each other's company, thoroughly forgetting about everyone and everything but themselves. It was dusk when Simon suggested they get their gear from the boat and go to his grandparents. After a taxi drive through the downtown area, they drove south towards Point Pleasant Park, which they had passed as they sailed up Halifax Harbour. The home in which Simon spent his youth was a stately old house near the park, which exuded a graciousness that seemed to have long since disappeared from most cities and eloquently spoke of former days of prosperity. The street was tree-lined and bordered by sprawling lawns of huge homes; it was still an obviously well maintained and well cared for area. Erin drew in a breath when she finally stood before the massive archway that marked the entrance to the home of Simon's grandparents.

'Enter the portals of the rich, Erin,' he invited caustically. 'In answer to your to this point unasked question, yes, my family does have money, a lot of it. They live very comfortable lives and see nothing wrong with it. And no, I do not share the wealth, as it comes mostly from my parents. I won't touch a penny of it, ever. I'm comfortable on my own. Nevertheless, despite the obvious dislike that you now know I hold for my parents and the money they seem to ooze from their very pores, you will find my grandparents to be basically loving and kind people, real people, in fact, and that's something it's not easy to find in any day and age, especially this one.'

Sarcasm sharpened the tone of Simon's voice and Erin was hurt by it. She shook her head sadly and murmured, 'I don't know why you're always so angry all the time. Just when you seem to start to relax and enjoy yourself, it's as if you realise what you're doing and you set out to punish yourself and others for the feeling. I couldn't help but notice the opulence of the place, Simon, but at least I wasn't practicing inverted snobbery or whatever you might want to call it. I don't look down on your grandparents nor your mother for having money. And I do wish you'd stop trying to tell me what my feelings are!'

She felt a little embarrassed when Simon's only response was silence. He stood leaning against the wrought iron railing that led up long carpeted steps to the oak front door. 'Yes, I'm bitter, and probably with more than enough cause. I've seen and experienced too much to have it otherwise.' He placed a firm hand on her elbow. 'Shall we go in now, or is there something else you'd like to tell me is wrong with my attitudes?'

Erin did not speak again but nodded to him to indicate that she would follow him inside. They went up the long line of steps and into a massive hallway. A butler met them at the entrance.

'Why, good evening, Mr Grayson. Your grandparents are in the library. It's good to have you home again, sir, it's been quite a while. I'll take your things to your room.' He picked up their suitcases and waited for them to pass.

'Could you show Miss McCourt to her room, Roger? I think she would probably like to freshen up before she meets my grandparents.'

'Of course, sir. I've prepared Miss Nadine's old room, if that will be adequate?'

'Thank you, Roger, it'll be just fine, I think.' With these cold words, Simon walked away, neither speaking to nor looking back at Erin.

When at last she was comfortably settled in Nadine's

room, Erin was glad of the privacy, glad to escape the tension that again had come between her and Simon. When she thought about it, she realised that Simon vacillated between times of being an honestly warm and kind person and a man driven by some anger and bitterness that he seemed unable to control. What a strange man he was, one she felt she would never come to understand. She wondered why he had even bothered to ask her to accompany him this weekend, for it seemed that he basically preferred his own company, not the irritation of her or anyone else's presence.

She scolded herself for worrying about it and slipped out of her clothes and into a hot shower. Afterwards, she put on a warm and comfortable corduroy jumpsuit with simple lines that accentuated her slim body and gentle curves. But despite the warning she gave herself, she found she was nervous about meeting Simon's grandparents. She walked quietly down the plushly carpeted stairway, for an instant giving way to a fit of giggles as she had a mental picture of herself sliding down the banister with laughing abandon. She heard voices coming from the library and moved in their direction, only to see Simon standing by the French doors that opened out into a stone patio that overlooked the rolling lawns. He had changed into a dark velvet evening suit and was cradling a drink in restless fingers. From the tone of his voice it appeared to Erin that he and his grandparents were having a disagreement about something. They did not see her standing in the doorway but continued their discussion oblivious of her presence.

'It's not that we disapprove, you know that. It's just that we don't know this young man, Allen, and we've never heard of his family,' said the older woman who sat nestled in a huge green chair.

'I told you, he's a good man and he's been good to her and for her. I feel certain that if they do decide to marry, it would be a solid and sound match.' Simon spoke with feeling, obviously striving for understanding from the two older people. 'He may not be from a moneyed family, but he's honest and hardworking and they love each other.' He paused and added, 'And I think they'd be happy together.'

He took a long drink and turned to look at them. 'After all, doesn't at least one of Selma and Richard's offspring deserve a bit of that elusive stuff called happiness?'

There it was again, the anger and hurt that simmered always beneath the surface and bubbled over to sear those who were with him, even those he loved as dearly as he did his grandparents. Erin gathered that they were discussing Nadine's friend Allen Beaumont; Nadine had been dating him regularly, Erin knew, and she now felt embarrassment for overhearing a family discussion. She cleared her throat to indicate her presence.

Simon straightened and walked towards her, lightly taking her hand in his and leading her into the room. 'Albert and Mary, this is the young woman I was telling you about—Erin McCourt. Erin—my grandparents.' She had been presented to a white-haired man almost as tall as Simon, not as broad in the shoulders, but who had surely in his youth been as handsome; and a small frail-looking woman, in whose eyes could be seen the shining light of kindness and contentment as well as an inner core of steel-like strength. Simon had apparently inherited much from these two persons who had figured so greatly in his youth and upbringing.

Simon did not let go of her hand after he had made the introductions, not even after the conversation continued into other channels. She felt her body afire from the merest touch of him and wanted desperately to withdraw her hand from his. And too, she realised that something within her wanted just as desperately to feel comfortable with his hand holding hers.

Dinner was more enjoyable than Erin expected. Simon's grandparents were wonderful people who loved and respected him and they made Erin welcome in their home. She found herself feeling a part of a family again, which made her realise just how much she actually missed her own parents in Montreal.

Simon had apparently come by his love of the sea naturally, for his grandfather had, in his younger days, captained a schooner out of Halifax. Simon and the older man seemed to share a camaraderie and closeness that one

usually saw between a father and son. This observation
jolted Erin into remembering that for all practical purposes,
Albert Grayson was in fact a father to Simon. But in spite
of this fact, and despite the love that they held for each
other, the older man had not been able to erase the pain
and scars of Simon's betrayal by his parents.

It was nearly midnight when Mary indicated that it was
well beyond their bedtime. She smiled and spoke softly.
'At our age, you seem to need more rest, somehow.' She
kissed Simon and Erin and began to leave the room. 'Come
on, Albert, let these two have some time alone.'

Albert turned to them before leaving the room. 'You have
a long trip back tomorrow, so you'd best be getting some
rest too.' He grinned, a friendly glint in his eyes. 'And I
nearly forgot, son, there's a change in the forecast.
Weather's going to close in about mid-afternoon tomorrow,
higher winds than you expected and rain squalls. Maybe
you'd best get an earlier start tomorrow than you planned.'
With his he turned to Mary and they left the room. Erin
heard the sound of their footsteps echo on the wooden hallway, growing slightly faint until they disappeared.

She turned, to realise that Simon was staring at her,
staring almost blindly. And for a few moments he did not
seem to be aware that she was now looking at him. Then
suddenly he started and said jerkily, 'I'm sorry ... I ...
don't know where my head was.'

Erin smiled faintly but said nothing. He put his empty
glass on the sideboard and walked steadily towards her.
Standing at last before her, he hesitated, then started to
speak. 'Erin, I ...' but whatever he was going to say, he
changed his mind and turned from her abruptly, moving
quickly to the French doors.

'Is something the matter, Simon?' Erin asked tentatively,
unsure of what was wrong but feeling certain that something was bothering him.

'No, nothing. Go to bed. I'll waken you early in the morning.' With these sharp words, spoken with his broad back
to her, he flung open the doors and disappeared into the
cold night.

Despite her tiredness, Erin did not sleep well. She lay

awake for hours until she finally heard Simon's footsteps in
the hallway and the soft click of his door closing. She lifted
herself up on her elbow and flicked on the light to check
the time. It was nearly two o'clock. Frustrated with her in-
ability to sleep, even when she was desperately tired, she
turned off the light, punched the pillow and determinedly
closed her eyes, demanding that sleep claim her. And it did,
but it was not a peaceful sleep. She tossed and turned, the
weight of the bedclothes heavy on her slim body.

Dream images fused with one another: Peter, his face
fluid, unfocused and angry, floated before her eyes. She
tried to run, to get away, but movement would not come to
her. She strained against the force that kept her chained to
inertia and cried out in the enfolding darkness, 'No, Peter,
no! Please let me go ... I want to go ... No ... No ...!'
Her pleas mingled with tears that filled her throat and
streamed down her face.

'Erin! Erin, wake up.' Strong arms lifted her up from
the bed. 'Wake up, Erin. You're having a dream. It's all
right.' Words soothed and comforted her as she shuddered
and buried her face against Simon's chest.

'Oh, Simon,' her voice quivered, 'I'm sorry. I must have
wakened the whole house. I don't know what happened.'

Simon sat down on the edge of the bed, still cradling
her in his arms, holding her small tense body to his. His
lips brushed her tangled hair. 'Ah, Erin, what in God's
name did he do to you? You've got to try and forget him.
Let it be and go on from here. God knows you can't live
with the past and expect to stay sane. It can't be done,
Erin.' Anger filled his voice and his body with its surging
power. 'I'd kill him if I could lay my hands on him!'

Erin shook her head, wondering at the strength and
passion of his outburst of anger. 'No, Simon, he did nothing to me. It's only me. I expect too much of people and I
expected too much of him. I was the fool and I got what I
deserved, I guess.'

'You're no fool to expect truth and honesty from someone you love and who claimed to love you. Your Peter Hall
was the fool, girl.' They sat for long moments in the darkness of her room, Simon's warm body held her close.

Finally he spoke, his voice husky in the darkness. 'Are you all right now? I think you'd better get some rest. It's a long trip and we should get an early start.'

She pressed closer against him, her voice drowsy and frightened that he would leave her. 'No, Simon, please. Don't leave me yet. Stay with me, just a while longer.'

He placed her on the bed and leaned over her, his mouth searching hers, gently at first and then increasing passion. 'Oh, Erin,' he groaned, 'do you know what you're asking of me?' She felt the tide of passion rise within him and the weight of his long powerful body move over hers, his hands seeking her breast through the filmy nightgown she wore. 'Erin ... Erin ...' he whispered.

She should have been frightened, but instead felt her passion responding to his, her hands pulling his face to hers. She felt the roughness of the mat of tight hair on his chest against her, but she did not want his gentleness now, she wanted his desire and she knew it. She wanted this man and not Peter. 'Don't leave me, Simon. Stay with me,' she pleaded.

No sooner had she spoken these words than he wrenched himself away from her. He pulled himself up from the bed, running his fingers through his rumpled hair, fighting for control. 'This is insane. There'd be nothing but grief in this for both of us, Erin. And I doubt if either of us could stand much more of that.'

She longed to call him back to her, to tell him of her feelings, but she could not stand the thought of his rejection. He had been carried away by a desire of the moment, he was doing what any man would have done. And she was ashamed of the feelings she had displayed. It was Peter she had loved, Peter whom she still loved, and yet her body had betrayed her. No man would ever again have the chance to hurt her as Peter had done. And so the voice Simon heard when she finally spoke was cold and distant. 'Of course you're right, Simon, it is insane, I'm sorry I permitted it to happen. Goodnight.'

The journey home was a silent one. They made good time, for the wind was brisk and *Early Summer* was a fine-lined and fast sloop. Nevertheless, despite their excellent timing, the sky became grey and darkened about mid-afternoon. To Erin the sea had become a threatening entity and fear welled within her. The fact that Simon was so withdrawn did nothing to quell her apprehension. He must have noticed this, for when he did speak he did so quite gently, trying to reassure her. 'It's all right, Erin, there's nothing to be afraid of. I've sailed in weather worse than this. We'll be home within the hour, I promise.'

In spite of Simon's reassuring words, Erin remained tense and frightened. The sea was no longer a sparkling and beautiful blue; in her eyes it had become a grey yawning monster and its change of rhythm terrified her.

Simon tried again. 'I'm sorry, Erin. We should have left Halifax sooner. It was my fault, but I thought you needed the sleep.'

Simon's words of apology eased her obvious reactions to some degree, for she did not want him to feel that she did not trust him. 'No, Simon, really, it's all right. I'm okay.'

He touched her hand lightly. 'Here, take the tiller for a moment, I've got to check the stays at the bow. You know what to do.' In her mind she wanted to scream no. She wanted him not to move, not to leave her any part of the responsibility for the boat, for it seemed too light and fragile on this vast moving sea. But she did as he asked and watched him as he moved steadily and easily forward to the bow. Long moments passed and she watched and waited for his return. He finished what he was doing and started back.

Then she realised that she had not been as careful as she should have been, for she had allowed *Early Summer* to change direction. She heard Simon call to her over the sound of the wind. 'Move the tiller! Move the tiller!' She quickly did as she was told, but in the wrong direction. The boom swung around suddenly and smashed into Simon, who was lowering himself into the cockpit. Erin heard herself shriek in terror as Simon's lips issued a low groan of pain before his body was flung over the side. But he was not swept away. Somehow, by some mad miracle, he had been able to grab hold of the side, and now he clung there, unmoving. For a moment Erin thought him to be unconscious, for his eyes were closed and his head swayed from side to side with the motion of the boat. She started to get up and move towards him, but his eyes opened and he said weakly, 'No ... stay where you are. Don't move. Just throw me that line ... and hurry.'

She did as she was told, fighting the impulse within her to rush to him and try and drag him back into the boat. His voice, still unsteady, barely rose above the wind. 'Hold her steady, Erin. Hold her steady.' For long moments after he had the rope tied around him, he stayed there, holding on to the side, his body half submerged in the icy water. He was obviously waiting and trying to gather enough awareness and strength to pull himself back into the boat.

'Please let me help you,' she called to him, frightened by his lack of movement and effort. 'Let me help!'

'No, I'm okay ...' And with a mighty surge he pulled himself up and almost into the boat. But not quite. In a swift second he had lost even the tenuous grip he had been able to maintain during these last moments. He sank back into the water and released his white-knuckled hold from the edge.

Erin screamed, 'No! Don't let go. You'll be drowned! Don't let go!' But the boat moved on and Simon's unconscious body was being swept away. Without stopping to consciously think about it, Erin secured the tiller with a rope and prayed that for the next few minutes the wind would hold, that there would be no shift. She crawled to the side and began to pull on the line, her hands burned by the rope, but she would not give in. 'You can't have him! He's going to live, do you hear me! He's going to live!' She was shouting angrily at some invisible and mighty force. She would not let him drown. Gradually she was able to bring him back to the side, not knowing how she would get him into the boat if he wasn't conscious to help her. His dark hair was a slick helmet on his head and she saw the purpling bruise on the side of his face—the result of her mindless and stupid mistake. She had almost killed him. The very thought that perhaps she couldn't get him into the boat, that after all this he could perhaps freeze to death in the icy water, squeezed desperate sobs from her. 'Please God, please don't let him die.'

But she could think of nothing else to do. Lifting his great weight was unthinkable and impossible. 'Simon, wake up. Please, Simon!' She held on to him until her hands were numb with the wet and cold, until she felt that she could hold no longer. Then he moaned and shifted slightly in the water. Somehow she knew that the movement belonged to him and was not just the movement of the sea against his inert body. His glazed eyes opened and he looked at her, unseeingly.

'Let go of me ... I ... told ... you ...' His words were slurred.

'Stop it, Simon. Don't frighten me. Just help me. Try to boost yourself in, I'll pull. Push yourself up. Please, you've got to try!' She begged and pleaded with him frantically. She felt the boat give a small lurch and thought wildly that now even the wind would forsake them, would conspire to destroy them. But she was able to cajole and threaten and drag Simon into the boat. As his sodden body lay on the floor of the cockpit, she knelt beside him, feeling the coldness that possessed him. It was then that the final irony struck her—she had saved him, but chances were they would both be lost, for there was no way that she could guide *Early Summer* into harbour, no possible way they could reach safety unless Simon regained consciousness. They would founder on the rocks at the harbour's mouth, within sight of shelter and safety.

'Simon, please wake up. Please, Simon!' Her voice was shrill with fear. She was sobbing, not knowing what to do next. She fell down next to him, cradling his head in her lap, her tears mingling with the cutting salt spray.

He stirred and moved slightly. 'Simon, Simon——' she called over the now howling wind. He opened his eyes and seemed to be aware of her and what had happened.

'How far ... how far have we come, Erin?'

'We're at the mouth of the harbour—Abbotsford ...'

'Help me up, please.'

She helped him stagger to the tiller, aware of the cost of this effort to him. Quickly he swung *Early Summer* around and they moved swiftly before the wind and into the safety of the harbour. Simon was able to bring the boat safely alongside the wharf before he allowed his body to relax and he sat slumped in the cockpit.

'Can you make it to the house?' Erin asked. 'Should I go and get someone?'

'No, I'll be all right. Maybe you could just give me a hand up to the house. I need to get warm, then I'll be okay.'

Erin walked stoically up the beach with him, Simon trying not to lean too heavily upon her. Somehow they managed to make it to the house, where he leaned against the wall at the entrance. 'Dear God, I think that was pretty damn close.' He put a tentative hand to his face and winced in pain.

'Maybe you should go to the hospital and have that checked. You could have concussion or something. It's badly bruised and it really looks awful. You shouldn't sleep after you've had a blow to the head or anything. Do you hear me, Simon? ...' Erin's words fell quickly as she began to release all the emotion she had pent up within her for the last hours.

Simon gently touched her face with his cold hands. 'Hush, Erin, it's over now. You're freezing, and needless to say, so am I. Go into Nadine's room and change your clothes and take a hot shower. Right now. Dr Grayson's orders. I'm about to do the same thing.'

Reaction set in when Erin was alone. She couldn't stop shaking and shivering long after the hot shower and long after she was warmly dressed in a pair of Nadine's cords and thick sweater. She couldn't move to go outside to see Simon, as all the fearful images of the experience swept back upon her. Simon found her curled up in a tight ball on Nadine's bed, dry sobs racking her body. She jumped at the touch of him. 'No! Don't touch me. Don't come near me. I want to go, I want to leave, right now. I want to go home!' Her voice rose as the hysteria mounted within her.

'Erin, stop it! You're all right now. You're safe.' His strong arms reached out and pulled her gently to him and held her. 'I'm so sorry about all of that,' he said evenly. 'It was my fault. I should have watched more carefully.'

The dry tears had turned to salt now and Erin was crying openly in his arms. 'You nearly died ... I nearly killed you. I ... in the water ... you were nearly lost and I ...'

He shook her gently. 'Stop it! You saved my life and you know it.'

'Yes, but only after I nearly took it from you. I was so stupid, I told you that you shouldn't have taken me with you. I'll never set foot in a boat again. Never ... never!'

'Don't be ridiculous. Of course you will. You'll crew with me again, wee Erin, believe me.' His lips gently brushed her hair and she turned a tear-stained face to his. He moaned and his mouth found hers, tenderly at first and then with increasing passion and desire. He lowered her to the bed, covering her with the length of his strong body, his hands moulding and holding her to him. They lay together for long moments, their bodies hungrily seeking the closeness and the passion of each other. His kisses became more searching and the pressure of his body on hers more demanding.

'Oh, Simon,' she whispered, her mind whirling in the sea of her emotions. Suddenly he pulled away from her, lying beside her with his hand covering his face.

'Dear God, what's happening to me? What am I doing to you?' He groaned with undisguised desperation.

Erin, desolate with this new abandonment, fought against the tears that stung her eyes. 'I think you should take me home, please, Simon, I just want to go home.'

He swung his long legs from the bed, turned and helped her to her feet. Shaking his head, he released a heavy sigh. 'Yes, it's time you went home, Erin.'

It was only a walk of mere minutes from Simon's place to hers and Erin contended that she could easily walk it, but it was raining heavily by this time and Simon insisted on driving her. They drove in silence, Erin once again wondering not only at her response to Simon but also at the strength and passion of her feelings. She was being a weak-minded fool who was letting herself be overcome with her loneliness and the fact that she was missing Peter. This would have to stop; she would have to seize control of her emotions and act accordingly. She must not let Simon Grayson take advantage of her vulnerability, for he was a hard and cruel man in spite of the faint glimmerings he sometimes showed that inside there was a man who was alone and who needed someone, perhaps as much as she needed Peter.

She was startled from her thoughts by Simon's impatient voice. 'Are you coming, or are you planning to daydream the rest of the evening alone in my car?'

She looked up quickly and saw that they had arrived at her home and Simon was standing at her side of the car, her gear in one hand, holding the door for her with the other. His hair was wet from the rain.

'I'm sorry, I ...' She mumbled her apologies and scrambled quickly from the car, ran up the steps before him, and flung open the door.

'Don't you keep your door locked?' he asked, his voice was still impatient.

'No, I ... seem to have misplaced the key and ——'

'You should get another made tomorrow. It's a lonely stretch of beach and you should be able to lock your door. You're a woman alone here, no sense being foolish.' He walked through to the kitchen and deposited her gear on the table. At that point the silence of the house was shattered by the shrill ring of the phone. Without hesitation, Simon lifted the receiver and answered it. 'Hello?' He paused, his face becoming a mask of clouded emotions that Erin could not interpret. 'No, she's here. Just a moment.' His tone was sarcastic and he glowered darkly as he held out the receiver, his hand over the mouthpiece. 'It's your lord and master, my dear, your precious Peter.'

Erin took the receiver from him, her hand brushing against his for a slim second. But it was long enough for her to experience again the electrifying feeling that overcame her whenever they touched. Her voice faltered when she spoke. 'Hello ... Peter?' Simon strode from the kitchen and she expected to hear the door slam to announce another angry departure, but he did not leave. She turned her attention to Peter. 'I'm sorry, the connection is bad. There's quite a storm here, so that must be it.' For a long while she listened to his angry tirade of accusing questions. Finally she broke in. 'How was I to know you were going to call this weekend? You have no right to expect me to be here to answer your calls whenever the whim strikes you to make them ... I'm sorry, I didn't mean to ... no, he's ... no one special ... he's just a friend ... please, Peter ... he's the brother of a friend of mine ... that's all ... yes, all right. Goodbye.'

She walked slowly from the kitchen to the living room. Simon was standing at the window looking out at the grey seas crashing against the shore. The clouds hung heavy and leaden grey, pushing down and threatening to suffocate them with the darkness that seemed to live in this very room.

'That was Peter Hall, my ex-fiancé,' she said quietly.

'I know who it was, he was very clear about who he was and about his relationship with you. He didn't mention the ex- part of it, however.'

'What do you mean by that?' Erin straightened as if to fortify herself for the attack but it didn't come. There was only an angry and accusing look.

'I asked you what you meant by that remark?' she repeated.

'What do you take me for, Erin, a fool? Your Peter Hall spoke as if he still had a claim on you and you seemed to act as if you felt he did too.'

'There you go again, telling me what I feel and how I am supposed to act. I'm sick of it, and I'm sick of you! Thank you for a very interesting and, to say the least, exciting weekend. Now will you please get out.'

'With pleasure, I assure you,' he said harshly. At the door he paused and turned, his eyes still dark with anger. 'But don't let this whole thing upset you too much, Erin. After all, I'm no one special ... just the brother of a friend.' The door slammed with a force that shook the house, and once again Simon Grayson left her feeling confused and hurt as he disappeared into the darkness.

CHAPTER FOUR

IT was nearly ten o'clock before Erin arrived at work the next morning, to be greeted by Nadine's laughing voice. 'Now, that must have been some weekend when you can't make it to work on time the next day! You and my brother must have really tuckered yourselves out doing the big city thing.' She stopped her friendly teasing long enough to interject a serious question—'Did you have a good weekend? Do you like him? What do you think?'

Erin raised a mocking, warning hand. 'Slow down, my friend, your questions are falling over one another!'

'Well, don't avoid them, tell me what you think,' insisted Nadine.

'I had a good weekend.' Erin shrugged mentally as she remembered the harrowing narrow escape that Simon had in the cold waters off Abbotsford and the distressing incident surrounding Peter's call. She wondered if 'good' was the word to describe the weekend.

Nadine put down a print she was examining. 'You don't sound so sure about that. Do I detect a note of hesitancy in the admission?'

'No, of course not,' Erin lied. 'Well, to be honest with you, he certainly isn't the easiest person to get along with, is he?'

Nadine laughed. 'Ha! Anyone who's ever met him once can tell you that. He can be very difficult to live with, believe me. But he's the best man I know.' She grinned shyly, 'Next to Allen, I guess.'

On that note Erin shifted the conversation to Allen.

'Things seem to be getting a bit serious in that quarter, don't they?'

'Umm ... yes, I hope so. I've liked Allen a long time. He's always been friendly with us and he's been a steady friend of Simon's, even when the trouble with his department made it—oh, what could you say—politically expedient not to be friendly with either Simon or his sister.'

'I don't understand—trouble with his department? What's that all about?'

'Simon's always gone his own way, no matter what the cost to him personally. He speaks his mind and he fights for what he believes. Outspokenness and truthfulness are not necessarily endearing qualities, Erin, and Simon always seems to be in the centre of some boiling controversy in the English Department. Actually, there's one particular professor, a Gerald Bendix, who has, for some reason that I can't fathom and neither can Simon, taken a violent dislike for him. In fact, I'd go so far as to say he hates Simon, really hates him, and that sometimes frightens me. I think that some day this man will take his chance and try to destroy Simon—somehow, I don't know how. All I do know is that it frightens me a lot when I see him; a few times, at a party, I've seen Bendix look at Simon, as if ... as if ... well, he had the look of a hunter waiting for the right time to kill.'

The intensity of Nadine's words and feelings created an ominous foreboding in Erin.

'And no matter what anyone says or believes about him, Erin,' Nadine continued, 'Simon is not a cruel man, he's more vulnerable than many might believe.' Her voice quivered and her eyes filled with tears. 'He deserves better than much of what's happened to him—first our parents left and then Adria and Elice were killed. He's always been bitter about Mom and Dad leaving us, but it didn't really control his life. But after the accident when *they* were killed, he just wasn't the brother I knew at all. For months he avoided all contact with anyone. Gradually he came back, but he's different, he's always a bit withdrawn now, and he's so much more cynical and harsh, so cold at times with people. Somehow I don't think he means to hurt those he loves or he's with, but I suspect that it's his strategy for survival.'

The two women stood looking at one another, Erin deeply affected by the love and concern Nadine revealed for her brother. She felt awkward and unsure of what to say. 'How long ago was it that his wife and daughter were killed?'

'Nearly eight years ago, a few years after we came to Abbotsford.'

'You lived with them then?'

'Yes, I wanted to come with Simon and he wanted me, and our grandparents didn't mind. I think Adria resented my being there, but Simon wanted me with him, so that's the way it was.'

They escaped into their own private thoughts and for a long time did not speak, but worked alone. Erin looked up at the clock and realised she had a class in fifteen minutes.

It was Nadine who broke the silence. 'I've got a bit of a problem, Erin.'

'Oh, what's that?' Erin looked up from her work.

'Simon asked me a few weeks ago to go with him to his cabin in the Sweet Mountains this weekend.'

'Oh—where's that?'

'In New Brunswick, a few hours' drive from here.'

'So what's the problem?'

'Well, Allen has asked me to the Octoberfest and the dance is on Saturday night. I want to go so much. I've wanted nearly two years for that man to notice me as more than "just a friend".' The phrase struck a sad note in Erin as she remembered when she had so carelessly and unthinkingly used it last ... 'And now he has noticed me—I think he has, anyway. And I want to go with him, but I don't want to disappoint Simon. I promised him I'd go with him and help get the cabin ready for winter. Besides, it's not good for him to be alone so much.' She dropped a print on the floor. 'Damn, what am I going to do? What would you do? Tell me honestly.'

Erin smiled. 'Simon would understand, Nadine, I'm sure. Explain the situation to him and you'll see. Really, I feel certain that he'd want you to go with Allen.'

'Do you really think so?' Nadine asked hopefully.

'Yes, I really think so—ask him anyway and find out, why don't you?'

'Ask him what?'

Both Erin and Nadine started at the intrusion of the deep masculine voice. They turned to see Simon leaning against the doorframe.

'Good morning, Simon.' Erin tried to make her voice friendly and betray none of the nervous flutterings that she was experiencing inside at the sight of him.

'Hi, Erin—Nadine. How are you both this morning?' Neither his voice nor his face showed any sign of the anger of last night. It was then that Nadine noticed the dark bruise on the side of his face.

'Simon! What happened to your face? Have you seen a doctor? What happened?' She reached out to touch the bruise.

'Don't touch, baby sister—it's still a little tender.' He gave a sideways glance at Erin. 'She's a very tough lady, that one, believe me.'

Nadine looked in confusion at Erin.

'What happened, Erin?' she asked, her frustration getting the best of her.

'Ease off, Nadine,' Simon interjected. 'A small accident aboard *Early Summer*, but nothing to get so excited about. We'll tell you all about it some day soon,' he glanced at his watch, 'when we all have more time.'

'What are you doing here so early anyway?' asked Nadine. 'You're usually not in until one o'clock at least on Mondays.'

'I have an eleven o'clock meeting with one of my thesis students and I just dropped in to say "hi" to my favourite sister and her good friend.'

Erin looked up quickly, afraid that his comment reflected some angry feeling from last night, but Simon's tanned face was pleasant and smiling. 'Now what do you have to ask me, sister of mine?'

'Oh—nothing, really ... it's not important. Just forget it,' Nadine stammered.

'Well, from all indications it would seem that my sister has some kind of problem, for only on such occasions, Erin, does she find herself at a loss for words. For, as you undoubtedly have noticed, talking a lot and loudly is definitely her favourite pastime.'

Erin laughed in the midst of this healthy camaraderie shared by Nadine and her brother. It was evident that they loved and cared a great deal for each other.

'Now, what is it, Nadine? I've only got about ten minutes, so tell me outright and don't play little games with me.'

Nadine pouted, but was not suffering from hurt feelings; she seemed, on the other hand, to be totally enjoying the joking and attention she was getting. 'Well, Allen has asked me to the Octoberfest this weekend and I promised you that I'd help at the cabin and now I don't know what to do,' she explained quickly, barely stopping for a breath.

Simon winked at Erin. 'Erin, do you think this gal's mind is in as much of a jumble as her tongue?'

'I fear sometimes that it may be, Simon, but there's a note of hope—her heart is definitely in the right place.'

'Stop it, you two! Stop teasing me so. Before there was only Simon—now you're in on the deal, Erin. I can handle Simon, but not both of you!' Nadine threw a wet sponge at Simon, which he caught and quickly returned, not missing his mark.

'Look, Nadine, I've got to run, but don't worry about it. Go with Allen and enjoy yourself. I can handle things at the cabin.'

Erin began gathering her papers, getting ready for class. 'I'll be back in about an hour, Nadine, and maybe we could have lunch together if you like. 'Bye, Simon.' But before she could leave, Nadine's excited voice called her back.

'No, wait. I have a brilliant idea.' She turned to Simon. 'Why don't you take Erin with you this weekend? She'd love it up there, and she could help you ...'

Erin sensed Simon's immediate and cautious withdrawal. 'Slow down, Nadine.' He shook his dark head. 'Erin probably doesn't want to come. She ...'

Nadine turned quickly to Erin. 'Well, what do you think? Do you want to go? It's really so beautiful there, you'd love it, I know you would. I just know it.' Nadine's excitement was infectious and Erin had to admit that she had caught some of it. But she was hesitant, unsure of Simon's feelings about the suggestion and unsure whether she was up to spending another weekend with him and his fluctuating moods.

'I don't know, Nadine, I ...'

Nadine interrupted her again to add more weight to her argument. 'Erin, take your photography equipment. It's the chance of the century, it can be a working weekend for you as well. Believe me, the Sweet Mountains in October are the absolute best!' She nudged Simon. 'Go ahead, persuade her. Tell her what it's like there.'

Simon stared steadily at Erin and for a moment she thought he wasn't going to speak at all. When he did, his voice was quiet. 'You'd be a welcome guest and work partner this weekend, Erin.' He hesitated, then added, 'But don't let Nadine persuade you to do something you don't want to do. Think about it and let me know later in the week.'

Erin startled herself with the suddenness and sureness of her response. 'No, I don't need to think about it any longer. I would like to come with you.' She blushed slightly at this outspoken expression of her feelings and under the warmth of Simon's gaze.

'Good, we'll leave Saturday morning and be back on Sunday. Now I've got to go, no delaying it any longer. 'Bye, Nadine.' And he kissed her lightly on the cheek. Nadine, smiling like the proverbial Cheshire cat, was obviously satisfied with the way things had turned out. Simon touched Erin's arm. 'Come on, I'll walk with you, part of the way at least.'

They only walked a short distance before Simon stopped at the building which housed his office. 'Are you going to the faculty reception tonight, Erin?' he asked.

'Yes—yes, I am. Another of Nadine's persuasions,' she added jokingly.

'Listen,' he started seriously, 'I ... I want to apologise for the way I acted yesterday. You're right, your life is none of my business. I had no right to say anything.' She looked into his eyes and saw some emotion she could not define. 'I appreciated what you did for me yesterday, saving my life and all.' She couldn't believe it, the cool and controlled Simon Grayson was actually uncomfortable, saying these things to her. She glanced again at her watch, aware now that she was five minutes late for class.

'I've got to go, Simon, I'm already late. I'll probably see

you there tonight.' Over her shoulder she called back to him, 'That is, if you're going.'

She ran across the spacious lawn, her long black hair flying in the wind, unaware that Simon stood on the steps of the Arts Building and watched her until she disappeared into the Art College.

That evening Erin went alone to the reception held in the faculty club. She was not comfortable at affairs of this nature and as she expected she found that she would have preferred a quiet evening at home. But Nadine had persuaded her that it was her duty as a new member of the faculty to attend and meet fellow staff members. 'Besides,' Nadine had assured her, 'they always have good food.' And so Erin found herself, by mid-evening, staring into a blur of faces still no more familiar to her than at the beginning of the evening. She had spoken to Nadine for a few moments before she was reclaimed by Allen and had been introduced to Dr Haley, the President of the college. But most of the time she spent feeling quite awkward and out of place, searching the crowd for a glimpse of Simon's face. But as the hours slowly melted away, he had still not appeared.

A flurry of activity and loud laughter erupted at the entrance to the club and served to announce Francine Haley's arrival. Erin inwardly chastised herself for reacting as she did about the very thought of this girl; after all, she hardly knew her. A sharp pang of jealousy was added to her feeling of dislike, however, when she saw Francine was escorted by Simon Grayson.

Fighting to control her inexplicable feeling, Erin counted herself a fool. How could she possibly let this man affect her so, time and time again? Hoping that she could avoid being seen by him, she moved quickly away from the group and into the shadowed quiet of the faculty reading room. Strangely enough, the sight of Simon with Francine brought disturbing tears to her eyes. She stood staring out the window into the darkness of the night, confused and yet compelled by this strange and strong attraction that somehow, outside her control, had developed within her for Simon Grayson. She stood there in the shadows, not aware of the passing time; the faint tinkle of glass and the distant mumbling of voices reached her but did not intrude on the feeling of isolation.

Suddenly she became aware of movement at the door and she drew back deeper into the shadows of the corner of the room. She wanted to be left alone, the farthest thing from her unhappy mind at this moment was the thought of having to carry on a shallow and banal conversation with someone who couldn't really care less about her. All she wanted to do now was to go home to the security of her own place. But whoever it was had entered the room, perhaps with the same intention of escape.

She quietly turned from the window, still concealed from sight in the shadows, and saw that it was Simon who had come in. Her heart leapt and she drew a quick breath. He dropped heavily into a chair and drank deeply from the glass in his hand, running his fingers through his thick hair. His shoulders drooped as if he were too tired to be here. Just then an older man, whom Erin had noticed earlier in the evening, entered the room, evidently seeking Simon out. But Simon stood immediately and headed for the door.

'Well, well, Dr Grayson. I trust you're well and enjoying this evening. I expect also that you're ready for our staff meeting tomorrow.' The man waved a careless hand in the direction of the crowd outside. 'If you're looking for Francine, she's not here. She's mingling, as a good hostess should.'

'Hello, Gerald.' Simon's greeting was emotionless and brief and again Erin sensed his cautious withdrawal as he began to move past the older man to the large room. So this was the Professor Gerald Bendix of whom Nadine had spoken. Erin saw Bendix's hand grip Simon's arm in a manner that could not be construed as friendly, his upper lip curling in dislike when he spoke.

'Oh, don't run away, Simon. You and I have a few things to say to each other, I think, before tomorrow's meeting.' Bendix's hand remained on Simon's arm, and when Simon spoke it was with steely reserve and control.

'We have nothing to say to one another before tomorrow, Gerald. I'm surprised that you deluded yourself into thinking that there was even a slim possibility of lobbying successfully for my support. You know exactly where I stand on the issue and the others will know tomorrow.'

'Now don't be a fool, Simon, you know as well as I do that this time I shall be department head. I ...'

'Take your hand off my arm, Gerald, and bring this so-called amiable conversation to an end,' Simon ordered.

Bendix slowly withdrew his hand, but he made no attempt to end the discussion. 'I've had it with you, Grayson, it's time you fell into line with everyone else. You and your reputation do nothing for this college, and I'm tired of your slanderous attacks on me during departmental meetings.'

Simon's voice revealed the tenuous hold he maintained on his temper. 'Is that what you call it, Gerald? Slander? The hell it is! My courses may not be organised the way you think they should be, but by God, do you think they're designed by mere whim? I've researched carefully, and I have sound and logical support for what I'm doing. Can't you see that I'm not attacking you when I defend my own philosophy of teaching, my own research?' Simon moved away. 'And if you can't see it, you're more paranoid than I thought you were.'

Bendix was not to be stopped; his voice rose, shrill and angry. 'Damn you, Grayson! I'll see you removed from this department and this college, in disgrace. People will know the truth of what you are, I'll see to it. I owe it to Abbotsford!'

'Don't be ridiculous—you're not doing this for Abbotsford and you know it. You're on the bandwagon for Gerald Bendix, who never was able to accept the fact that he was passed over for the chairmanship of the department last time. Wake up and face the truth for a change.' Simon gave free rein to his anger. 'And I'm sick of the whole thing, if you really want to know the truth. You've managed to turn a solid English Department into warring camps just because you can't stand me as a person, because my work here threatens you and your chances of being the next department head. This place should be able to function in a healthy way with more divergent philosophies than ours,

Gerald. But no, you won't be satisfied until you tear it apart.'

For a single breathless moment, Erin saw Bendix move suddenly as if he intended to physically strike Simon. 'I wouldn't try it if I were you,' Erin heard Simon caution.

'I'll see the end of you yet, Grayson. Your kind can't last here,' Bendix rasped. 'You——'

His latest tirade was interrupted by the entrance of Dr MacIntosh, the head of the English Department, to whom Erin had been introduced earlier in the evening. 'Good evening, Gerald—Simon. It would appear that you two are having a pleasant evening—and another of your *friendly* discussions. Don't you two ever weary of your armed battles?'

Bendix, his face flushed and sweating, turned and headed for the door. 'I'll leave you to talk some sense into this ego-tistical fool. He won't listen to a word I have to say.' He added sarcastically, 'It would seem that our famous Dr Grayson can't make himself see beyond personalities.' With these biting words, he left the room.

Simon finished his drink and wearily moved as if to follow.

'No. Stay a moment, please, Simon. I'd like to talk to you about an important matter, if you don't mind.' Kevin MacIntosh smiled at him and added in a soothing tone, 'I promise not to be as hard on you as Gerald has un-doubtedly been.'

Erin drew deeper into the shadows. Escape was impos-sible, for if she emerged now Simon would know she had heard his argument with Gerald Bendix. He would despise her for remaining concealed in the shadows and overhear-ing such an intensely personal and painful conversation. Guilt swept over her and also the strange feeling of want-ing to protect and ease the struggle of this man who was so adamant about defending his principles. Simon's voice in-terrupted her thoughts.

'Need I ask about what, Kevin, or is it the chairmanship again?'

'Stop being so difficult, Simon. Admit it. It's important to you too.'

'Yes, it's important to me. What is there to admit? My teaching is important to me, you know that already, everyone I work with knows it. There's nothing more to admit, as you say.'

'Damn it, boy, be reasonable.'

'Look, Kevin, I don't happen to think I'm being unreasonable.'

'Simon, you've been with this department for eight years, ever since Adria and Elice were killed, and you've been the devil to work with for every single one of those years, and you damn well know it.'

'That's too bad, isn't it! It's just too bad if people like Bendix can't stand to be questioned if they consider a man openly defending his work and philosophy as being "unreasonable".'

'Now who said anything about Bendix? I didn't even mention his name.'

Simon shrugged impatiently. 'Stop playing games with me, Kevin, I've had one hell of an afternoon in meetings with that man, and I'm just too tired to run the course with you. Say what you've come here to say.'

'All right, I will.' Dr MacIntosh drew in a long breath and began. 'I want you to stop being so bullheaded and aggressive in your attacks on Bendix and his supporters. I want you to ease off. Must you always fight Bendix? Can't you learn to compromise?'

Simon replied roughly, 'If I ease off, he'll turn this department into a farce, a comedy that will be more absurd than humorous. There'll be no room here for anyone who doesn't agree with the policies and directions of Bendix and his people. You don't seem inclined to fight him lately, but I have no intention of letting up. I don't compromise. Never.'

Kevin MacIntosh pointed a warning finger. 'All you young people are the same. You think the only way to fight something is out in the open. I'm fighting Bendix, but I'm doing it my way. Do you think I'm unaware of what it would mean to the department if he got the chairmanship when I retire at the end of the year? Whatever you might think of me, son, I'm not a fool.' He shook his head impatiently. 'I want you to be the next head of the department. I want to be able to give my support to you, but you've got to stop being so outspoken and arrogant. What's the matter with you, can't you see there are more astute ways to fight men like Bendix? You're just too young and too outspoken.'

'Damn it, Kevin, I'm thirty-eight years old, and I've lived in this town for thirteen years. It's my home and I know the people. I know how they think and I know how men like Bendix think. Do you believe I've lived this long wrapped in some kind of protective covering? I've lived and I've seen a lot. I will not sell myself for the chairmanship, nor will I sell myself for the sake of popularity with the department members. I'm doing the work the way I believe it's right for me. I live for me.' Simon's body was tense as a coiled spring. 'And I'll continue to do it that way as long as I can breathe, so you might as well accept it.' He paused and added with a note of finality, 'So maybe we'd better just drop the whole thing once and for all. I'm just not the man you're looking for.'

Hidden in the darkness, Erin wished desperately that she had never entered the room. She wanted nothing more but to escape and hear no more of Simon's strained conversation with Kevin MacIntosh. But she had stayed too long; she had to wait until they left.

Dr MacIntosh's pleading voice continued, 'All right, but if it means anything to you at all, you'd better fight to stay here—and become head of the department. Can't you see that people hate to be told so often and so loudly that you don't agree with them? Your behaviour is plainly unorthodox at this college and I'm asking you, for the sake of your career and your place here, to stop going out of your way to alienate people.' He paused, waiting for Simon's agreement or acceptance of his words, but Simon shrugged and said nothing. Dr MacIntosh uttered an angry oath. 'You're a fool, boy. Can't you see I'm trying to save your career?'

'I can see, Kevin, that you're trying to save the department—perhaps at my personal expense,' snapped Simon.

'Sometimes I think that what you really want is to be punished, to be destroyed, to see people tear down everything you've worked so damn hard to build. Where do you get all the guilt you must be carrying inside you, if that's the case?' He raised an impatient hand. 'And don't interrupt me, keep quiet and listen for a change. I suspect you really may be challenging them to try and get you.' He shook his head, as if to indicate that he had at last discovered a saddening secret. 'I'm right, aren't I, Simon? You won't bend until they break you, will you?'

'I don't know, Kevin, I honestly don't know,' Simon responded slowly. 'Maybe you're right. After I lost Elice, my teaching and my writing were all I had left, all I wanted. I ... they were the only things that were still important in my life, but even at the cost of losing them I couldn't give in, not an inch, to a man like Bendix.'

'What do you mean when you say they "were" important to you?'

'I mean that now I think they've never really been enough to survive on, although maybe I've been able to fool myself into believing they were.' Simon rubbed the back of his neck and stretched his tired muscles. 'I've lived alone for eight years now and God knows, I'm so very tired of being alone.'

The older man placed a hand on Simon's shoulder. 'Then don't be alone. Marry Francine.'

Erin gasped inwardly at the suggestion. Everything within her screamed in defiance of this horrifying prospect and she strained to see Simon's response, but she could not. His back was to her.

'Think about it,' she heard Dr MacIntosh continue in a tone of hushed conspiracy. 'Not only are you used to each other, you've known each other for years—so it would be a comfortable union; and right now, believe me, it would be the wisest thing to do, politically. Marry her, Simon, and you might even end up with the presidency of this college one day.'

'Dear God, Kevin ...' Was that a note of unbearable sadness mixed with Simon's evident weariness? Erin couldn't know for sure. A rustle at the door interrupted anything that Simon might have said, and Francine moved to Simon's side, placing her hand possessively on his arm, her voice smooth like silk. 'Ah, there you are, Simon, darling. Come on, join the others. Everyone is wondering where you two escaped to. Don't tell me there's some conspiracy going on right under our noses!'

What was left of the evening passed for Erin like a dull ache. Somehow she was able to force herself to remain, to circulate, and meet people, and to engage them in light chatter. She believed herself successful in her task to hide the sadness and the hurt which filled her at the sight of Simon and Francine laughing together, Francine flaunting her close relationship with Simon.

When Erin felt that she had put in enough time and could now leave without raising comment from anyone, she went to gather her wrap from the small sitting room. A warm hand touched her shoulder as she leaned to pick up her shawl. Startled, she turned quickly, only to find Simon standing behind her. 'Oh, Simon, hello. How ... are you?' Why did she always feel such a loss of composure when she was near him? He had the power to turn her into a tongue-tied schoolgirl.

'I'm fine, Erin, thanks. Are you having a good time?'

She laughed nervously. 'I'm afraid this isn't exactly my idea of what you'd call a "good time". I never do well at affairs like this. I'm about to make good my escape.'

'So I see.' He helped her on with her shawl, his hands lingering on her shoulders. Slowly he drew her small body back against him. 'You look lovely tonight, Erin. A bit paler than usual, but lovely nevertheless.' His hands held her tightly at the sides of her waist. They were alone in the room and the buzzing of chatter from the reception area faded as the rhythm of his breathing filled her ears. The warm masculine smell of him dominated her senses as she became aware of desiring nothing more but to melt into the arms of this tall, dark man.

He turned her round slowly to face him, his fingers gently exploring the back of her neck, her face, and the fine curves of her throat. 'Erin, Erin ...' he muttered, as he pulled her towards his hard, muscular body. His mouth sought hers, passion increasing the strength of its demand, as his lips hardened. They clung to one another with an

almost desperate fervour, until a cold voice from the doorway made Simon move abruptly away from her.

'My, my, my ... what have we here?' Gerald Bendix's
menacing voice continued to drip venomous words. 'This
is certainly a pleasant little scene, dear Simon. Sorry to be
the interloper—heaven only knows what I may have interrupted.'

Simon's body tensed visibly. 'What do you want,
Bendix?'

'My coat, of course, Simon. Just my coat,' Bendix said
smoothly. With pedestrian slowness, he gathered his coat,
scarf, and hat and moved at an equally snail-like pace towards the door. 'Perhaps you shouldn't resume things just
now, right here, Simon, you know how jealous Francine
can be when one she considers to be "property" behaves
in ... well, after all, you know all about the wrath of that
young woman, don't you? ...' Bendix did not finish his
statement but left it as the implication he had intended it
to be.

Now Erin knew the truth of Nadine's words, for she had
seen the look of desired destruction in Bendix's eyes as he
glared with hatred at Simon. The degree of his undisguised
hostility for Simon would undoubtedly drive him to find
his time of action. He was the hunter in this game of his
own design.

Erin shivered, not with cold, but with repulsion at what
she had witnessed and with actual fear of what she felt certain Bendix would try to do. Simon spoke softly, gently.
'There's still a while left for this so-called party and I
should be here, but I'll take you home and come back.'

'No—no, please, I have my car here. You don't need to
do that. You should stay.'

He sounded worried about her. 'Are you all right, Erin?
Look at me.'

She did as he bid her, the fear in her eyes evident. He
spoke with startled surprise. 'You're not afraid of Bendix,
are you?'

She nodded hesitantly.

'Well, don't be. The man is so eaten up with his impotent

bitterness and hatred, he's eventually going to burn himself out.'

Erin wanted desperately to believe Simon, but somewhere deep within her she harboured the disturbing belief that he was underestimating Bendix. 'But ... he hates you, Simon.'

'I know that, but there's nothing for you to fear because of that.'

'But why? Why should any man feel that way about another?'

Simon smiled at her and shook his head gently. 'God, I've found myself a real innocent, haven't I?'

She wriggled away from him. 'Stop it, I'm serious. I don't understand.'

'Neither do I, Erin, but I'm not going to lose sleep worrying about it. One thing I do know is that hatred, like love, doesn't always need a logical reason to explain its existence, believe me. Now come on, I'll take you home.'

'No, Simon. I want to go alone.'

'Are you sure you're all right?'

'Yes ... fine.'

He bent down and kissed her on the lips. 'See you Saturday morning. Goodnight, wee Erin.'

CHAPTER FIVE

THE phone rang on Friday evening while Erin was gathering her things for the weekend. As usual she hesitated before picking up the receiver, wondering if she would hear Peter's voice, no longer entirely sure whether she wanted to or not. So when she finally said, 'Hello,' her voice was hesitant, unsure of itself.

With a surge of pleasure she heard Simon's deep tones at the other end of the line. 'Hello, Erin. We didn't arrange when I'd pick you up, did we? It's about a four-hour drive ... how good are you at getting up early in the morning?'

There was an underlying thread of amusement in his question.

'If I don't have to talk to anyone before I've had my first cup of coffee, I'm fine!' she chuckled. 'Why, what ungodly hour are you thinking of leaving?'

'Six?'

She groaned theatrically. 'I thought this trip was supposed to be for fun!'

'Six-thirty?'

Laughingly she relented. 'Six will be fine. I'm just getting ready now. Am I allowed to take my camera, or will I be spending the whole weekend chopping down trees and hauling wood?'

'Oh, I think a camera would be permissible. I can always use it to take pictures of you chopping down trees! Have you ever done that, by the way?'

'Never.'

He gave a sigh of mock resignation. 'Hired help isn't what it used to be!' Then, suddenly serious, 'I'm looking forward to the weekend, Erin, I'm glad you're coming.'

Disarmed, she said shyly, 'I'm glad you invited me.'

'I'll see you bright and early tomorrow, then.'

'Well, early, anyway!'

He laughed and rang off. A smile playing on her lips, Erin carefully zippered up her camera bag and put her boots and raincoat on the little pile of belongings by the door. Now she'd wash her hair and get to bed early ...

By some miscalculation her alarm rang fifteen minutes late the next morning, so when Simon tapped on the door and let himself in, she had only just had her shower. She came to meet him in a flowered caftan that subtly hinted at the ripe curves of her body; her hair was loosely pulled to the top of her head by a ribbon, although a few damp tendrils clung to her cheeks. She greeted him with a smile, as always bemused by the intensity of his grey eyes, the sinewy hardness of his big body. He was wearing a checked shirt, open at the neck to reveal the dark hair curling on his chest, and a pair of lean-hipped jeans, laced leather hiking boots on his feet. As always there was the impression of leashed power, of sensuality held in check only by intellect.

He stepped closer to her so that she could feel her limbs tremble in anticipation. One hand fell heavy on her shoulder, the other slid to her waist and pulled her nearer still. Blushing, she knew he must now be aware that beneath the long gown she was naked. And then she was crushed against his chest, his hands exploring her pliant figure as his mouth sought, found, and held hers in a kiss of ever-deepening passion. In utter surrender she melted against him, her lips parting under the pressure of his.

Eventually, reluctantly, he released her, twin flames blazing in his eyes, his breathing harsh. With one finger he slowly traced the rounded fullness of her breast to its hardened tip, then laid his palm against her heart, its frantic drumming echoed in the pulse at the base of his throat. There was a long moment of wordless communication between them before he said huskily, 'You'd better get dressed, little mermaid, or the only place we'll be going is to bed.'

Scarlet colour poured into her cheeks, but even so she managed to say wickedly, 'And that would never do!'

He grinned and gave her a rude slap on the rear. 'Get dressed, Erin. Can I help myself to a cup of your delicious-smelling coffee?'

As she pulled on jeans and a close-fitting knit shirt of royal blue, Erin's heartbeat slowly returned to normal. Deliberately she quelled the rational, cautious voice that was inwardly warning her that the last place she should go was a mountain retreat alone with Simon Grayson. That she was helpless to resist his sensuality she knew only too well; it was he who had so far kept matters under control. Equally well she knew she would defy the cold-blooded advice of her conscience, and go with him. To the ends of the earth, she thought recklessly, shoving the caftan in her case and throwing her white nylon jacket around her shoulders.

When she went outside, she was amused to see Robbie filling the tiny back seat of Simon's car; the dog's long pink tongue licked her ear in rough greeting. Simon drove fast but competently, the Mercedes eating up the miles; they stopped for a late breakfast near Truro but soon were on

their way again. Completely relaxed in his company, Erin
leaned back against the seat and imperceptibly drifted off to
sleep. Nearly two hours passed before she became aware of
someone squeezing her arm, and of a voice close to her ear
saying, 'Wake up, Erin. We're almost there.'

With a start she sat up, realising in some confusion that
while she slept she had fallen against Simon, her fingers
curled warm on his thigh. Straightening, she avoided his
eyes and murmured, 'Sorry, I didn't mean to fall asleep.'

'That's all right. But I woke you up to admire the
scenery. I think this is one of the prettiest parts of New
Brunswick.'

She looked around with increasing pleasure. They were
driving along a narrow dirt road on the crest of a hill, the
sweep of the valley to their left, the rounded silhouette of
more hills on the far horizon. Through the valley meandered
a rock-strewn stream, its banks overhung with trailing wil-
lows and alders; in a cleared field a herd of Holsteins grazed
peacefully. Dark patches of spruce and jackpine stained the
slopes, already mottled with the extravagant scarlet and
orange of maples, the gold of birch and poplar; nature's
autumnal palette splashed on in vivid abandon. Erin gave
a sigh of satisfaction. 'It's beautiful!' she breathed.

'Those hills are called the Sweet Mountains. Very aptly
named, as it happens. There are vast tracts of sugar maples
growing on them, and the boiling down of maple syrup is
a valuable source of income here.'

'I've heard about that, but I've never seen it done.'

'You'll have to come here next spring,' he said, casually
assuming that next spring she would still be in Abbotsford.
'Every year I have a sugaring-off party. We boil the sap
until it turns to syrup and then make toffee and maple
butter. Gorgeous stuff! I'll take you up to the sugar shack
this weekend, so at least you'll see where it's done.'

The road had wound down the hillside and now was
faithfully following the bends of the river. In a few minutes
Simon turned on to an even narrower track, bordered by
gnarled maple and beech trees. They bumped over a stone
bridge and crossed a wide expanse of open field before
climbing a perilously steep incline. As they crested the rise,

Erin saw his cabin and gave a spontaneous exclamation of delight. 'Simon, it's lovely!'

He was obviously pleased by her response. Stopping the car, he let Robbie out and then came to stand beside her; Erin let the silence of the patient hills waft over her. They could have been alone in the world, she thought, in a place as akin to paradise as could be imagined. And in a surge of primitive emotion she knew she wanted to be Eve to his Adam.

She glanced up at her companion, whose eyes were wandering over the hills as though greeting long-lost friends. The spot where they were was cradled by the hills, a rolling tapestry of autumn colours, their hues brightened by the sunshine and the clear blue sky. To her left an orchard rambled up the hillside, the tang of near ripe apples carried to her on the breeze; from the laden branches came the warning chirp of a robin, to which a squirrel chittered a cheeky response. And behind her, nestled into the side of the hill, was Simon's cabin, solidly built of handhewn logs, its roof of old-fashioned slate, its chimney of the same grey granite that formed the skeleton of the hills.

'I built it myself, seven years ago,' he said quietly.

With swift compassion she realised that must have been shortly after his wife and daughter had died; perhaps, in the desperately hard physical labour of constructing this haven of wood and stone, he had been able to blunt his grief. 'It must have taken a long time.'

'The best part of two years.' Then, almost curtly, 'Would you like to see the inside?'

'Mm, please.' The interior of the cabin was as pleasing as its outside, for it was panelled throughout in varnished pine, mellow as honey, with hooked rugs scattered on the polished board floors. There were two bedrooms, each charmingly decorated with colonial antiques, and, Erin was relieved to see, a very modern bathroom. But the kitchen had an old-fashioned wood stove, its surface rubbed to a dull black sheen; an orange and green Tiffany lamp hung over the refectory table and benches, while matching crisp gingham curtains framed the square-paned windows that overlooked the valley. The morning sun glinted on the row of copper pots dangling from the beamed ceiling, interspersed with bunches of dried herbs. Ivy trailed gracefully from a pottery vase. 'It's all so spotlessly clean,' Erin marvelled.

'I'd like to be able to tell you I keep it that way myself! But the truth is, a couple from Pleasantvale keep an eye on things for me. They came here yesterday and cleaned and aired the place. I'll get your case in, then shall we go outdoors for a while before lunch?'

Shortly afterwards they set off up the hillside together, Simon carrying a chain saw, Robbie padding at his heels. He pointed out the dead trees among the birch and spruce, chose one, then showed Erin how to use the saw. Under his guidance she made a V-shaped notch in one side of the trunk, followed by a clean slice on the other, so that the tree fell down the slope away from them. She felled two more, gaining confidence in her ability to handle the noisy machine, although its vibrating made her arms and shoulders ache, and she was soon ready to pass it over to Simon. He cut the wood into manageable chunks, which between them they carried down the hill to the chopping block by the cabin.

After they had worked steadily for two hours, Simon turned off the motor of the saw. 'Ready to eat?'

'Do you know, I'm starving!' She looked proudly at the untidy pile of logs waiting to be split. 'We did a lot, didn't we?'

'We' was the right word, she found herself thinking, for they had worked as a team, Simon giving her an equal share of the labour. How different from Peter, who by treating her as fragile and feminine, had at times caused her to feel both useless and helpless. She tucked this away in the back of her mind for further consideration, and then, suffused with a glow of well-being, she stretched unselfconsciously to get the kinks out of her back. The thin fabric of her shirt was pulled taut across her breasts, and as she relaxed, she caught his eyes on her, sparks of light in their grey depths. Flustered, she stammered, 'What are we having for lunch?'

Putting down the saw, he advanced on her with deliberate slowness. 'How hungry are you?' he asked, his gaze moving from the tumbled silk of her hair to her mouth, where it lay, as possessive as a caress.

Almost suffocating from his nearness, she heard again that inner warning voice. Suddenly afraid, she backed away, her sooty lashes masking her eyes. 'I—I'd like to eat now,' she murmured, side-stepping his body to walk to the door.

'What are you frightened of?' he demanded shortly.

'N-nothing. What makes you think I'm frightened?'

He had caught up with her and now turned her around to face him. 'You're as flighty as a deer.' With an utter seriousness that soothed her fears as rough lovemaking would not have, he went on, 'I won't hurt you, wee Erin, I promise you that—I'll never hurt you.'

With a rush of confidence Erin felt she truly could depend on him, sensing again that rock-like integrity beneath the chiselled features and firmly held mouth, the strong chin and straightforward grey eyes. A shy, sweet smile curved her lips, her eyes wide and vulnerable with new-found trust.

He gave a rough exclamation. 'God! Don't look at me like that! I'm only human, Erin.' Entwining his hands in the sweet-scented weight of her hair, he tilted her face up to his and kissed her gently, as though sealing the promise he had just made to her. It was a moment Erin was to remember to the end of her life, and one which she would often re-live in the long, bitter days to follow. Happiness shimmered in her eyes and there was a new pride in her bearing.

Snapping the tension between them, Simon gave her an uncharacteristically clumsy bear-hug. 'Let's eat! And then I'll take you up the mountain to the sugar shack.'

They started out an hour later through the dried grass and the red-leaved blackberry canes that cloaked the hill. The golden rod had been withered by the frost, but tiny mauve asters still bloomed among the poplar saplings. When the track entered the forest, its floor was soft and springy underfoot. The trees enclosed them in their own kind of silence, the unobtrusive sigh of wind in the high boughs, the thin cheeping of a flock of chickadees, the scrape of one dead branch against another. The path was steep, and Erin was the first one to stop for breath, using as an excuse the sight of a single young maple in a clearing, its scarlet leaves tipped with fire by the sun's rays. She focused her camera and snapped a picture, knowing she wanted something tangible with which to remember this day.

As she caught up with Simon, she wished there was some way she could commemorate on film the Indian-like grace with which he moved, the impression he gave of being totally at home in an environment that for all its beauty could be both dangerous and deadly. It was he who pointed out to her a set of moose tracks imprinted deep in the peat by the edge of a bubbling creek, showed her rabbit runs among the undergrowth, and found her edible mushrooms and wild watercress. Encouraged by her intelligent and enthusiastic interest, he talked of woods survival, displaying a depth of knowledge that impressed her. Before she knew it, the spruce and pine had given way to a tall-trunked stand of maples, their leaves a gold and orange canopy, dappling Erin's uplifted face with shadow. The sugar shack, built of weathered boards with its roof moss-covered, was almost indistinguishable from the forest itself; in her imagination Erin blanketed it with snow, smoke curling from its chimney, steam from its vented roof ... it would be a place of romance, and sharply she longed to be here next spring when the sap rose in the trees.

'Are you tired? Or could you manage another ten-minute hike?'

'Where to this time?' she laughed. 'You surely can't take me anywhere better than this.'

'Wait and see,' was all Simon would say. He held out his hand, and as she took it, she felt inexplicably content to have his fingers laced with hers. Hand in hand they wandered among the stark grey trunks, their feet scuffling through the dead leaves. There was a steep scramble over some rocks, encrusted with lichen, before they came to a rough-hewn bridge of logs over a rushing stream. Down the opposite bank, a steady roar growing ever louder in Erin's ears ... even so, she was unprepared for the sylvan loveliness of the scene that met her eyes.

The bed of the stream had narrowed to a cleft between two great boulders, so that the water burst through and foamed down a fifteen-foot cliff into a deep pool, dark and mysterious even on this day of bright sunshine. Enraptured, Erin could find nothing to say, but her enchanted smile was enough for her companion. Finally she said softly, 'Thank you for bringing me here, Simon, I don't think I've ever seen anywhere more beautiful.'

'I found it by accident a couple of years ago. I think I'm the only person who knows it exists ... I've never seen anyone else here.'

Leaving his side, she clambered down the rocks to the water's edge and dipped her fingers in. It was icy cold but oddly invigorating, and she splashed some on her warm face.

With a rattle of tiny stones, Simon thudded to the bank beside her. 'Want to go for a swim?'

'I'd love to!' she exclaimed, for the rocks had cupped and held the sun's heat to an August warmth, and she was perspiring. 'But'—disappointed—'I can't. No swimsuit.'

'There's no one else here but us—and you must have something on under your jeans and shirt?' His words were a challenge and recklessly she responded to the devil-may-care glint in his eyes.

'If you promise not to look!'

'I'll turn my back until you're in,' he countered, not promising anything at all, she noticed. Slipping into the waist-high bracken, she took off shoes, jeans and shirt, so that she was clad only in her lacy nylon underwear. Then, taking her courage in both hands, she waded quickly into the water. The rocks dropped off steeply and almost immediately she had to swim. Instinctively she headed for the base of the waterfall, where the foam splashed and rolled. Playful as a porpoise, she dived, surfacing in a sheltered crevice behind the tumbling sheet of water. She shook her wet hair back, fascinated by the illusion of security of the curtain of spray, and feeling every nerve of her body tingle with life.

In a moment of utter clarity she knew she had never experienced a day such as today with Peter, had never enjoyed such a synthesis of body and soul as when Simon had kissed her. She and Peter had rushed from party to party, one glamorous and exciting event after another; they had never wandered hand in hand through the woods, or worked side by side at a common task, or exulted in nature's beauty together. They had, she realised now, rarely been alone with each other, but instead had surrounded themselves by crowds of other people ... had they been subconsciously avoiding the shallowness of their relationship, she now wondered, afraid to acknowledge to each other how little they actually had in common?

She was so deep in thought that she gave a visible start when Simon's head broke through the water beside her. 'Sorry—I didn't mean to startle you.'

'It's all right. I—I was thinking,' she stammered.

'What about?' he rapped, his eyes narrowing.

With disastrous honesty, she said, 'About Peter. I was remembering——'

'What the hell are you thinking about him for?' he demanded violently, seizing her bare shoulder with cruel fingers. 'Don't tell me you're still in love with him!'

'I was only——'

'How many times do I have to tell you he's not worth the time of day?'

Answering anger sharpened her voice. 'And how many times do I have to tell you it's really none of your business?'

'Does this make it my business?' With brute force he pulled her towards him. Clasping the back of her neck, he fastened his lips on hers with bruising strength. Her head was forced back and water ran into her nostrils ... terrified, remembering all too clearly the suffocating weight of the sea so short a time ago, she kicked out at him, thrashing free of his grip. Then with the sinuous speed of a silvery fish, she flashed under the spray and stroked towards the shore.

She almost made it. Painfully her elbow scraped bottom, as with her toes she fought for a purchase on the slippery rocks, wanting only to feel solid ground under her feet. But as she gained the safety of the bank she heard the scraping of stones behind her. With a tree trunk at her back, she whirled at bay, her eyes blazing with a mixture of panic and defiance.

Then he was upon her. She tried to scratch his face, but with one hand he pinioned her wrist, with the other clamping her writhing form against his big body. She felt herself thrust backwards and cried out in fear. Although the bracken cushioned her fall to the soft forest floor, the breath was knocked from her body by his weight, and her puny efforts at resistance were of no avail. Her breast heaving, she lay beneath him, helpless. 'I hate you!' she spat.

Astonishingly Simon threw back his head and laughed, then surveyed her with an air of forbearing amusement that she found well-nigh intolerable. 'Hate is the opposite face of love, didn't you know that?'

'I don't love you,' she cried, wishing she could strike the mocking smile from his face. 'I love Peter.' Somehow her words sounded hollow in her ears, but she shut her mind to the implications of this.

'How can you be so stupid?' he demanded, anger again hardening his features. 'You're not in love with that weakling, and you know it.'

'You don't know anything about it!'

'So he's romantic and buys you flowers and treats you like a piece of Dresden china—do you think that's what love's all about?'

'Since you seem to be an expert on the subject, why don't you tell me what's it all about?' she flared, fury dissipating any vestige of caution.

'I won't tell you—I'll show you.'

Their eyes clashed, sapphire against granite. He began kissing her, rough in the heat of his anger. Desperately, Erin tried to steel herself against this new onslaught, her muscles rigid, her mouth tight and hard with resistance. But deep within her she was achingly aware of the masculine hardness of his body on her almost naked flesh, and with every ounce of her willpower fought for self-control.

Abruptly he released her. 'You can't fool me, Erin! I know only too well you're not frigid. Not with me, anyway.'

Burning with humiliation as she recalled how easily and wantonly she had responded to his earlier caresses, she cried, 'Let me go! You're so damned conceited you think all you have to do is kiss me and I'll fall at your feet. Your precious Francine might be like that, but I'm not!'

'Leave Francine out of this.'

'Why should I? You can say anything you like about Peter.'

'That's different and you know it.' His mouth thinned implacably. 'Come on, Erin, admit the truth ... Peter never once aroused you as I can, did he?'

His question was far too near the truth. Wanting only to evade the searching scrutiny of his eyes, she dug one heel into the ground and with all her strength tried to lever her body free of his. As she twisted sideways, a sharp stone scraped her ribs and she cried out in pain, involuntary tears flooding her eyes.

'What's wrong? Are you hurt?'

Blessedly, he had rolled off her. In a childish gesture she rubbed her eyes with her knuckles, leaving a streak of dirt across her face. Even though his fingers on her bruised skin were now incredibly gentle, she winced away from his touch. 'Just leave me alone,' she quavered, still able to muster defiance against him.

'It's only a scratch,' he said coldly, pulling her upright.

Erin glared at him in mute rebellion, too proud to let him see how shaken she really was. 'No thanks to you!'

He took a step towards her. Although desperately afraid, she stood straight and tall, the green fern fronds swathing her legs, the sunlight gleaming iridescently in her hair. 'Get dressed,' Simon ordered with barely concealed contempt. 'I'll wait for you by the bridge. And don't try and find your way down the hill alone, you'll only get lost.'

Since this had been exactly her intention, she flushed with irritation. The wretched man could read her mind! He gave her an ironic little salute, wheeled, and disappeared through the trees; in a few moments she heard the scrape of his hiking boots against the rocks. Then silence fell over the forest.

Slowly she walked over to her heap of clothing and began pulling on her jeans. One thought dominated her consciousness, looming over her like a cloud of fear, blotting out all the carefree pleasure and excitement she had anticipated for this weekend; she was committed to spending the night in an isolated cabin in the company of Simon Grayson.

Now that he was no longer here to see her, she allowed herself to subside on a fallen trunk, as she dispassionately studied the trembling of her hands; had he continued to kiss her, she knew, she would have weakened, and been swept up in that tide of desire he could so easily evoke.

She did up her shirt, hiding the red patches on her shoulders and arms that would soon darken to bruises, and considered her various alternatives ... she could try and reach the cabin before him, take the car and drive to safety. But she would probably be unable to locate the cabin again, for she had not been paying attention to landmarks on her way up; furthermore, she didn't know where the car keys were kept ... she could follow him down the hill and tell him she wanted to leave immediately—but what if he refused, as seemed only too likely? ... or she could bide her time, keep her eyes peeled for the keys and simply drive off without him the first chance she got.

Of the three, this last seemed to her the best plan. Strengthened by her decision, she padded through the woods, past the roar of the falls, over the mossy boulders. He was waiting for her, indolently leaning against a beech tree. When he saw her he turned and started off towards the sugar shack, not even bothering to see if she would follow. Her lips tightened angrily at this further sign of his arrogance; it would give her great pleasure to take his car and abandon him to his own devices! Blind to the beauty that had earlier so pleased her, she followed him, jogging to keep up with his long, loping strides.

Simon had banked the fire so skilfully that blue smoke was still lazily drifting from the stone chimney. He held the door open for her, not meeting her eyes, and she preceded him into the room, instantly—and fruitlessly—scanning the shelves and table in the kitchen for the key ring. Refusing to be discouraged, she turned to face him, and said with an assumed coolness she was far from feeling, 'After that little debacle, what's next on the agenda?' Goading him sarcastically, she added, 'you could always chase me around with the axe for a while.'

His mouth thinned to an ugly line. 'I think a more interesting alternative would be a spot of rape,' he drawled, moving casually so that he stood between her and the door.

In spite of herself, Erin blanched. 'You must be joking, I'd scream the place down,' she said shakily. 'Besides, I know you wouldn't do that.'

'You have such touching faith in me, my dear,' he replied silkily.

She bit her lip. Had it not been for that terrifying interlude up the mountain, she would never have considered him forcing himself upon her; yet now she could not be sure of anything. Shivering, she would have given almost anything to hear another car, the sound of other people's voices ... the utter silence was unnerving.

But then he spoke with a smile that did not quite reach his eyes. 'Of course I'm joking, Erin. Your opinion of me may be low, but surely you're not silly enough to think of me as criminal.'

He hesitated and she had the oddest sensation that in the past few minutes he had arrived at some kind of decision, a decision that would affect her. 'I shouldn't have frightened you like that,' he said smoothly. 'I'm sorry.'

She stared at him, a puzzled frown furrowing her forehead. 'You frightened me far more up at the waterfall,' she said, unwilling to accept his almost too facile apology.

'Did I? Then you must forgive me for that too.'

Again it seemed too easy, and although his mouth was smiling at her, his eyes were watchful on her taut face, yet he must be sincere, she thought in confusion. Why should he be otherwise? Because Peter had proved untrustworthy, she should not allow herself to become sceptical of everyone's motives. And she remembered as though it had just happened, that moment of trust and reliance she had felt in Simon earlier in the day ... had that been meaningless? Her mind cried out a denial. So once again she decided to put herself at his mercy, to depend on him, putting her faith in what she knew of him; so little and yet so much. She took a deep breath and spoke the ordinary little words that were yet momentous. 'It's all right—but you won't do it again?'

'No.'

With this brief reply she had to be satisfied.

'Well,' he said, obviously wanting to bring the conversation to a more mundane level, 'why don't we eat? Nadine made a meat pie and I brought some vegetables from the garden. And she gave me one of her chocolate cakes ... guaranteed to make a glutton out of anyone!'

Erin smiled faintly, accepting his words as a peace offering. Simon found a vegetable peeler and gave her some carrots, while he chopped up broccoli and put potatoes on to boil. The wood in the stove snapped and crackled cheerfully as the mouth-watering scent of the pie drifted from the oven. Somehow the casual domesticity of their occupations calmed Erin's fretted nerves, and the harrowing scene at the waterfall faded to the back of her mind.

Simon began telling her about the various ski trails on his land and soon she joined in; from there the conversation covered the Olympics, modern music and the theatre. Despite their different backgrounds they had many common interests, so their talk was lively, and Erin thoroughly enjoyed herself, stimulated by Simon's wide range of knowledge and the acuteness of his observations. This was the Simon she knew and liked, she thought, smiling at him with unselfconscious warmth as she sat down to eat. But as she did so, she caught him off guard, assessing her response with a sharp intelligence in his expression. Startled, she gazed at him in enquiry. But then he was smiling back, a smile that did funny things to her heart and left her wondering if she had imagined the incident.

By the time they had cleaned up the kitchen, it was dark. 'Put on your jacket and let's go for a walk,' Simon suggested. 'We can go up the valley.'

The track was just wide enough for two of them, the alders and spruce catching at Erin's sleeve like questing fingers. The moon had risen over the hill, silvering the trees with luminous light, casting eerie shadows on the grass. From high on the mountain an owl hooted, repetitive, far away, indescribably lonely. They came to a turn in the path and Simon laid his hand on Erin's arm. 'Shh,' he whispered, 'go as quietly as you can.'

She did as she was told, seeing how the trail widened to a clearing on the edge of a bubbling brook. Etched in the moonlight, ears pricked, nostrils quivering, eyes dark as velvet, were two deer who had been drinking at the stream. The buck swished its white-furred tail, tensing to spring. Pointed hooves dug in the ground, and the graceful creatures leaped the bank, disappearing into the anonymity of the shadowed forest.

Erin let out her breath in a tiny sound of wonderment. 'You knew they would be here, didn't you?' she whispered.

'I hoped so. I've often seen them here.'

'That was perfect—thank you.'

His arm had somehow found its way around her shoulders. His lips slid across the sheen of her hair until softly, tenderly, they found her mouth. Just as slowly he released her. 'You've bewitched me,' he said huskily, 'with your black hair and your moon-pale face and your eyes like blue flames.'

She could only gaze at him wordlessly, looking every bit as fey and alluring as he had said. Suddenly he broke the spell, seizing her hand in his as though reassuring himself that she was indeed flesh and blood. 'Let's go home,' he said. They were simple words, thought Erin, yet with a wealth of meaning to them; words a husband would say to his wife at the end of a day, or a lover to his beloved when he wanted to be alone with her. Abandoning herself to the delight of his presence, she allowed him to lead her back along the path.

He had left a single lamp burning in the cabin, its golden halo beckoning them from the hillside. Once inside, Erin was all of a sudden overwhelmed by tiredness from all the exertions of the day; she had a quick, reviving shower and changed into the flowered caftan, leaving her hair loosely gathered in a knot on the crown of her head. When she came back into the living-room, Simon too had changed, into his suede trousers and silk shirt. He had just put a match to the heaped paper and logs in the fireplace and had mixed them each a drink, the ice clinking against the sides of the glasses. Erin knelt on the fur rug by the hearth, watching him as he selected a record and put it on the stereo ... a Beethoven sonata. 'The Moonlight?' she asked with a gamine grin.

He laughed. 'No, "Les Adieux". Sorry!'

Sipping her drink, a tangy concoction of rum and fruit juices that coursed pleasantly through her veins, she did not even notice that Simon had switched off the kitchen lamp, enclosing them both in the circle of light cast by the flickering flames. He came and sprawled beside her on the rug, leaning on one elbow, his long legs stretched out, his head only inches from her arm. She held tightly to her glass, knowing only too well how her treacherous fingers longed to stroke his hair, to bury themselves in its thick waves. The music rippled and sang, and Erin surrendered herself to a trance of blissful contentment, wishing these moments could go on for ever ... she had completely forgotten her earlier intention of taking Simon's car and fleeing the cabin.

Simon got up to put another log on the fire. Secretly she admired the long line of his back, the play of muscles under the thin fabric of his shirt. He turned to look at her and she blushed, remembering how once before he had read her mind. 'No woman should be as beautiful as you are now,' he said softly, letting his eyes wander over her in a caress as natural as the touch of his hands. Glorying in the blurred tenderness of his features, she sat statue-still, only the slightest quiver of her lower lip indicating how he was affecting her.

He reached out in a leisurely fashion and removed the drink from her unresisting fingers, putting it on the stone hearth. A pulse began to flutter at the base of her throat. He knelt beside her and carefully undid the ribbon in her hair, so that it tumbled in raven-black curls to her shoulders. 'I've been wanting to do that ever since you sat down,' he muttered, picking up one thick strand and letting it fall across his palm, where it gleamed almost with a life of its own. Then she was crushed against him, one arm tight about her waist, the other tilting her chin. He kissed her, his mouth hard and demanding as he sought the very essence of her. All her normal restraints gone, she felt her lips move against his and part under their probing. Her hands moved to his chest, undoing the buttons of his shirt to expose the curling dark hair, sliding across the warmth of his flesh and over the arch of his ribs. An inarticulate groan came from deep in his throat.

His weight fell on her, so that she lay back on the fur rug, her hair spread in a coal-black fan, her arms locked around his neck. Again their lips fused in mounting passion. Simon slid one hand inside the V-neck of her gown, spreading it apart, exploring the smoothness of her skin, the delicate hollows of her throat. She was distantly aware that he was fumbling with the row of tiny buttons below the neckline and cried out in delight as his fingers found the ripe curve of her breast, holding its softness while she moaned with pleasure. With every nerve of her body she sensed his passion, his masculine hardness, the thrust of his leg between her thighs. She was powerless to resist when he picked her up and carried her into the darkened bedroom, lowering her on to the bed.

Her caftan had slid above her knees, so that her limbs gleamed palely. Her cheeks were flushed, her eyes dark pools of desire. When he began kissing her again, his hands roaming over her quivering body, she ached for a final consummation. She had never made love before, yet even in her innocence she knew that Simon too longed for this ultimate possession.

Consumed by the fires which he had ignited, she opened her mouth to say the only words which could adequately express the mingled tenderness and passion which were overwhelming her; the three simple words that had such a wealth of meaning ... I love you. But before she could speak, she felt a shudder run through his body.

Roughly he pulled himself free of her embrace. Stunned, she fell back on the pillows, gazing at him in consternation. He was breathing in harsh gulps of air, his chest heaving, his eyes flintlike, merciless. 'What's wrong, Simon?' she cried. 'Are you all right?'

'Oh yes, I'm all right.' He gave her a wolfish grin. 'How about you, my dear?'

'I don't understand what you mean ...'

'I asked you how you were feeling. That seems a straight-forward enough question to me.'

Where love had burned in her body, anger now flared as

uncontrollably. 'Stop playing games with me, Simon!'

'Yes ... the game's over, isn't it?' he said in a voice heavy with meaning. 'And I proved my point beyond the shadow of a doubt.'

'What the hell are you talking about?' In one lithe movement Erin stood up, her fists clenched at her sides.

'It's very simple. I wanted to prove to you, once and for all, that you are no longer in love with Peter ... if indeed you ever did love him. I would say I succeeded, wouldn't you?'

Lightning-swift she struck him across the face. One tiny part of her brain registered the whip-like crack her palm made against his cheek, and the spreading red imprint of her fingers. Smothering any remorse she might have felt, she spat, 'How could you! What a loathsome thing to do!'

'Come now,' he drawled, his voice at odds with the twin devils flaming in his cold eyes, 'it's time someone ended this illusion of yours that you're undyingly in love with someone who's not worth loving. You should be thanking me. After all, I need not have stopped when I did.'

She gasped in mortification, hot colour flooding her cheeks. Then, wanting to salvage what pride she could from the ruins of the day, she drew on all her reserves and said with a steadiness that privately amazed her, 'You're drawing some sweeping conclusions from very little evidence— you've never met Peter, so how can you tell what he's like? And it so happens you're quite wrong. He's well worth loving.'

'Five minutes ago you knew damn well you wanted me to make love to you,' he said with brutal frankness. 'And you can still say you love someone else?'

Too deeply hurt to care what she said, she let the words fall from her lips with icy precision. 'Surely you're not so naïve as to equate the purely physical response I felt towards you with love, Simon? Or are you still living in the Victorian era, when women were scarcely supposed to know sex existed, let alone enjoy it?'

His breath hissed through his teeth. 'You promiscuous little bitch!'

'I don't think you're in any position to call names.'

But he did not seem to have heard her. 'God! You make me sick. You talk of loving one man and in the same breath of sleeping with another.'

He had finally penetrated her defences. 'I wouldn't have slept with you!'

'You'd have a hard time convincing me of that.'

'I've never slept with anyone——'

'Do you expect me to believe that after tonight?' His laugh grated on her nerves, so devoid it was of amusement. 'You're the epitome of modern liberated womanhood ... totally selfish and totally amoral.' He raked his fingers through his already disordered thatch of hair. 'I've had enough of this. I'm going to bed—and believe me, I'm going alone.'

'So you were planning on doing otherwise?' she pounced.

His lips thinned, and she quailed before his ferocious stare. 'Don't push me too far, Erin. You can sleep in here. And I suggest we leave first thing in the morning. The sooner this charade is over, the better!'

'I couldn't agree more.'

He gave her one last contemptuous glance, as cutting as the flick of a whip. 'Pleasant dreams ... of Peter, of course.'

Her chin tilted defiantly. 'Goodnight.'

He shut the door with a perceptible snap, and Erin could hear his footsteps moving to the adjoining room. She pressed her hands to her hot face and inadvertently caught sight of her reflection in the mirror above the dresser; tangled black curls feathering pain-filled blue eyes and temper-flushed cheeks. Then the mirrored image wavered and blurred as tears finally spilled over her lashes. She sank down on the bed, then flung herself full length, her face buried in the pillows to muffle the sobs that threatened to choke her. Trust, love, tenderness ... the words were ashes in her mouth. She could no more trust Simon than Peter.

CHAPTER SIX

ERIN woke with a start. She was lying flat on her back in the blackness, her heart pounding in her breast ... what could have woken her? Could it have been Simon? She strained her ears, but the cabin lay in utter silence. As her eyes became accustomed to the dark, she could see that she was alone in the room. The illuminated hands of her watch pointed to two-thirty; at least five hours before she could get up. She turned over on her side and with grim concentration sought the oblivion of sleep again.

An hour passed before she confessed that she was beaten. Although her eyes itched with tiredness, she was becoming more and more wide awake, tossing and turning restlessly as she tried to find a comfortable spot in the bed. The confines of the room had become claustrophobic, and suddenly she knew she had to escape. She sat up, pulled on her fur slippers and tiptoed over to the door. She opened it with infinite caution, but the hinge still squeaked and tensely she waited to hear Simon stir. But all was quiet. Without further mishap she found her long suede coat and managed to close the front door behind her. Swiftly she moved away from the cabin to stand in the middle of the clearing.

Silence pressed against her ears; not a breath of wind, not a leaf stirred. The moon had climbed in the sky until it was directly over her head, where it cast a silver radiance over the sleeping valley. Stars spangled the velvet blackness, distant, cold, and uncaring.

Something of the scene's unearthly beauty spoke directly to Erin's unhappiness. Looking like some sylvan spirit, she glided across the open grass to the lane that sloped down the hillside between a tangle of unpruned apple trees. Solitude beckoned her; pulling her coat around her for warmth, she slowly wandered down the path, not realising she was now hidden from sight of the cabin. A few late apples still clung to the branches; she seized a low-hanging limb and shook it vigorously, so that three apples plummeted to earth, one bumping her shoulder.

But simultaneously, and so loudly that her heart stopped in fear, came a wild snorting and trampling from the impenetrable depths of the undergrowth. Petrified, she backed away, a sharp cry of fright leaving her lips. A black shadow broke free of the trees and leaped down the hill ... for the second time that night she saw the flash of a white tail: a deer, a huge buck, his antlers silhouetted in the moonlight as he plunged into the shelter of the valley.

A heavy fall of running footsteps down the lane—Simon. Almost Erin forgot the bitterness of their quarrel as she made an instinctive move towards his solid, comforting bulk. But his voice stopped her as surely as a stone wall would have.

'What the hell are you doing?'

She thrust her hands deep in her pockets so he would not see their trembling. 'I couldn't sleep. So I came out for a walk.'

'Don't you realise it's dangerous to wander around at night by yourself? You could fall and break a leg, or get lost —and I wouldn't have any idea where to look for you.'

'As you can see, I'm perfectly all right. I'm sorry to disappoint you,' she said with heavy irony.

'It didn't sound as though you were all right a minute ago. You screamed as if you were scared out of your wits.'

'The deer frightened me, that's all,' she said coldly. 'I really came out here to be alone.'

'Well, you're not staying out here. Come on.'

'Don't be silly,' she cried, venting her exasperation. 'You're treating me like a child. I'm quite capable of looking after myself.'

'I think that's debatable, but it's really beside the point. I said you were going in, Erin, and I meant it.'

'And I said I'm not!'

He took a single step towards her. The moonlight shone down on his face, shadowing its hollows and delineating its carved lines. His eyes were as black and as subtly menacing as the surrounding forest. He looked tough and formidable, capable of anything; nervously Erin retreated.

'Are you going to come quietly, or do I have to pick you up and carry you? It's because you're acting like a child, Erin, that I have to treat you like one.'

Her nostrils flared wth impotent fury; she knew only too well he would carry out his threat. With cold dignity she capitulated. 'I would prefer to walk.'

She brushed past him and walked swiftly up the lane, her mind a turmoil of frustrated anger. Because she was not watching where she was going, she tripped over a clump of grass and would have fallen had it not been for Simon's restraining hand on her arm. She shook it off impatiently, not looking at him and certainly not thanking him.

In the cabin she hung up her coat, and with her back to him said tautly, 'I'm going to bed.'

'Aren't you forgetting something?'

Because his tone of voice was entirely natural, she turned to face him in surprise. 'No, I don't think so.'

She was given no time to guess his intention. His arms were steel-tight around her before she could move, and his lips claimed hers in a brief hard kiss. Just as abruptly he released her, his features a satanic mask. But again his voice was perfectly under control. 'Goodnight, Erin.'

Not trusting herself to speak, she stalked into her room and slammed the door. The man was a devil, she thought, his emotions as cold and inhuman as the distant stars . . .

She did finally fall into an exhausted slumber, only to be roused what seemed like minutes later by Simon knocking on her door. 'Breakfast is ready.'

She stretched wearily, wishing she could curl up again under the warmth of the blankets. But she knew better than to do that, for she was sure he would forcibly haul her out of bed if it suited him. The meal was strained and uncomfortable, their conversation restricted to monosyllables, and Erin was glad when they finally locked up the cabin and drove away, neither of them looking back; at least in the car she could legitimately close her eyes and ignore her hostile companion.

Four hours later Simon pulled up in front of Erin's house; she had never been more glad to have a journey end in her life. Stiffly she got out of the car and reached in for her coat and handbag, giving Robbie a farewell pat, while Simon carried her overnight case to the door. For the first time that day she looked him square in the face; it was with an unbidden shock of concern that she saw how tired and haggard he looked; for an instant his eyes had been unguarded and bleak with a private unhappiness. But then, as though shutters had descended, all feeling was erased from his face. 'Goodbye, Erin,' he said.

There was such finality in this brief phrase that she felt herself flinch. Yet what else had she expected? Determined to match his own indifference, she too said, 'Goodbye.' Sarcastically her ungovernable tongue added, 'Thanks for the lovely weekend.'

'Don't worry, it won't be repeated.' And he turned on his heel and went back to the car. Quickly Erin busied herself with the door key, so that she did not have to watch him disappear up the hill.

That evening, craving some work to keep her mind from re-living all the disastrous details of the past two days, she walked to the college. In her office she selected a couple of books and some papers from her desk, wishing Nadine was free; she felt badly in need of some female company. She left the Fine Arts building and took a short cut across the lawn, emerging from the trees to the macadam surface of the road. Round the bend came a glare of headlights, the well-bred purr of a car engine, and instinctively she stepped back on the shoulder, as a sleek sports car came into view. Transfixed by the two beams of light, she saw Simon at the wheel, a very different Simon from the man who had left her this morning, for he was now dressed in a dinner jacket and frilled white shirt, and was laughing at something his companion must have said.

With a stab of pain Erin saw that Francine was with him, elegant in a silver lamé evening gown, her hair elaborately coiffed, jewels gleaming at her ears and throat. And then the car had swept past her, and with a kind of dumb gratitude she was sure neither of its occupants had seen her. They must be going to Halifax, she thought, wondering dully why she cared; after all, Simon Grayson had proved to be as cruelly unreliable as Peter, and far more threatening to her peace of mind. She trudged down the hill, not knowing that was to be her last glimpse of Simon for many days to come.

Soon November had gripped the countryside with cold fingers. The blaze of maples had given way to the brilliant yellow of poplar and birch, the rust of beech. But they too had faded, and now the trees raised skeletal brown branches to the leaden sky. The first snowfall came, melted and was gone; a foretaste of the long months of bitter weather to come.

At the university Erin threw herself into her work and was rewarded by an increasing sense of self-confidence and a growing rapport with her students; she was warmly praised for her contributions to a photography exhibition at the gallery. But busy as she was, she could not make work occupy all her waking hours, and despite her growing friendship with Nadine, she of necessity spent many hours alone. Occasionally Peter phoned, his manner as debonair and charming as ever, but in the secrecy of her heart Erin had to admit she had difficulty in keeping a picture of him clear in her mind; she could no longer recall the exact cadences of his voice, nor summon his face in her memory. Another face, another voice, had ousted Peter from her dreams; a rough-hewn face with cold grey eyes and untidy dark hair, a harsh, demanding voice. Subconsciously whenever she was on campus, or doing errands in Abbotsford, she was watching for him, but this secret surveillance went unrewarded, for she never saw him; he had dropped out of her life as abruptly as he had entered it.

Often she wished she had never met him, decrying the hold he had over her; once she had allowed herself to trust a man, and it was impossible not to conclude that she had only her own foolishness to blame for her present unhappiness. For unhappy she was; there was no question of that. She felt restless and unfulfilled, her body disturbed by a yearning whose source she did not understand.

She fell into the habit of walking on the beach almost every day, her slight solitary figure wandering along the empty stretch of sand. The breakers fell monotonously, the sea as grey as the clouded sky. The terns and the sand-pipers had flown to warmer climates, leaving the gulls to scavenge the beach. On the shore the spruce trees huddled together against the biting wind, which rustled the dry brown eel grass ... a desolate scene that matched Erin's mood, her ache of loneliness, her longing for the carefree and delightful companionship she had so briefly shared with Simon.

Even when with Nadine she could never quite dispel her sense of isolation. But it was from her that she finally learned of Simon's whereabouts. Nadine had come for supper one evening, and driven by a need she would scarcely acknowledge, Erin said with assumed casualness as she took the casserole out of the oven, 'I haven't seen Simon around the campus lately. I hope he hasn't caught the 'flu that's on the go?'

'Didn't he tell you?' Nadine said in surprise. 'He's been away at a European conference—he went right after the weekend the two of you were at the cabin. He should have been back in a couple of days, but I just got a telegram to-day saying he'd been delayed, so it'll probably be early December before he'll be home.'

'No, he didn't mention it,' Erin replied, busying herself with the salad so that Nadine's shrewd eyes could not see her telltale features; illogically she was wounded that he could have gone so far away without letting her know. She changed the subject hastily, for she had never told Nadine the truth about that disastrous weekend in the Sweet Mountains, and certainly did not want to now. 'We really did well with the exhibition, didn't we?' she said, sure that this would distract her friend from the subject of Simon, for Nadine had also shown some of her work at the gallery.

'Mm,' Nadine agreed abstractedly, as she helped herself to the salad. 'This looks delicious, Erin! You're such a good cook. You're wasting your talents living on your own, you should be married!'

More warmly than she had intended, Erin exclaimed, 'No, thanks! Once bitten, you know ...'

Thoughtfully Nadine replied, 'Not all men are as undependable as your Peter.' In a seeming non sequitur she added, 'I'm worried about Simon, Erin.'

Erin felt a tension inadvertently sharpen her voice. 'Why? Is he getting married?'

Nadine raised her eyebrows in surprise. 'No. At least as far as I know, he's not. Unless Francine finally managed to get her claws in him. No, it's something else altogether ...'

It was not like the happy-go-lucky Nadine to look so worried. 'Tell me about it,' Erin suggested, in her heart of hearts pleased to be talking about Simon with the sister whom he loved; it made him seem less far away, less unattainable.

'All right, I will. I need to talk to someone and I know you won't tell anyone else.' The two girls smiled at each other, Nadine's features momentarily lit by an elusive likeness to her brother's, the resemblance causing Erin a pang of painful emotion. 'He shouldn't be away right now,' Nadine went on. 'It would have been bad enough if he'd returned on time, but now he'll be delayed at least two more weeks. I know I'm Simon's sister, so I'm prejudiced, but just the same I'm convinced he's the best man to be the head of the department. He's always worked so hard and he gets along tremendously well with the students ... he's really responsible for putting the English department on the academic map here.' She buttered a roll thoughtfully. 'But Bendix wants the job too, I'm sure you already know that. Erin, I don't like to be critical, but Gerald Bendix would be the worst possible choice. All Simon's good work would be undone in no time, I just know it.'

'Would he really be that bad?' Erin asked sceptically.

'Yes! Apart from anything else, he hates Simon and will do anything he can to discredit him. There's a lot of backroom politics going on right now; Simon should be here to fight it, instead of being in Europe.'

'But Dr MacIntosh is on Simon's side, surely?'

'Up to a point. But he's such a diplomat, and besides, as retiring Head he only has so much power to wield.'

'I think you're worrying too much. They won't make the appointment until after Christmas, and Simon will be back long before that.'

'I guess you're right. But if Bendix did get the chairmanship, I know the first thing he'd do is get rid of Simon—by fair means or foul. This place has been part of Simon's life for so long ... he met his wife here, you know—she was a student. And their daughter was born here. He has so many memories tied in with Abbotsford and the college, I don't see how he'd ever want to leave.'

Obscurely hurt by this turn in the conversation, Erin said flippantly, 'Maybe he will marry Francine after all, and end up president.'

'I'm sure there's nothing Francine would like better! He's been seeing quite a bit of her these last few months, too. Goodness, I wouldn't like her for a sister-in-law.' Nadine made such a comical grimace that Erin couldn't help laughing, and the subject of Simon was dropped. But in the days to come Erin often thought about this conversation, so much of it disquieting to her peace of mind. Inevitably, too, once the date of his arrival back in Canada came and went, she began to hope against hope that she would hear from Simon himself. But the phone remained obstinately silent, nor did she see his tall figure striding around the campus, although subconsciously she was always watching for it.

Indeed it was because she was thinking of him when she should have been concentrating on her driving that she got herself in trouble one snowy day early in the month. Three inches of heavy, wet snow had fallen in the night and the continuous traffic on the narrow campus roads had packed it into a glaring sheet of ice. Backing out of her parking lot, Erin turned the car down the hill, incautiously putting on her brakes as she came to the turn. The car began to skid inexorably towards the fence on the opposite side of the road. She wrenched at the wheel and put her foot to the floor on the brake pedal, but to no avail; helplessly she gripped the wheel as the front bumper struck a metal fence post and the car came to a complete stop. Her lip banged against the steering wheel with painful force.

'Oh, damn!' she exclaimed, glad she had come to no more serious harm, but nevertheless still trembling slightly with reaction. It had been a nasty experience watching the car slide closer and closer to the fence and not being able to prevent a collision.

Someone tapped on her window. Startled, she looked up, automatically winding down the frosted glass.

It was Simon. Greedily her eyes traced his features, noticing a new tautness to his mouth, lines in his face that had not been there a month ago. 'Hello,' she said lamely, through lips gone suddenly dry.

'Haven't you got snow tyres on?' he demanded unceremoniously.

'No. I haven't got around to it yet.'

He gave her one scathing look that spoke volumes, and she flushed with mortification, knowing only too well how foolish she had been to delay having them installed.

'Put it in reverse,' he ordered, 'and I'll give you a push.'

She did as she was told. Simon put his shoulder to the hood, bracing his feet, and with a shrill whine of spinning rubber, pushed the car back on the road. Brushing the snow off his bare hands, he asked, 'Where are you going?'

'To the post office and then home.'

'Move over. I'll drive you as far as the post office.'

'You don't need to do that——'

'Move over, Erin,' he repeated with exaggerated patience, his cold eyes surveying her impersonally. 'Next time you might do worse than bruise your mouth.'

Her fingers touched the sore spot gingerly. In a disconcerting flash of memory, she remembered how his mouth had moved against hers, the searching, hungry passion of his kisses. No such recollections were bothering him, she thought bitterly, as she shifted to the passenger's seat. 'How was your trip?' she asked, unable to think of anything more intelligent to say.

'Fine,' he said noncommittally. With considerable skill he guided the car down the hill, between the two gateposts, and on to the main road, which had been both ploughed and salted and was consequently ice-free. He said nothing more, and it was humiliatingly plain to Erin that he had no desire for her company, nor the slightest interest in even maintaining a civilised conversation with her. She stared down at her gloved hands, sick at heart.

He drew up outside the post office. 'I'd advise you to go straight to a garage and get those tyres put on. Besides your own, you're also endangering other people's lives as well.'

'Do stop ordering me around,' she snapped, wishing he did not always bring out the worst in her.

'I don't plan to make a habit of it.'

She glared at him from mutinous blue eyes, her fall of black hair framed by the white fur on her winter coat. 'I'm not asking you to.'

He flicked her cheek with his fingernail. 'You've lost weight. And those circles under your eyes don't become you. What's the matter? Can't you pin the estimable Peter down to a wedding date?'

No prospect could have been further from her mind, but she would be the last one to tell Simon that. 'That's my affair, surely?' she said with assumed coolness.

He laughed contemptuously. 'Affair is certainly the appropriate word!'

Her expressive eyes flashed with temper. 'Your European trip doesn't seem to have improved your disposition,' she remarked waspishly.

'I'm sure we both have better things to do than sit here trading insults ... goodbye, Erin.' In one lithe movement he was out of the car, his hand raised in sardonic salute.

'Thank you for helping me,' she faltered tardily. But he had gone, and she was sure he had not heard her. She waited for a moment before she got out of the car, wanting no further contact with him.

There was only one letter for her at the post office, the envelope addressed in her mother's familiar handwriting. It was probably finalising their plans for Christmas; Erin had booked her flight to Montreal over a month ago. A few days away from Abbotsford in the familiarity of her old home sounded like heaven, particularly now, with the constant abrasions to her spirit that Simon seemed to cause ... she tore open the envelope and began to read.

She skimmed the letter first, then went back and read it more slowly, sharply aware of a growing disappointment. Her parents had been offered the unique opportunity of

flying to Hawaii for Christmas with close friends of theirs;
her mother hoped Erin wouldn't be too upset by this change
of plans, it really was a once-in-a-lifetime chance . . .

For her parents' sake, Erin was genuinely pleased, knowing how her mother in particular loved to travel and rarely
had had the opportunity. But for herself, it was a little
different . . . where would she go for Christmas? She might
have spent it with Nadine, but that would inevitably in-
volve Simon, so that was out. Peter had airily informed her
he would be in Vancouver with his own parents and had
not invited her to accompany him—not that she would have
anyway . . . She could feel tears of self-pity gathering at the
backs of her eyes and angrily blinked them back; something
else would come up, she thought, stubbornly. And not for
anything would she let her mother and father know how
their change of plans had affected her.

'Hi! Not bad news, I hope?'

Erin looked up. 'Hello, Nadine. No,' she lied, for how
could she tell Nadine she had nowhere to go for Christmas,
'everything's fine. Are you going back to the campus?'

'No, I've got a bit of shopping to do—decorations and
presents for the staff children's party tomorrow. Why don't
you come along this evening and help me decorate? It's
always fun, and the more the merrier.'

Erin agreed to this plan, and so at seven that evening put
on slim-fitting grey slacks and a soft angora sweater and
drove to the big reception room in the faculty club. She
knew almost everyone there, for they were largely the
younger members of the staff; and in no time a glass of
rum punch was thrust in one hand and some thumb tacks
in the other, and she was perched on a ladder pinning tinsel
chains across an archway. A few mothers had brought their
children and she could hear their excited shrieks mingling
with the Christmas music from the stereo. Later she volun-
teered to set up the crêche scene on the oak mantel, and was
soon happily absorbed in arranging the carved wooden
figures among fragrant boughs of pine. There was even a
five-pointed star, painted gilt . . she would need a ladder
to fasten it to the rough-hewn stones of the fireplace.

'Let me help.'

The star slipped through her nerveless fingers and would have shattered on the hearth had Simon not grabbed it. 'Thank goodness you caught it!' she exclaimed, her thick eyelashes hiding her expression.

Before she could gather her wits, a little voice from behind them piped, 'Uncle Simon! Are you coming to the party? Santa's going to be there.'

The voice belonged to a dark-haired little girl of about four with a captivating smile. She was charmingly dressed in a red velvet pinafore and a frilly white blouse.

What an enchanting child! Erin thought, wondering if she really was related to Simon, or if 'uncle' was a courtesy title. She glanced at him and her heart skipped a beat. His fingers were gripping the edge of the mantel for support, for he was swaying on his feet. The colour had drained from his face, leaving it ashen grey, while his eyes were naked with a pain so intense she felt she was seeing into his very soul; he was a man lost in some private hell.

'What's the matter, Uncle Simon? Don't you like my new dress?'

With an immense effort Simon took a deep breath and managed to say with a semblance of naturalness, 'I wasn't expecting to see you, Cheryl. Of course I like your new dress. What do you think Santa will bring you for Christmas?'

'I asked him for a doll,' the little girl whispered confidingly. 'Oh, there's Mummy, I've got to go.' Her chubby legs carried her across the floor to her quiet-faced mother, whom Erin recognised as the wife of one of the History professors.

She turned to face Simon, the noise and confusion around them fading into the background until they could have been alone in the room. He was staring after Cheryl; the suffering on his face made her want to weep. 'Simon,' she said quietly, 'tell me what's wrong.'

He dragged his eyes away from the child's figure and looked at her. All the defences were down. His vulnerability roused in her a surge of compassion, and with calm certainty she placed her fingers on his sleeve. 'You must tell me what's wrong,' she repeated patiently.

'I had a daughter once ... her name was Elice,' he said tonelessly. 'The last Christmas before she—died, she had a dress almost identical with Cheryl's. She was about the same age too, and looked not unlike her, dark hair, chubby. Perhaps all little girls are at that age, I don't know.'

'What happened to her, Simon?'

He looked into Erin's eyes, as though wanting to drown himself in their sapphire depths. 'She was killed in a car accident early in January. The car went out of control on an icy road.'

So perhaps that was why he had been so tense and angry this morning when she had foolishly skidded on the ice, Erin thought in swift comprehension. But she allowed none of this to show, for she did not want to distract him; somehow she sensed in him a desperate need to unburden himself of the intolerable pain he had carried alone for far too long. 'Were you driving?' she asked, wondering if it was guilt that was haunting him.

'No. I wasn't there. Her mother was driving—she was killed too.'

Feeling her way with infinite care, Erin said, 'You lost them both at once, then.'

He stood quite still, bleak grey eyes trained on the lovely young face raised to his. For a moment his gaze dropped to her slender, ringless fingers still resting lightly on his sleeve. Then, as though he had made a difficult decision, he said, 'That's what all my friends thought. A double tragedy, they called it in the newspaper. And everyone said how sad it was that I should lose wife and daughter in one blow. Little did they know——'

He broke off. In the dim light from the Christmas tree bulbs she could see sweat beading his forehead. Her heart ached for him, but resolutely she persisted, 'Know what?'

'I've never told this to anyone before, Erin.'

'Then it's time you shared it. You've kept it locked away too long.'

'Yes ...' He raked his fingers through his long hair. 'My wife was leaving me. The marriage had been a mistake from the beginning ... we mistook infatuation for love. It didn't take long for the truth to dawn on both of us, but by then

Elice was on the way, so we stayed together. Adria—my wife—bitterly resented the pregnancy; I don't think she ever loved Elice at all. It was all very simple to her; Elice was the means whereby she was trapped in a marriage to a man she hated.'

'Couldn't you have divorced her?' Erin murmured, appalled by the understated desolation he was exposing to her view.

'I could have, yes. But although she hated me, she loved my money and the easy life she led—so she had no intention of letting all that go. She told me point blank if I ever tried to divorce her, she'd take Elice and I would never see her again.'

'But that's dreadful, Simon——'

He glanced at her, noticing the distress in her face, the way her hand had tightened on his sleeve in unconscious sympathy. He patted her fingers, a wintry smile lightening his features. 'Don't look so upset, it's all a long time ago.'

Knowing there was worse to come, Erin said quietly, 'You didn't love your wife, but you loved your daughter.'

'Oh yes, I loved Elice. I would have done anything for her. She was so tiny and so beautifully made. She always seemed to be laughing and chattering away about something; she never stopped from morning until night.' He sighed heavily. 'She was my Achilles heel, and well Adria knew it.'

'So in the end, she took Elice with her?'

'That's right. I suppose it was inevitable that sooner or later Adria would meet someone with more money than I. She flaunted her affair with him so blatantly to me that we had one hell of a row—I threatened to cut off her allowance if she didn't behave herself. So when I came downstairs that Tuesday morning, there was a note waiting for me, saying she'd gone to the man she loved, and that she expected her allowance from me to continue—and just to guarantee that I would send her the money, she had taken Elice with her. . . . She was driving to the airport when the accident happened.'

'And no one other than you ever knew why she was going away?'

'No.'

'Not even Nadine?'

'Not even Nadine.'

'Thank you for telling me, Simon,' Erin said finally. 'You can be sure your secret is safe with me.'

Again that fleeting smile broke through his strained features. 'I know, Erin, you don't have to tell me that.'

Delicate colour tinged her cheeks, for she treasured Simon's rare compliments. As they stood gravely regarding one another, Cheryl again came over to them. 'Goodbye, Uncle Simon,' she piped. 'Will you be at the party?'

He knelt down and gave the child a quick, hard hug. 'Yes, I will be. I hope you get your doll.'

'Me too. 'Bye!'

As Simon straightened, Erin could see that a hard-won resignation, a kind of peace, had settled on his face; he looked both younger and yet more mature. Without ceremony he said, 'The staff Christmas party is the night after the children's party—will you go with me?'

She did not pause to think. 'Yes,' she said simply, 'I'd love to.'

'Good! And now maybe we should join the others.' He paused, then added softly, 'And Erin—thanks.'

CHAPTER SEVEN

WHEN Simon arrived to get Erin for the party, she had just put the finishing touches on her appearance. She walked out into the hall to meet him, the soft radiance of the light from the living room falling on her. Simon closed the door behind him, slowly pulling off his gloves, as in one all-encompassing glance he took in every detail of her slender figure.

She was wearing a full-length evening gown of dark red velvet, its low neckline moulding the curves of her breast, its rich sheen in sensuous contrast to the creamy pallor of her skin. Her hair she had arranged high on her head, bar-

ing the delicate column of her neck; a gold necklace set
with garnets encircled her throat, and matching droplets
sparkled at her ears. In the shining coils of her hair she had
cleverly woven a bracelet, the stones a barbaric red against
the filigree of gold. Excitement had flushed her cheeks and
darkened her eyes; she looked as poised and graceful as a
medieval princess, yet as vivid and alive as a gypsy.

The silence stretched into minutes. Nervously Erin
smoothed back a stray tendril of hair. 'Is anything wrong?'

'Far from it.' He gave a crooked little smile, his eyes in-
scrutable under dark brows. 'You look—breathtaking.'

She looked at him uncertainly, for it was impossible to
read his expression, yet he was surely sincere. Giving him
the benefit of the doubt, she swept a low curtsey, her sleek
head bowed in a gentle parody of humility. 'So do you,' she
countered, for his black dinner suit and immaculate white
shirt-front suited his saturnine good looks to perfection. But
she couldn't help noticing he looked tired.

'Then we must agree we are a handsome couple,' he said,
with that gleam of self-mockery that she so enjoyed in him.
'Shall we go, little mermaid?'

It was a long time since he had called her that, she
thought, with an unbidden catch of happiness in her throat.
She picked up her long black evening cloak and Simon
placed it about her shoulders, its loose folds enveloping
her slender body. When they entered the faculty lounge,
more than one head turned in their direction, and Erin was
conscious of a surge of pride in her escort.

But when she saw the receiving line she felt the first
qualm of disquiet, for beside the President and his wife
stood Francine, accompanied by, of all people, the red-
haired Gerald Bendix. Erin greeted Dr and Mrs Haley
politely, and she and Simon chatted with them for a few
moments. While Simon was still deep in conversation with
the president, Francine said sweetly, 'Why, Erin, how nice
to see you. How charming and old-fashioned you look. You
know Dr Bendix, don't you?'

Erin acknowledged the Professor, wishing Simon would
join her.

'How nice of Simon to invite you,' Francine went on

smoothly. 'He was so disappointed when he found out I'd already accepted Gerald's invitation.'

Could this be true? Erin wondered with a sickening little lurch of her heart; after all, it had only been three days ago that Simon had invited her. Perhaps it had been for him a second choice, a last-minute decision to go with her rather than stay at home or go alone. The perfect shine of the evening already seemed tarnished.

'Simon and I are very close, as I'm sure you know,' Francine went on archly. 'I wouldn't want you to misinterpret your date with him this evening.'

Belatedly Erin found her tongue. 'You're making sure that I don't, aren't you?' she retorted, even as her mind wrestled with the implications of Francine, who wanted Simon as head of the department, attending the staff party with Gerald Bendix, Simon's sworn rival. What was the president's daughter up to? It was with deep relief that she finally sensed Simon's presence beside her; she smiled up at him more warmly than she had intended. He held out his hand to Francine, who pulled him closer and stood on tip-toe to kiss him full on the mouth. 'That's an early Happy Christmas, darling,' she exclaimed gaily. 'Do you remember what a good time we had here last year? You must dance with me, Simon, Gerald isn't very keen on that.' And she pouted full lips at her escort.

'By all means,' Gerald said heartily. 'I'd be glad of the chance to get to know Erin a little better.' He bent over her hand, imprinting a moist kiss on her wrist.

It was as much as Erin could do not to snatch her arm away, and it was with dismay that she heard Francine say to Simon, 'You and Erin will join us at the head table, won't you? It's all arranged, so don't say no!'

Simon murmured something which Erin could not catch, and Francine's bell-like laugh rang out. 'We'll see you later, then, darling.'

Simon procured cocktails, then he and Erin joined a group of professors and their wives; among them Erin recognised Cheryl's mother. Too proud to show how the brief exchange with Francine had upset her, Erin chatted about Christmas plans and the prospect of snow for skiing, even as she came gradually to believe that Simon had indeed invited her as his second choice; otherwise, would he have agreed so readily to sharing a table with Francine and Gerald Bendix? But if there was a brittle quality to her laugh and a faint reserve in her manner when she addressed Simon, he did not appear to notice.

At the dinner table Francine skilfully engineered it so that she sat between Bendix and Simon with Erin on Simon's other side, and throughout the meal she managed to monopolise the conversation; inevitably Erin felt left out ... and even more convinced that Simon would have preferred to attend the party with Francine. But when the band arrived and took their places on the decorated stage, it was Erin whom Simon led out on to the floor. The lights had dimmed and as his arms went around her and their hands clasped, a little of the evening's magic was restored for Erin. Simon danced superbly, having an innate sense of rhythm combined with the grace of a natural athlete. Erin gave herself up to the music, temporarily released from the tensions the past couple of hours had engendered. But all too soon Gerald Bendix tapped Simon on the shoulder, and with a shaft of pure jealousy Erin watched Simon and Francine dance away, the blonde girl's head on his shoulder, her body in its pencil-slim sheath provocatively pressed against his. She forced a smile to her lips and for the next three dances made somewhat stilted conversation with Bendix as they circled the floor; he held her uncomfortably close, his breath fanning her cheek, openly flirting with her in a heavy-handed manner that made her thoroughly uncomfortable. It was a relief when they finally sat down, although with a sinking heart she realised Simon and Francine had disappeared from the dance floor. The slow minutes dragged by, then with a suddenness that startled her, Simon spoke from behind her. 'It's time you and I danced again, Erin. If you'll excuse us, Gerald?'

She turned to face him, noticing a grimness to his mouth, a shadowed strain about his eyes. She stared resolutely at his shirt front as they danced, her body unconsciously rigid in her embrace. Not for anything would she ask where he had been, she thought with fierce resolve.

'Relax, Erin,' he chided, his arms drawing her closer.

Treacherously her body yielded to the pressure of his hands, her cheek against the smooth cloth of his lapels. She closed her eyes, drifting in the limbo of a physical closeness that was marred by vivid mental images of him and Francine together.

He danced in silence, his fingers gently rubbing the tension out of her shoulder-blades. When he did speak, his question was commonplace enough. 'Are you going to your parents for Christmas? They live in Montreal, don't they?'

'No and yes,' she replied with a rueful laugh, wishing he had asked anything else, and hoping that he would drop the subject there. 'I forgot to ask whether you went to the children's party—did Cheryl get her doll?'

'Yes, I did, and yes, she did, and you're changing the subject,' was his calm reply. 'Where are you spending the holidays, then, Erin? With Peter?'

'No!' she exclaimed, more vehemently than she meant to, and bit her lip in vexation. 'My parents are flying to Hawaii with some old family friends,' she continued matter-of-factly, but in spite of herself there was a tinge of loneliness in her voice. 'It will be the first Christmas in my life that I haven't spent at home.'

'Nadine and I are going to the cabin for Christmas. Why don't you come with us? I know she'd like that almost as much as I would.'

Afraid to trust in his words, Erin looked up at him, her doubts faithfully mirrored in her mobile face. With painful clarity she recalled his grim features a few moments ago when he had come back with Francine—had he asked her to spend Christmas with him and had she refused? Yet why should she? Unutterably confused, she faltered, 'I don't know, Simon. Christmas is a family time, a time of happiness, and you have to admit my only other stay at the cabin was hardly happy.' Although it had taken considerable courage for her to be this honest, she was glad that she had been; not for anything could she endure such disillusionment as that weekend again.

'I promise that will never be repeated,' Simon said with deep seriousness. 'I would like you to be a part of our family for Christmas, Erin.'

Joy kindled a small steady flame within her. 'Then I

accept with pleasure,' she said, the formality of her words cloaking a depth of emotion that even she scarcely recognised. Armoured by the inescapable sincerity of his invitation, she drifted through the rest of the evening, her beauty illuminated and made vulnerable by happiness.

They were among the last to leave and when Simon took her home it was nearly two in the morning. He escorted her to the door and waited until she had unlocked it. With a bittersweet tenderness his lips brushed hers, lingering all too briefly. 'Goodnight, Erin. Sleep well, dear.'

'Goodnight,' she murmured, longing to delay his departure yet not daring to. The house seemed very empty after he had driven away, but she fell asleep to the warming anticipation of Christmas in the Sweet Mountains with Simon.

Nadine had been seeing a great deal of Allen Beaumont lately, and two days after the staff party she burst into Erin's office, accidentally knocking over a pile of books on the chair as she did so. 'Erin! Guess what?'

'What?' Erin laughed, gazing with affection at her friend's wind-flushed cheeks and blown hair.

'Allen's asked me to spend Christmas with him and his parents,' Nadine crowed. 'Erin, I think he's going to ask me to marry him, I really do!' She hesitated, her eyes anxious. 'Do you think Simon will mind very much—about Christmas, I mean, not about Allen marrying me?'

'Surely not,' Erin said reassuringly. But happy as she was for Nadine, she couldn't help wondering how this would affect Simon's plans; perhaps he wouldn't want to go without Nadine. Now that it was threatened, she realised how much she had been building on the prospect of Christmas with Simon, what bright images had formed in her mind of carol singing and skiing, of trimming the tree and wrapping presents. But she successfully hid her worry from Nadine, not wanting to spoil the other girl's pleasure.

A couple of hours later, when she was absorbed in marking some term papers, a knock came at the door. Expecting one of the students, she called, 'Come in,' and finished reading the paragraph. She looked up, pushing the hair back from her face. 'Why, Simon, how nice to see you,' she said with spontaneous pleasure, before realising the errand he must have come on. She braced herself for the inevitable disappointment and said brightly, 'Would you like a coffee?'

'No, thanks.'

'Well, sit down. If you can find room, that is. I really must clean up this office, it's a disgrace.' Realising that she was chattering nervously, she fell silent. There was an awkward pause.

'Have you seen Nadine?' Simon asked.

'Yes, she was here a little while ago.'

'Apparently she's been invited to Allen's for Christmas.'

Wishing that he'd come to the point and end her suspense, Erin said, 'She sounded pretty happy about it. You may soon be adding a brother-in-law to your family!'

'I couldn't ask for a better one—he's a nice guy. Nadine's known him for quite a while too. I'm sure they're well suited, and they're both old enough to know what they're doing.'

'That doesn't sound very romantic!'

'As I told you, I had all the romance knocked out of me several years ago,' he said drily. He had perched himself on one corner of the table, and picked up a book, leafing through it absentmindedly.

Convinced that he was trying to let her down gently, Erin heard herself say, 'It's all right, Simon—I realise this changes your plans for Christmas. You don't have to feel you're committed to taking me, now that Nadine can't go.'

The book dropped to the floor and he swore lamentably. 'Who said I didn't want to take you?' he demanded.

'Well—I did.'

'You can stop putting words into my mouth. I was afraid you wouldn't want to come without Nadine.'

'Oh. We seem to be at cross purposes,' she said blankly.

'We do rather.' He grinned crookedly, with a charm so real that she longed to reach out and touch him. 'Let's begin at the beginning. Erin McCourt, I would like the pleasure of your company for Christmas.'

Matching his banter, she inclined her head formally. 'Dr Grayson, it gives me great pleasure to accept your invitation.'

'Phew!' he exclaimed boyishly. 'I'm glad that's over. And I promise I shall behave impeccably, Erin. After all, we can always take Robbie as a chaperone!'

Suffused with relief that she was to have her holiday after all, Erin smothered the cold inner voice of caution that was muttering, 'So you're going to trust him again? Look at what happened last time ...' This time it will be different, she told herself, and said outwardly, 'We'd better talk about food and decide what we'll need.' Within half an hour they had settled all the practical details and had agreed they would start out early on Christmas Eve.

Three days before Christmas there was a blizzard that lasted twenty-four hours, so that when Erin and Simon arrived at the cabin, it was tucked under a blanket of sparkling white. The driveway had been ploughed and a path shovelled to the front door, but other than that the snow stretched in pristine perfection wherever they looked, the boughs of the evergreens weighted down with their icy burden. An incongruous cap of snow topped the chimney, while the roof was jagged with shining icicles. 'We'll get the fire started, then we'd better cut a Christmas tree,' Simon announced, his face relaxed and happy as he surveyed his domain. In an excess of high spirits, he seized a handful of snow and lobbed it in Erin's direction; more by luck than good judgment it hit the collar of her coat, sending a shower of icy particles down her neck. She shrieked and fired an answering snowball at Simon, while Robbie lost his sense of dignity and capered about them, barking hoarsely. With lazy grace Simon ducked and it flew past his shoulder. But she had sent another after the first, and this one hit him full in the chest. He staggered so theatrically that she collapsed against the side of the car, laughing until the tears ran down her face. Surreptitiously she filled her mittened palms with snow, and when Simon came incautiously to stand only a foot away from her, she reached up and rubbed his face with the wet snow. His grey eyes warm and vibrant, he began to chuckle so infectiously that she couldn't help joining him; their laughter echoed over the empty valley. Then he lowered his snow-streaked face to hers and kissed her, a kiss more of comradeship and shared happiness than of passion. She grimaced at him cheekily. 'Your lips are cold and wet,' she complained.

'Whose fault is that?'

'You started it!'

'And I will again, unless you behave.' They smiled at each other amiably and Simon exclaimed, 'I'm glad we're here.'

'Me too,' she agreed ungrammatically.

'Such language—you're forgetting I'm a professor of English!' Somehow their lighthearted repartee set the tone for the rest of the day. They unloaded the car and Simon started fires in the kitchen and living room, while Erin put away their belongings. Again the cabin was immaculately clean and she was glad to notice the registers for electric heat in every room, so they were not totally dependent on the fires for warmth.

On snowshoes they climbed the hill behind the cabin, trying to break a trail for the dog, who was so heavy that with every step he sank to his shoulders. They selected a shapely young fir tree; the woods echoed with the bite of Simon's axe and the tree swished to the ground. With a pen-knife Erin cut a few pine boughs and some orange rose-hips to make a wreath for the door. As they emerged from the forest into the clearing she stood still for a moment, inhaling the crisp cold air. The scene looked, appropriately enough, like a Christmas card—the white-clad hills outlined against a bright blue sky, the groves of spruce like silent dark sentinels, the brook, as yet unfrozen, a metallic band of silver in the valley. Its serene beauty filled her with wonderment; she glanced at her companion and without words saw that he shared and understood her mood.

Erin cooked supper while Simon erected the tree by the big window overlooking the valley, and laced the boughs with tiny coloured lights. After they had eaten, they decorated it with shiny ornaments, strings of scarlet cranberries and tendrils of tinsel; a handpainted wooden angel watched them with a quaint air of dignity from her perch on the tip.

Night had fallen, and Simon switched off all the lights. Turquoise and green, gold and red, the tree lights glowed in the dark, shimmering in the silver bells and gleaming foil. Unconsciously Erin clasped her hands in delight, her face reflecting all the magic of Christmas.

Simon came and stood beside her, casually putting an arm around her shoulders. 'Like it?'

'It's lovely,' she said, her pleasure completed by the warmth of his embrace.

'Shall I help you with the wreath?'

'All right, thanks.' They made a circle of the pine boughs and studded the needles with clusters of rosehips and with pine cones dipped in silver paint; a bow of red ribbon anchored the wreath to the door.

'It's nearly eleven,' Simon exclaimed. 'They're having a midnight carol service at the little church down the road ... if you'd like to, I thought we could ski down rather than taking the car. There's enough moonlight that we should be able to see where we're going.'

'That's a wonderful idea,' she said, glad that he had suggested they go to church, for it had always been a part of her family's Christmas.

Their skis hissed through the light snow as Simon went ahead to break the trail, his tall figure moving with deceptive ease, his ski poles leaving the two rows of tiny punctuation marks. The exercise had brought colour to Erin's cheeks and she had tied her jacket around her waist long before they arrived. There was a line of cars parked outside the church and even horse-drawn sleighs, gold bells jingling on the midnight air.

The service was simple, proclaiming the age-old message of peace and hope; the flickering candlelight illuminated the straw-filled crêche holding the newborn infant. Erin's ears were still ringing with the exultant music of the carols as they skied their way home. She and Simon sat contentedly in front of the fire with glasses of hot spiced wine, until eventually he pulled her to her feet, stretching and yawning, 'Time for bed, wee Erin.'

She smiled at him, her eyelids drooping with drowsiness.

With infinite gentleness Simon put his arms around her. His face was smoothed of care, his grey eyes as open and vulnerable as on the evening he had told her about his wife and daughter. When he spoke his voice caressed her.

'Happy Christmas, Erin,' he said softly, and touched his mouth to hers.

'And the same to you, Simon.'

One last squeeze of his arms and they separated. Although her body always clamoured for his touch, never seeming to get enough of him, tonight she was almost glad of his restraint, sensing that he was telling her that she could trust him. On impulse she stood on tiptoe and kissed his cheek, murmured goodnight and went to her room. Pervaded by a vast contentment, she fell asleep almost instantly.

When she awoke she was dimly aware of noises in the kitchen; the metallic clatter of the woodstove, the crackle and spit of flames, the gush of the tap. She snuggled deeper into the cocoon of blankets, secure and warm, drifting back and forth between sleep and waking. A tap came at her door and sleepily she called, 'Come in.'

When Simon entered, balancing a tray of two steaming cups of tea, she had hoisted herself on one elbow and was rubbing her eyes. Her thick black hair fell down one bare shoulder to lie across her breast, whose curves were faithfully outlined by the clinging silk nightgown. She smiled at him, and discovered in his face that which caused her to pull the sheet over her body, a rosy glow on her cheekbones. And then she remembered what day it was. 'Happy Christmas!' she cried.

Setting down the tray on her bedside table, he bent and kissed her, supporting himself with one hand on her pillow, his big body leaning over her. He was wearing light blue pyjamas and a velvet dressing gown that brought back to her a flood of memories—how long ago it all seemed, their first tumultous meeting! He released her and said prosaically enough, although a pulse was throbbing at the base of his throat, 'Cup of tea?'

'Thanks. Are you going to join me?' He sat on the bed beside her, and she felt a delicious confusion envelop her. 'Have you been up long?' she asked hastily.

'An hour or so,' he said, and she knew perfectly well he had seen through her gambit. 'The turkey's in the oven, and the bacon is frying for breakfast.'

'You're spoiling me.'

'It's not that difficult to do that, Erin,' he said, and before she could think of an answer, sat up. 'I'd better go and check on the breakfast. Take your time—there's no hurry.'

They spent a leisurely morning preparing the dinner, bringing in armloads of wood from the shed, and unwrapping their presents; she had given Simon a briefcase of soft tooled leather, for she had noticed how shabby was the one he used on campus; and he had given her a cashmere turtleneck sweater of palest blue. Delighted, she put it on with a gathered skirt she had brought with her, and paraded in front of him in a parody of a model's long-legged stride. 'It looks a lot better on you than it did in the box,' he said drily, laughing as she pulled a rude face at him.

They ate a traditional dinner of stuffed turkey and cranberry sauce, with homegrown vegetables and a delicious dry white wine, followed by a plum pudding with brandy sauce, and coffee and liqueurs in front of the fire. Simon groaned loudly. 'If I don't get some exercise I'm going to fall asleep. How about it, Erin—want to go for a walk?'

'Let's—I ate far too much, but it was all so good. I'll change into my slacks.' In her room she hesitated before pulling on her two-piece ski suit over her slacks, an act she was later to be deeply grateful for. Grabbing her fur mittens and hat and lacing up her mukluks, she joined Simon outdoors. Today there was no brilliant blue sky, only a heavy unbroken greyness that presaged snow. A light wind ruffled Simon's hair as he bent to lace up his snowshoe harness, his broad shoulders straining at his heavy lumberman jacket. 'We've got time to go up to the sugar shack if you'd like to?'

They set off up the hill, the snow swishing over the rawhide bindings of their snowshoes. Robbie started after them, but soon Simon ordered him home. 'Go back, Robbie! You'll wear yourself out, you silly old dog.' Robbie subsided on his haunches, his massive black head tilted on one side as though he understood every word, then in as dignified a manner as was possible in the snowdrifts, jogged back down the hill towards the cabin.

Erin laughed. 'He's a nice dog. Have you had him long?'

'Yes, he's getting old for a dog; I've had him nine years.' He smiled reminiscently, with none of the corroding bitterness that had eaten away at him for so long. 'Elice loved him; she used to ride on his back as though he were a pony.'

'He would have been as big as a pony to her!' Erin chuckled. 'How old was she when you got him?' By asking further questions about Elice she encouraged him to talk about her, her intuition sensing that for far too long he had kept his memories of his daughter locked away.

She was breathless by the time they clambered up the bank of the creek to the sugar hut; the tall tops of the trees were swaying in the wind, which sighed through their naked limbs like the sound of the sea. A few snowflakes were falling, blown this way and that by the capricious gusts. It was a landscape painted in grey and white, desolate and subtly threatening. Erin shivered, hurrying to reach the weathered shack, its man-made roof and walls offering a sanctuary from the winter's bleakness. Inside, Simon lit a fire, filled a billycan with snow, and produced packages of pre-mixed cocoa. Erin cupped her fingers around the cup and sipped its steaming contents gratefully.

'Cold?'

'A little,' she admitted. 'The wind's come up quite a bit even since we left, hasn't it?'

'Yes.' He cast a knowledgeable glance out of one of the windows and his voice sharpened with quick anxiety. 'We'd better not stay too long. It looks as though it's settling in for a real snowstorm. It's only four and it's nearly dark.'

That he should betray anxiety was enough to frighten Erin, for she had a healthy respect for his knowledge of the outdoors, knowing it had been gained through years of experience. Hurriedly she gulped down the last of her cocoa and replaced her boots. When she left the shack to get her snowshoes, she was horrified to see how thickly the snowflakes were falling now, whirling downwards as though driven from the sky; by the time she had tightened her bindings her fingers were red and numb with cold.

'Ready?' Simon shouted.

She nodded, her eyes apprehensive.

He wasted no time in reassuring her, for he was as worried as she. 'Stick close behind me; we'll go as fast as we can.' He swung off down the trail, a curtain of whiteness immediately almost obscuring him from view; quenching her nervousness, Erin set off after him. He set a cruelly fast pace, which for a few minutes she was able to maintain. But then she stumbled and had to clutch at a tree for support; when she straightened Simon was out of sight and she was alone in a claustrophobic world of swirling snow. Panic-stricken, she held on to the tree trunk with desperate fingers, for it represented at least a semblance of stability; twice she called out Simon's name, the wind snatching the words from her mouth and tossing them away into the storm.

A dark figure materialised out of the gathering night and with a sob of sheer relief she saw it was Simon. Against the wind's keening, he shouted, 'What happened?'

She clutched at him with both hands, finding his solid bulk infinitely reassuring. He held her tightly for a moment, sending her an unspoken message of comfort. 'I'll go slower —and don't worry, we'll get home safely.'

Again they started off, Erin at times almost stepping on the backs of his snowshoes in her haste to keep up with him. She had no idea how he knew which way to go, and followed him in blind trust. The biting cold had penetrated the fur and leather of her mittens, and she clenched and unclenched her fists to stimulate the circulation, only too aware of how quickly and insidiously frostbite could set in; her temples were aching with the cold and her cheeks felt numb.

Ahead of her Simon halted and she almost bumped into him. She swung her arms to keep warm as he stared around him at the trees, as though seeking a landmark. 'I think we're okay—the trail should bear to the left shortly.' He came as close to her as he could, trying to shield her from the worst of the blizzard's fury with his body. 'Are you all right?'

She nodded, giving him a gallant little smile.

'Good girl!'

Sure enough, in a few minutes the trail did bear to the left; immeasurably encouraged, Erin lurched onwards, keeping her chin tucked into her chest, in a vain effort to protect her face from the pain of the stinging ice crystals. The step-by-step movement of her snowshoes had become automatic, and just as automatically she kept her eyes glued to Simon's broad back, drawing strength from the sight of him, noting how often he looked back to make sure she was following. She was getting very tired, and a stitch in her side stabbed her with every step. Her legs felt like lead, her feet ached with cold. It began to seem like a never-ending nightmare, that she should stagger through a blizzard after him, never able to stop, yet never quite reaching him.

When she fell, it happened so quickly she had no chance to prevent it. The path seemed suddenly to vanish. Her left snowshoe came down, not on level snow, but on a steeply sloping drift. Thrown off balance, she fell sideways, grabbing at the branches of a spruce in a frantic effort to save herself. But the needles slid through her wet mittens even as a long-dead branch, broken and sharp, scraped her cheek. She cried out in pain and tripping on her own snow-shoes tumbled down the bank, her body thudding against a tree trunk with bruising force, driving the last vestige of air from her lungs.

'Erin, where are you?' Simon's voice came thinly through the blizzard. She tried to call out, but not a sound came from her lips. Then he was sliding down the bank towards her; he pulled off one glove to touch her cheek, brushing away the clinging snow. 'You're bleeding—what happened?'

His face was only inches from hers; her eyes were so accustomed to the semi-darkness that she could see the intolerable anxiety that lined his features; his fingers were not quite steady. 'I'm all right—it's only a scratch,' she gasped. 'Can you help me up?'

His steady hands pulled her to her feet, and for a moment she leaned against him, her heart pounding in her breast with delayed shock; she felt dizzy and bitterly cold, long shudders shaking her frame. Simon put his mouth near her ear. 'We're nearly there,' he said. 'Can you manage another few minutes?' He kept an arm around her and half pushed her up the bank, back on to the trail. She held on to him, still needing his support, and together they staggered down the hill.

He was right; within only a few minutes they had left the shelter of the forest and emerged on the open hillside. Momentarily, Erin caught a glimpse of light beckoning them from the cabin window; she did not think she had ever seen a more beautiful sight in her life. But now they were struck by the full force of the gale, as it swept unimpeded up the valley. By the time they reached the cabin Simon was half carrying her, shielding her as best he could from the knife-like stabs of the wind. Somehow he got the snowshoes off their feet and lifted her over the threshold into the blessed warmth and brightness of the cabin. Banging the door shut behind him, he leaned against its panels, his breathing ragged and uneven. He still had Erin in the circle of his arm; she huddled against him, scarcely able to believe that they were safe. With wondering eyes she saw every detail of the room, the mellow pine walls, the glow of the coals in the hearth, the sparkling Christmas tree, and tears of thankfulness spilled over. They were safe!

She had no strength left to struggle when Simon picked her up and carried her over to the armchair by the fire. He stirred up the embers, adding more wood so that the flames leaped up the chimney. Then he knelt by her chair and pulled off her snow-encrusted hat and her frozen mittens, chafing her cold hands in his. Although she protested weakly, he insisted on helping her out of her wet snowsuit and wrapping her in the eiderdown from her bed. Warmth began to spread through her body, ousting the chill from her bones, and finally she was able to say, 'Simon, you must look after yourself—please.'

'Starting to give me orders again, wee Erin?' he said gruffly. 'You must be feeling better!'

'It's you I'm worried about,' she answered, knowing his roughness was a measure of his concern for her, and in her heart cherishing his concern. In a few moments he came back in the room, having changed his trousers and sweater, and bringing with him two bowls of thick soup, piping hot. It was only as she finished it that Erin realised what had subconsciously been bothering her for some minutes now.

'Where's Robbie?' she exclaimed. 'We didn't see him outdoors anywhere.'

Simon looked at her in consternation. 'I'd forgotten all about him.' His face relaxed. 'He's probably in the shed—I have an outdoor kennel built into one side of it. Although it's funny he didn't hear us when we got back—I know he'd far rather be in here than outside.'

'Maybe you'd better check,' Erin suggested, even though she dreaded the thought of him having to venture out into the storm again.

'Okay—I'll be back in a minute.' But when he came back, one look at his face told her Robbie was not in the kennel. 'I went all round the cabin and called for him; but there's no sign of him. Where on earth could he be?'

'Maybe he's just curled himself up in a snowbank somewhere,' she suggested, not very hopefully.

'No, he'd head for home, I know he would. I'll have to go and look for him, Erin—I think something must have happened to him.'

She had known he would make that decision—apart from everything else, the dog was his only link with the past, with his lost daughter. But in spite of herself, her voice trembled. 'Be careful, Simon.'

'Don't worry, I won't go far—but I can at least look for him in the vicinity of the cabin.' Even as he talked he was pulling on his sheepskin boots again and zippering his parka, putting a flashlight in his pocket. He hesitated a moment, seeing only too clearly the fear on Erin's face. One quick hard hug, and he was gone, swallowed by the storm. Knowing she would be unable to sit still until he returned, Erin banked the fire with birch logs, the bark crackling merrily into flame, then went out into the kitchen and doggedly started to wash up their dinner dishes—it seemed an aeon ago they had eaten. But not even that activity could last for ever; when the kitchen was as neat and tidy as she could make it, she put more wood in the kitchen stove and went to stand by the living-room window, staring out into the impenetrable, windblown blackness, her heart crying out for Simon to come home.

With a suddenness that frightened her, all the lights in

the cabin flickered, brightened, flickered again and then went out. She caught her breath in dismay—a power failure, and little wonder in such weather. Fortunately there were red Christmas candles in silver candlesticks on the coffee table; she lit one and put it in the window, carrying another to Simon's bedroom in the hope that its feeble light would guide him back to the cabin. There was nothing more she could do now but wait ...

For many years afterwards Erin would remember that wait as the longest hour of her life. She paced the floor, stoked the fires, wandered from window to window and ceaselessly in her mind reiterated one prayer, 'Simon, come home—please, Simon, come home!'

Behind her the door burst open. She whirled. 'Simon! Thank God you're back!' Running to him she saw that one hand was clenched in Robbie's collar; the great dog was limping badly, his black face rimmed with frost, his fur matted with lumps of frozen snow. Then to her horror Erin realised that the fingers around the leather collar were bare—Simon must have lost his glove. The flesh was dead white, icy cold to her touch. 'Simon!' she cried sharply, but although he looked in her direction, his eyes did not seem to be focusing properly. He was swaying on his feet, his pallor indicating total exhaustion. Her hands clumsy with haste, she unbuckled Robbie's collar; the dog padded to the hearth, sank on to the fur rug and began to lick his wounded paw.

It took every bit of Erin's strength to guide Simon to the armchair; he collapsed into it, his head bowed, his hands resting stiffly on his knees. Distant memories of a first aid course she had once taken filtered back into Erin's mind. 'Slow steady warmth to restore sensation gradually.' She unbuttoned his shirt and gently put the injured hand under his armpit, knowing that his own body heat was the best cure of all. The eiderdown was still over the back of the chair; she tucked it around his shoulders, and kneeling in front of him took off his heavy boots. He smiled at her dazedly. 'Sorry,' he muttered, 'I'm being a lot of trouble.'

'Don't be silly,' she said, too overwrought to be anything but totally honest. 'I'm just glad you're back.' And for a moment she rested her forehead on his knee, her hair tumbling across his thigh. With his good hand he clumsily patted her head.

'Erin,' he said, each word an obvious effort, 'I had frostbite once before, so I know what to expect. When my fingers start to thaw, it'll hurt—don't worry, okay? It won't last long.'

She stared at him, her eyes huge, her face pale. 'Let me see it.'

He gave her his hand; a little colour seemed to have come back to the skin.

'It's starting to tingle,' he said ruefully, pushing it back under his shirt. 'Why don't you make us something hot to drink?'

She got up, knowing he was trying to spare her distress. She had filled the kettle with water and put it on the stove while he had been gone; she added tea, and poured milk into the mugs. But the still figure by the fireside drew her like a magnet. His forehead was resting on his other hand and from the taut line of his shoulders she knew the pain had started. On silent feet she approached the chair, and knelt beside it, helpless to offer anything more than her presence. From between her lashes she swiftly glanced up at him; his eyes were closed, his mouth tight-held, lines of pain already scoring his face. She leaned her cheek against his knee and felt his hand come down hard on her shoulder.

The next ten minutes told Erin more truly than any passionate lovemaking that she loved Simon Grayson, for she felt his agony as her own, and ached to bear it for him. All she could do was wipe the beads of sweat from his ashen forehead, and try not to flinch as his fingers bit into her shoulder. It went on too long, and twice he groaned aloud, so that helpless tears of compassion flooded her eyes.

But gradually the pain abated, as he had said it would. He sat up a little straighter in the chair and loosened his grip on her shoulder; she knew her skin would be marked from the bruising pressure he had unconsciously exerted. 'I'm glad that's over,' he muttered, for the first time seeing the tear marks on her face and the blue shadows under her eyes. 'I thought I told you to stay in the kitchen.'

She gave him a tremulous smile. 'Yes, you did. But I couldn't leave you alone——'

'I'm glad you didn't. It was a help knowing you were there.' His words brought a flush of happiness to her face, and deliberately, it seemed, he changed the subject. 'Where's that tea?'

She got up, stretching her cramped limbs gratefully. 'I'll get it.'

Not long afterwards they banked up both fires for the night, and Simon found and lit two oil lamps for the bedrooms. Outside Erin's door he surveyed her sombrely from unreadable grey eyes. Cupping her face in both hands, he tilted it to his as his mouth found hers and drank of its sweetness. 'Goodnight, Erin,' he said huskily.

'Goodnight. I'm glad you're safe.'

Tonight it took her some time to get to sleep, for although her body ached with tiredness, her mind could not rest but scurried actively over the events of the day again and again. And outside, a perpetual reminder, the snow beat against the window pane, while the merciless wind lashed the cabin.

The cold seeping through her blankets awakened her. She curled up into a ball to keep warm, pulling the eiderdown over her shoulders, but sleep eluded her. And then a tiny sound from the next room made her sit bolt upright in bed. It was Simon, moaning in his sleep. She slid out of bed, finding her slippers and her long robe. In the living room the fire was almost out and the chilled air made her shiver; hurriedly she added more wood and soon had the satisfaction of seeing the flames curl hungrily around the logs. She did the same in the kitchen, and then crept back to her room; the activity had warmed her and she thought she would be able to sleep again. But even as she pulled off her caftan, from Simon's room again came the low moan of distress.

On bare feet she tiptoed to his door and eased it open. His room was cold, so she pushed the door as wide as it would go to let the heat circulate from the fireplace. In the light from the leaping flames she could see he must have tossed the covers back from his bare shoulders; she went closer, reaching out a tentative hand to touch his flesh—it was cold, and she could feel the constant shuddering that rippled through his muscles. For a minute she stood in silent indecision, but she knew there was only one way to warm him. She lifted the blankets and slid into bed beside him.

His eyes flew open. 'Erin?'

'Ssh! Go back to sleep.'

'The fires——'

'I looked after them. They'll be all right until morning.'

He was shivering again, and she pressed her body to his, burrowing her face in his shoulder, an arm falling across his waist. His skin smelt clean and masculine; the hair on his chest was rough against her cheek. He gave a sigh of contentment, inhaling the scent of her hair, one arm pulling her closer. His thigh fell across her legs. 'You feel nice,' he murmured drowsily, and with a naturalness that disarmed her he kissed her goodnight.

Imperceptibly she relaxed, knowing that her own warmth had spread to him, hearing his breathing become deep and even as he slept. Although outside the blizzard raged unabated, she felt utterly secure, knowing she was in the safest place in the world—in Simon's arms.

CHAPTER EIGHT

It was the silence that finally awakened Erin, the silence and the warmth of Simon's body next to hers. He had been restless part of the night, his long frame racked by fevered chills, but had finally relaxed his tense body and had lapsed into a quiet sleep.

She moved slightly, torn between the desire to stay with him, to continue to feel the warmth and rhythm of his quietly breathing body, and the embarrassment that was beginning to rise in her and take control. Simon moved slightly, drawing in a breath and moving closer to her, his arm carelessly flung over her breasts. She lay there quietly, trying to figure a way to get up without awakening him to her presence; probably he wouldn't even remember that she had slept next to him for the last hours of the night.

The fires must have gone out, for Erin could feel the icy chill in the room, made visibly evident by the white breath she expelled when she moved her face above the covers. The wind outside had died down and perhaps it had ceased to snow as well, she thought. As she gathered together courage to face the coldness of the room and get up to start the fire, Simon spoke softly as he lay beside her, his eyes still closed and looking for all the world to still be asleep.

'What are you thinking of, wee Erin, getting up and leaving this patient of yours to the ravages of the cold?'

'Oh, Simon, you're awake,' she murmured.

'No, I'm talking to you in my sleep, and you must never ever awaken a sleeping talker, Erin.' He smiled contentedly, his eyes still closed. 'You wouldn't leave this comfortable man just yet, would you, as you seem to be intending to do?' He moved even closer, drawing her slim body into his strong arms, drawing her face close to his.

'Please, Simon, I have to get up and start the fire, it's cold in here. You need warmth. You . . .'

'Stay here, Erin. We have warmth already.'

'Simon, please!' She shivered at the touch of his fingers on her lips and was too shy to look into the depths of grey eyes that now gazed seriously at her.

'Please what, Erin McCourt? Please me and stay.'

She turned her face from his in an effort to hide her confusion.

'I'm sorry, Erin, I didn't mean to tease you.' Still she did not turn her face to him. 'Hey, wee Erin, look at me.' She felt her throat tighten and tears begin to sting her eyes. What would he believe of her? She had never slept with a man before, but would he believe that?

Simon lifted himself up on his elbow now and leaned over her. 'Erin, I want you to look at me. What's the matter with you? Don't you feel well?' He gently turned her face to his and saw the tears in her eyes. 'God——' he whispered. 'I was only teasing you, gal. I didn't mean to hurt you. What's wrong?'

'Nothing,' she gulped, closing her eyes. 'It's just that ... just that ...' she couldn't continue.

'Just what?' he insisted softly.

'Just that I don't want you to think that I ... that I ... I mean I've never slept with a man before and I didn't want you to think that I ...'

Simon murmured, 'My silly Erin! Don't be so foolish. I know you haven't slept with a man before. There's no shame in what we did last night, none at all.' He gently wiped the tears from her cheeks and drew her close to him, his body insistent for possession of her. 'I want you, Erin,' he groaned, 'I want you.' His mouth claimed hers with a demanding ferocity, his hands moving possessively over the gentle curves of her body, seeking to know every inch of her. Her body cried out for a completeness that could only come with their union, as her passion rose and responded to his. Suddenly Simon drew away from her. 'Oh God, Erin, we can't,' he grated. 'As much as I want to, we can't —not now.'

He didn't leave her but lay beside her, struggling to control his desire for her, his ragged breathing gradually returning to normal. They lay together for a long time, watching the early morning sunlight flood the cabin with shafts of gold, not speaking but lying quietly in each other's arms. Silence and peace filling her world, Erin was suddenly overcome by the joyful realisation that it was love that she held in her heart for this man. It was love that had been growing and stirring and waiting for the time of its birth from the first moment of their meeting those long days ago, back in the last days of summer. It was not Peter Hall whom she loved at all, foolish woman that she was; the love she thought she had borne for Peter was but a slim and pale shadow of the feeling she now recognised existed within her for Simon, this man who had at first appeared to be harsh and cold but instead was a man of warmth and caring and strength and integrity. Simon was the man she loved. Of this she was certain, and this realisation filled her heart to the point of bursting.

So quietly did she rest against Simon that he wondered if indeed she had not fallen asleep. He stirred, pushing back a straying hair from her face, and asked quietly, 'Are you awake, Erin?'

She stretched luxuriously and snuggled closer to the muscled hardness of his chest, revelling in the rough feel of the dark hairs on his naked chest. 'Yes, I'm awake.'

'You're very quiet. Are you all right? I didn't frighten you, did I?'

'I'm fine—the finest I've ever been, in fact.'

'Don't you think it's time you got up and got some food for your man?' he teased.

Her heart lurched at his reference to himself as 'her man'. Oh, lord, yes, her heart cried out. He's all I've ever wanted, he's all I'll ever need. If only he was 'my man'.

With the grace of a mountain lion, despite the size of his huge frame, Simon moved quickly out of bed. He pulled on his brown cords and put on his thick wool sweater, the muscles of his bronzed back rippling. 'I'll get the fire started and maybe you could make us a bite to eat, while I see what it'll take to dig us out of here,' he said briefly.

The door of the cabin closed behind him and he left Erin alone with her excited thoughts and soaring feelings. 'I love you ... I love you ... I love you ... Simon Grayson,' she said over and over again to herself. '*I love you!*' She felt like dancing, running, and shouting it to the sky, the trees, the whole world.

By the time Simon returned, stomping the snow from his boots at the door, Erin had made the beds, tidied the cabin, and breakfast was hot and waiting. She set the food on the table and sat down, feeling more than a little proud of herself. They ate, chatting comfortably with each other, and eventually Simon leaned back, sipped his hot coffee, and patted his lean stomach. 'You'll make a fat man of me, Erin, if I have too many breakfasts like that.' He looked relaxed and content, more than he ever had in the months she'd known him. He looked years younger, in fact, with none of the tight lines of worry and strain creasing his face. She hoped fervently that it was because of her. She wanted desperately to be the source of as much happiness for him as he was for her.

'We'll have to snowshoe down to the village to arrange

for someone to plough us out. There's about two feet of fresh snow out there.'

'Why?' she asked playfully. 'Why don't we stay here until it melts?' Part of her question was a wish.

He pulled her roughly to him and hugged her. 'Because, wee Erin, if you even suggest such a thing again, I'm apt to take you up on it, because it wouldn't take much to break down my defences. All I seem to want right now in this entire world is here in my arms. And,' he added quickly, 'we've got to go back to Abbotsford this afternoon—I've got a lot of work that's waiting for me at my office, a desperate thesis student who didn't even want me to take Christmas Day, a meeting with Kevin that's prime on his list if not mine, and an important personal matter in Halifax to attend to.'

She could not conceal her disappointment. It swept over and through her and made itself painfully visible in her eyes, that filled with regret. Seeing this, Simon said, 'I hate to go back too, Erin, believe me, but I don't really have a choice. We'll escape to our cabin in the Sweet Mountains again soon—I promise.'

He turned to check the fire, then walked to the door. 'We might as well let the fire in the stove go out, we'll be leaving as soon as they can plough us out. Cheer up and come down to the village with me. It's a beautiful day.'

'I'll tidy up here and pack some things and then I'll be right with you,' she responded, trying not to show sadness in her voice. She was surprised at her own feelings, surprised that her emotions could dip so low and so quickly as soon as he had said that they would be returning; she wanted to be with him, she wanted to revel in the peace and joy he brought to her. 'You're a selfish spoiled woman, Erin McCourt, and it's time to grow up,' she scolded herself for forgetting so easily that Simon had other things in his life besides her that were important to him.

It was a winter wonderland. And Erin was made breathless by the beauty of the scene that surrounded her. The branches of the trees were heavily laden with snow that was inches thick, perfectly sculpted in a fine white powder. The sky was a brilliant blue, with only the faintest wisps of white cloud appearing in its wide expanse. What must it have been like to forsake civilisation for a life alone in these mountains? For a moment she wanted such a life, but knew that, like Simon, she needed more. This was an escape, a place to which they could come and rest and revitalise, but there was another life and a whole world beyond this place; they both had important and meaningful things to do out there.

The walk down the mountain was fun. They tried to throw snowballs at each other, but the snow was too fine and too powdery, so they ended finally by showering each other with snow crystals. At one point, Erin carefully manoeuvred Simon under a tree and then with wild abandon and oblivious to any retaliation he might take, she tugged on the overhanging branch and covered him with snow.

He squirmed as it went down inside the neck of his sweater. 'You're a heartless, fiendish woman, Erin, and now I need your help. Come here and get some of the snow out of the back of my sweater before it melts and drenches me.' He looked so serious that she came back to him and told him to turn around. He laughed the laugh of a theatre villain and grabbed her. 'No one, man or woman, ever gets away with dirty business like that, Erin McCourt. There's a snow bank waiting for you.'

He lifted her easily, as if she were no heavier than a puff of air. She struggled and held tightly on to his neck. 'No, Simon, I'm sorry—don't! Don't throw me into that snowbank ... I didn't mean to, really I didn't!' Her words were punctuated with her laughter, but no amount of begging on her part could persuade Simon to abandon his intention. The next moment she felt herself moving in mid-air and she landed softly, face down, in a mound of snow.

She didn't move a muscle, suffocating her laughter with effort. She heard Simon's voice, teasing at first and then concerned by her lack of movement. 'Erin, are you all right?' Then he was kneeling beside her, gently turning her still and relaxed body over. 'For God's sake, Erin, are you all right?'

Suddenly she lifted her arms and flung a fistful of snow

into his face, grabbing him and catching him off balance and pulling him down into the snow beside her. They tumbled and rolled, laughing and struggling and relishing the feel of each other, then finally lying still, side by side, breathlessly exhausted by their play.

The man at the garage in the village looked at them, a stern smile growing on his face. 'What did you two do? Roll down that blamed mountainside?'

'That's exactly what we did, Angus,' Simon laughed, hugging Erin affectionately, 'that's exactly what we did.'

Late that afternoon they drove home. Once he started the job, it had not taken Angus long to plough the road while Simon and Erin had quickly loaded the car with all they needed to take back to Abbotsford with them. All too soon as far as Erin was concerned, they were on the highway that crossed the flat marshlands marking the provincial boundary between New Brunswick and Nova Scotia.

Erin must have slept against Simon's shoulder, for she wakened finally when he nudged her gently. 'Wake up, sweetheart—journey's end.' She opened her eyes, surprised that they sat outside her house with everything enveloped in darkness. She shivered as she opened the door of the car and stepped out into the damp coldness.

'There's a heavy snow coming our way, I'd say,' Simon muttered as he sniffed the air. 'In the next day or so, I'm thinking.' He took out her overnight bag and carried it inside.

For a moment Erin was nearly overcome by the coldness and emptiness of her bungalow, and by the prospect of being left alone in a few moments. She looked awkwardly at the floor, unable to meet Simon's eyes.

He touched her hair, running his strong fingers lightly through the silken length of it. 'I didn't want to come back either, Erin, if that means anything to you,' he said quietly, almost tentatively. He then bent and kissed her lightly on the lips, before moving to the door. 'I'll be in Halifax in the morning, but I'll try and get over to see you in the afternoon if you're around. See you tomorrow, wee Erin.'

And then he was gone, leaving Erin to the pulsing emptiness of her house and a feeling of futile aloneness and separation. For a moment she could almost feel again the warmth and tenderness of his body next to hers the night before when she had slept in his arms. Whatever might become of them and their relationship, Erin knew with a blinding certainty that she had found, at last, the man who would have her love. There would never be room for anyone but Simon in her heart.

The next day Erin was amazed by the startling blueness of the sea. It was like a summer blue, she thought, as she breathed deeply of the salt air and gazed with wonder out to the harbour's warmth. It certainly wasn't going to snow today, regardless of Simon's prediction. Almost, in her mind, she could visualise the white sails of *Early Summer*, skimming and cutting her way through the sheet of blue. *Early Summer* racing with the wind, with Simon standing tall and strong at the tiller, his bronzed face smiling and laughing, happy to be alive. In her mind she could hear him call to her, clear and strong over the space of blue, 'Erin . . . Erin . . .' And she felt for a moment that he had called her to join him.

She smiled at herself for indulging in such fantasies. 'Erin McCourt, you're nothing but a foolish teenager, dreaming of your special beau.' She looked up quickly as she heard her name again, this time not in her mind. She turned to see Simon's tall figure walking towards her on the beach, his footsteps punctuated with the cracking of crusted snow. He had returned from Halifax.

'Hi, wee Erin,' he said tenderly, his eyes warm with some secret smile. 'Have I told you today that I think you're beautiful?'

'Ah, and you, my Simon Grayson, you are one fine cut of a man, even if I do say so myself,' she retorted, a giggle escaping her lips.

He ruffled her long black hair, as she gave him a push that caught him off balance and sent him sliding on the hardened snow. 'Don't tease! I'm always serious when I pay the man . . .' She stopped suddenly, aware that she had nearly said 'the man I love', and quickly changed her words, 'the man with whom I'm speaking a compliment.'

But the catch in her voice, slight and almost imperceptible, did not escape Simon's notice and he quickly regained his balance, caught her by the arm and said softly, 'Walk with me, Erin, down the beach a piece.' There was something in his voice that made her look up, made her search the grey depths of his eyes, but there was nothing there that she could understand. He returned her gaze. 'Please,' he said again.

'Of course I'll walk with you. It's a beautiful day, a blue and yellow day, and I love it.' She ran ahead of him, trying to scoop up snow to throw at him, but all she could scrape were a few hardened ice crystals. She sprinkled them in his hair, laughing and admonishing him for walking along an icy beach in the dead of winter 'at his age'. 'You know, dear old Simon, at your age with hair as white and frosty as yours, you should really be inside sitting by that fireplace in your rocking chair.'

'Laugh at an old man, will you gal? I should throw you into the sea for making fun of a poor, unloved man.'

They were standing at Simon's dock now, *Early Summer* rising and falling in the water, the sound of the waves slapping against her side echoing in the silence. A sudden tension filled the air. Her voice barely audible, Erin reached out and touched Simon's face, touched his eyes and cheeks with her slim fingers. 'Not ... not unloved, my dearest Simon.' Her hands were trembling and Simon gathered her into his arms. He stared into her eyes and she could hear the quickening of his breath.

Embarrassed by the words she had just uttered and uncomfortable under Simon's unflinching stare, she laughed self-consciously. 'You know, Simon, a few minutes ago I was dreaming, before you came ... day-dreaming, of course ... but I thought for a moment that it was summer and I could see you out there.' She raised her arm and pointed out to the mouth of the Harbour. 'Out there, sailing in *Early Summer*, and I could hear you, all the way from summer to here, calling my name, and I could see your face, just as plain, even over this distance, and ...' She was talking quickly, trying to hide her embarrassment. '... And you called to me and you wanted me to come with you, and ...'

'Erin,' Simon's voice broke her mad rush of words, 'when you saw me out there and heard me call to you, did you want to come with me?'

She stood stock still, with only the sound of her ragged breath and the squealing of a seagull marking the silence.

'Did you want to come to me, Erin?' he repeated, and she turned to him.

'I don't know ... I ...' She twisted her fingers together nervously, afraid that he would laugh at her if she told him the truth, afraid of his rejection if he didn't feel for her what she bore in her heart for him. 'I feel strange, Simon, I think I want to go home, please, I ...'

'What are you frightened of, Erin?'

'I'm not afraid. Don't be silly, Simon, there's nothing to be afraid of. I'm tired, that's all.'

'Are you afraid of me?' He turned her to face him, his hand gently holding her chin and tilting her face to his. He bent and softly brushed her lips with his. 'Are you afraid of me, Erin?' He repeated his question, as he held her face firmly, not permitting her to escape his searching eyes.

'No. No! I know you'd never hurt me, not on purpose, anyway.' A sob broke from her lips; all she wanted to do was escape and be alone. He was a man of experience and maybe he would laugh at her and count her love for him as merely infatuation, and she could never stand that. She pulled herself away and turned and began to walk down the beach towards her house.

Simon didn't come after her, but called to her, just as she had heard him do in her dream, moments before, 'Erin!'

Looking back, she saw that he beckoned her to return to him, his hand held out to her. Still she could not move, hot tears searing her face. He waited for her and slowly she walked back to stand before him.

'You're not frightened of me. Are you, Erin?'

'No.' She hesitated. 'I fear the feelings you arouse in me. I've never felt this way about a man before. But I'm not afraid of you.'

With these words she walked into his arms. He held her tightly to him, nearly crushing her small body with the ferocity of his passion. 'Oh God, I love you, Erin. I never thought it possible to love anyone as much.'

She was weeping openly in his arms now, the joy of hearing these words unleashing all emotion. 'Please don't cry, Erin. Trust me. I'll never hurt you, never. Don't be frightened of this thing we share.' He gently stroked her hair. 'Will you marry me, Erin? Will you let me love you for the rest of our lives?'

She turned a tear-stained face to him as he gently wiped the tears from her face. 'Oh, Simon, yes. A thousand times yes!'

Simon reached into the pocket of his jacket and took out a small box. Taking her small hand in his, he slipped on a ring, a brilliant blue sapphire surrounded by a circle of diamonds.

'Oh, Simon, it's beautiful,' she breathed. 'I've never seen anything as lovely!'

'I have,' he said. 'It's blue to match your eyes and blue to match the sea on a summer day. And ...' he added, 'on a particularly glorious day in December.' He drew her gently into his strong arms. 'I love you, Erin, and all I want to do is make you happy.' He hesitated, then continued, as if finding the rest of what he had to say difficult, 'Will I be enough for you? Can I make you forget Peter?'

Erin threw her arms around his neck and hugged him joyously. 'There's only you, Simon. Only you.'

'Come on, Erin, a drink to celebrate.' He led her towards his house, bounded up the steps and held the door for her. Then quickly lifting her into his arms, he carried her into the living room.

'Silly man,' she teased, 'put me down, you're only supposed to do this after we're married.'

'What?' he chided in mock seriousness, 'aren't we married yet?' He buried his face in her silken hair. 'Well, I for one, woman, have never felt more married in all my life.' He lowered her to the chesterfield and then lay full length beside her. 'Happy?' he asked.

'So happy that it scares me a bit.'

'There's nothing to be scared of, my love, as long as we're together.' His mouth sought hers and for a long time they lay together, exchanging kisses, talking, and caressing each other, united by a happiness as deep as the ocean, as joyously free as the sea wind.

Then as Simon moved his hand to stroke the soft skin of her neck he caught sight of his watch. 'Hell,' he said in annoyance. 'I'll have to run. I've still got a few things to do at the office and I've got a meeting with Kevin at five—I'm already ten minutes late.' He groaned as he buried his face in her silky tresses. 'I'm sorry, I don't want to leave you now, I want to stay, but I've got to go.' He got reluctantly to his feet and slowly tucked in his shirt. Erin, as comfortable as a sleek young cat, lay back on the couch.

'I'll stay here and wait for you.'

He sat down on the couch and drew her into his arms. 'It would probably be better if I dropped you at your place. I'll see you tomorrow, but don't forget we're invited to the Haleys' dinner party in a couple of days.'

She twined her hands around his neck, and pulled him closer.

'You Jezebel, Erin McCourt. If you don't stop it, I won't be able to leave.' He kissed her firmly on the mouth and then lifted her to her feet.

The fire in the fireplace was now just a few glowing embers and the house was in darkness. But the warmth that filled Erin melted the darkness and sharpened her awareness of everything around her.

'I love you, Simon,' she whispered to the darkness and to him, bathing in the feeling that filled her at the sound of the words.

'And I love you, wee Erin,' breathed Simon.

It was nearly nine o'clock when she heard Simon's footsteps on the veranda the night of the Haleys' party. He knocked and quietly let himself in. Her heart beat with the rhythm of thunder at the very sight of him, so tall and handsome in his black tuxedo. He managed a few disjointed words—'Sorry, I'm later than I thought ...' then fell silent and stared at her as she waited breathlessly for his reactions to her preparation for the party. She turned round slowly, showing him the dress she had chosen to wear, a long dress of deep blue satin with simply cut lines that highlighted her pale skin and her trim figure. Her thick black hair she wore up, with some curls straying purposefully at the side of her delicate face.

'Do you like it?' she breathed cautiously.

'Do I like it?' he said, surprised. 'Erin girl, you're the most beautiful woman I've ever seen in my life.'

In the next moment he was holding her close. 'And you're all mine.' He held her away from him. 'I'm almost tempted to suggest an alternative to the party, but I want everyone to see what a lucky man Simon Grayson is.' He picked up her coat and held it for her as she slipped into it, and drew her back against his hard muscular body. She could feel his uneven breathing. 'You've made me very happy, Erin,' he said huskily, 'in fact, you've given me the world.'

Francine's slim figure greeted them at the door. 'Why hello, Simon, darling,' Francine said silkily, exuding a social polish that seemed to Erin totally false and at the same time totally threatening, for some reason. The tone alone sent a chill of fear up her spine.

'We're so glad you could come, we missed you on Christmas Day.' Her eyes flicked distastefully over Erin. 'It's the first time in quite a few years that you didn't spend some part of Christmas Day with us. What kept you away?' She draped her hands possessively over Simon's arm and led him inside, leaving her father to take Erin's coat, and cruelly taking no pains to hide her displeasure at seeing Simon and Erin together. 'Why did you bring *her* with you, Simon?' she whispered harshly, but loud enough for Erin and others to hear. 'You should have come alone, darling. You knew I was waiting for you.'

'I've brought Erin for the best of reasons, Francine,' Simon replied to her angry enquiry calmly. 'We're going to be married soon.'

His words had the effect of an exploding bombshell. Francine's face, chalk white, stared in angry disbelief. 'You can't be serious! This is New Year, Simon, not April Fool's Day—it's time to end this foolish charade.' She spoke loudly, her voice tinged with a note of hysteria.

Erin, uncomfortable and shaken by the outburst, came to stand next to Simon, sliding her hand into the secure warmth of his. Simon stood looking darkly down at Francine, as if daring her to utter another abrasive word.

It was Francine's father who intervened and prevented a continuation of the crisis. He spoke firmly, brooking no arguments from Francine. 'I think you'd better go to your room Francine, and compose yourself before you return to our guests—after you've apologised to Erin and Simon.'

Francine glared in hatred at Simon and Erin, and uttering no word of apology, turned swiftly and strode across the room and up the stairs.

Dr Haley turned to Simon. 'I'm sorry, I apologise for my daughter's ungracious behaviour, Simon—and Miss McCourt.' He shook Simon's hand and took Erin's. 'I wish you both all the best, may you be very happy together.' He steered them into the living room. 'Come on, enjoy yourselves. There's plenty of wine and good food to follow.'

For Erin the incident left a blemish on the entire evening. What had started out as a joyful celebration all too soon had been marred by Francine's bitter words. After listening to her strained and monosyllabic responses to Allen's and Nadine's cheerful conversation, Simon drew her aside.

'All right, Erin, out with it. What's troubling you?'

She sighed, knowing that it was useless not to tell him the truth. 'It's just what Francine did,' she said in a hushed whisper. 'I have the most terrible feeling it's somehow like a bad omen.' She stared down at the floor, the words sounding foolish and superstitious, even to her own ears.

His eyes revealed the utter depths of his feeling for her. 'Just as it isn't April Fool's Day, Erin, neither is it Halloween.' He laughed easily and then added with mock contriteness, 'Forgive a pressured English professor his poor jokes.'

'Oh, Simon, you're impossible!' she muttered under her breath.

'Yes, sweetheart, I probably am, but are you going to abandon me because of that?'

Unconsciously, Simon's light bantering made her spirits lift, and she gradually relaxed and managed to smile up at him. 'No, never shall I abandon you, dearest Simon.'

'That's my girl!' He took her hand and squeezed it affectionately. 'Now, let's join some of the fun. Never let it be said that Simon,' he paused slightly, 'and Erin Grayson ever let a party pass them by.'

Nevertheless, and despite the friendly conversations they shared with friends and acquaintances, and despite the fact that Simon stayed attentively by her side for most of the evening, Erin was unable to shake off the sense of foreboding that had filled her as a result of Francine's behaviour at the beginning of the evening. This feeling only intensified as the evening wore on, and more than once Erin looked uncomfortably up from dinner to see Francine's watchful eyes surveying her, her expression hiding nothing of her bitter hatred of Erin.

After dinner, as they stood alone talking by the bookcase, Erin was astonished to see Professor Bendix seek them out. Simon stiffened at his approach and although Bendix slapped him heartily on the back, and to anyone looking on the relationship between the two men was friendly and amiable, Erin could feel the current of electric tension flowing between them.

'Well, well, my boy, I hear you're going to be making some big changes in your life—taking on a wife, no less.' He smiled suggestively at Erin. 'You'd better watch this one closely, Miss McCourt, hard as quicksilver to hang on to, I'm told.' He shook his head with mock sadness. 'A lot of women are going to be very upset, but I guess when you think about it it's probably best that you legalise this little escapade, eh, Grayson?'

Simon's face darkened as he spoke with steely control, a muscle twitching in his jaw. 'You say another word, Bendix, and so help me I'll make you wish you hadn't. I'm not going to ask you what you meant, I can guess. All I want is for you to walk away from us—now. I don't want to cause any trouble here.' He stopped, waiting for Bendix's retreat, and when he did not leave, but stood smiling evilly at them both, Simon uttered a harsh expletive. 'So help me, Bendix, don't push me . . .'

Still smiling, Bendix raised a hand to him. 'All right,

Grayson, I'm going, I'm going.' He turned to Erin. 'Many are probably offering you their congratulations. I'd be a hypocrite if I did, Miss McCourt. Our Dr Grayson here is well known for the number of women he's had. Don't fool yourself into believing that marriage will kill the habit in him.'

In a single blinding movement, Simon's powerful body lunged forward and with a hard fist he struck Bendix on the jaw. Bendix reeled and fell against the bookshelf, his lip cut and bleeding.

'Please, Simon ...' Erin pulled at his arm, 'let's go, I want to go.' He shook her hand impatiently from his arm and stood towering threateningly over Bendix's cowering frame. For a moment Erin feared that Simon would hit him again, but at last the tension in Simon's body relaxed and he drew a deep breath, winning his battle for control over his raw anger.

'No more, Bendix, I've taken all I'm going to from you,' he grated harshly. 'Stay away from me and what's mine.' He turned quickly, seizing Erin's hand and propelled her across the room. 'Get your coat,' he snapped sharply, then looking down at her pale face he muttered, 'God, I'm sorry, Erin. I didn't mean for that to happen.' He raked his fingers through his hair and turned her towards the stairs. 'Go and splash some cold water on that lovely face of yours and I'll get your coat. I really think it's best that we leave now.'

She did as she was told, walking slowly up the stairs to the powder room. She was unprepared for Francine's furtive entrance shortly after her. Francine quickly closed the door and flicked the lock before she turned menacingly to Erin.

Erin's eye widened in fear. 'What are you doing? Unlock that door at once! You have no right ...'

Francine glowered at her and ignored her frightened words. 'Quite the little scene downstairs—the mighty Simon defending his fair lady's reputation, no doubt. Don't let it fool you, Erin, it'll never last.'

'Open the door, Francine, we have nothing to say to one another,' Erin retorted.

'No? Well, I have a few things to say to you, you little fool, so you'd better listen, if you really care about Simon.'

'I don't know what you're talking about.'

'Then listen to me,' Francine responded petulantly. 'You can never hope to hold him, never. You think he loves you, just because he's slept with you?' She laughed harshly. 'He has slept with you, I have no doubt, but he's slept with a lot of women and he's married none of them. He wants a woman who can give him what he really needs—a career and position.' She moved threateningly close to Erin, who was leaning weakly against the wall. 'Simon wants to be chairman of his department and later the president of this college when my father retires. And you have nothing to give him that will advance that career in any way.'

'And I suppose you can?' challenged Erin.

'You know I can!' exclaimed Francine. 'If you go through with this marriage, I'll make sure that Simon loses the chairmanship, I'll make sure he's destroyed in this town. I want you to break the engagement—right away!'

Erin's hand smothered a gasp, but she could not disguise the pain in her eyes. Francine pushed her advantage, her voice cold and without feeling. 'If you do marry him and he discovers that he lost the chairmanship because of you, how long do you think he'll stay with you, anyway? He'd come to hate you because the price he would have had to pay to have you would have been too high. Either way, you're going to lose him.'

'No . . . Simon and I love each other, you have no right to interfere with that. He's not a stupid man, he'll see through your scheme . . . he'll . . .'

'It's up to you, Erin, to convince him that you don't love him.'

'He's a good man, and you have no right to do this to him!'

'No right to do it to you, you mean, don't you?'

'I mean to *us*. For God's sake, Francine, think of what you're asking. We love each other.'

'Ha! Simon's loved before. But have it your way if you want to about that. It's still really quite simple, all you have to do is decide how much *you* love Simon. Leave him or you'll see him torn to shreds before your eyes and you'll know that you were the cause,' Francine sneered threateningly.

'And you pretend to love him?' said Erin, a broken sob torn from her lips.

Francine laughed mockingly. 'God, but you are a naïve one, aren't you? I never for a moment pretended that I loved him, my dear. I can get him the chairmanship and maybe later the presidency, and he can give me what I want —position and status in this town.'

'You're disgusting!' Erin flung her words in angry and broken frustration, 'You're sick. You'd destroy a man to satisfy your obsession?'

'Yes, I would,' Francine responded bluntly. 'But the question you have to answer now is—would you?'

She unlocked the door and slipped quietly into the hallway, leaving Erin to the searing pain and conflict she had created. Erin leaned her face against the cool plaster wall.

'No . . . no . . . I can't leave him . . . I can't give him up . . .' Tears filled her eyes as she thought desperately of what to do. Realising that Simon was waiting for her downstairs, she quickly fixed her hair with trembling fingers and tried to compose herself.

But still Simon noticed that something was wrong. 'Have you been crying, Erin?' he asked with concern as soon as he looked at her.

'No . . . yes . . . never mind, I'm all right now . . . please let's just get out of here,' she stammered.

The drive home was a strained one, with Erin not responding to any of Simon's attempts to lighten her mood. Finally, as he drove into her driveway and turned off the ignition, he turned and said quietly, 'I know something's wrong, Erin.' He put a hand on her shoulder and prevented her from leaving. 'No, don't run from me. Stay and talk it out.' He waited and sighed as he suggested, 'Maybe we should go inside where it's warmer and discuss this.'

'No!' she said quickly. 'No. I want to be alone.'

'Erin, please, I'm trying to understand. Is it what happened tonight with Bendix? What he said?' He waited for her affirmation or denial, but she gave none. 'Is it what

Bendix said about me? Is that it?' He gently touched her face. 'Erin, I've been alone for nearly eight years and I have been with other women—you must have known that. I'm not a monk and I've never pretended to be. Can't you understand and accept that? For God's sake, Erin, it's you I've asked to marry, no one else. And it's not something I do lightly, I intend that it be a lifetime thing. I love you, Erin.'

Still she made no movement, no sound. He tried another tack. 'Look, I thought maybe we could drive up to Halifax tomorrow morning and tell Albert and Mary about us. What do you think?'

Driven to the point of desperation by his expression of love and his patient attempts to draw her out, Erin could contain herself no longer. She pulled herself from his touch and cried out, 'All right, all right. Anything you want ... but right now, I just want to be left alone, Simon. Just leave me alone!'

He leaned his head against the headrest and looked worriedly at her. 'All right, Erin,' he sighed, 'if that's what you want. I'll see you in the morning.'

She closed the car door, ran up the steps and into the house, slamming the door behind her. Before Simon was out of the driveway she had already collapsed on the bed in a desperate storm of inconsolable and bitter tears.

CHAPTER NINE

BUT Erin was unable to seek her escape from her misery in sleep. Early the next morning, after a night of fitful and intermittent sleep, the phone rang, loud and insistent. She rolled over on her stomach, reached for the receiver and answered, her voice husky with sleep. 'Hello?'

A voice, sharp and cutting, a verbal razor, responded sarcastically, 'Well, good morning, Miss McCourt. I do hope you slept well and I didn't awaken you.'

With dismay, Erin recognised Francine's voice. She

blinked and looked at the clock; it was barely seven. She sighed and said wearily, 'What do you want at this hour, Francine?'

'Now, now, Erin my dear, let's not be hostile. I just called to give you a little reminder and add one more small but important piece of information.' She paused long enough to make Erin think that perhaps they had been disconnected.

'Hello? Hello?' queried Erin.

'Oh, I'm still here,' Francine responded. 'I was just waiting, making certain you were listening carefully, Erin.'

'For heaven's sake, Francine, stop the stupid games!'

Anger spilled from the other woman. 'Oh, don't mistake this as a game, Erin. I'm very serious about all of it. This is no game, believe me.'

'Say what you called to say, Francine, and get it over with,' Erin snapped impatiently.

'Well, how strange, that's exactly what I called to say to you. You make sure that you tell Simon that it's over between you two and that you do it today.' Francine gave Erin no opportunity to interrupt or speak but continued, her voice a silky threat, 'If you don't want to see Simon brought to his knees, you'll do as I say and you'll do it soon. Remember this—Bendix knows about you and Simon and your sailing weekend and Christmas at Simon's cabin. He knows enough and he hates Simon enough to go after him, to destroy all that Simon's worked for and his place in this town. The people here are rather conservative, you know.'

Erin struggled to comprehend what Francine was getting at. 'Nothing happened between Simon and me ... we did nothing wrong ... Bendix can know nothing of ...'

Francine broke in, 'Never mind, you little fool, everyone knows Simon. Do you think people will believe you two spent nearly a week together and nothing happened, that he never touched you?' She laughed, 'Even I know better than that! People always believe the worst about anyone and they'll be very pleased to hear this about Simon. He isn't the humblest person I know of and he's alienated a good number of people in this town with his outspokenness, his arrogance, and his standoffish ways. No, Erin, they'll believe the worst of him and be glad of it.'

Erin, horrified at the lengths to which Francine would go, said nothing. Francine continued, purring menacingly. 'Bendix is prepared to use this information if I tell him to, so break the engagement and do it today. Believe me, I'll ruin him if I have to.' The receiver clicked and Francine was gone.

The morning passed in a blur of pain, with Erin avoiding acknowledging to herself what she knew she must do. Finally, she could do nothing but face it. Tears fell freely, but it could not be avoided. She had to sacrifice her happiness to save Simon; nothing must harm him.

It was a cold day, one of those days in winter when clouds scudded across the sky and the wind whipped the sea to a boiling frenzy. Sometimes the sun would break through and the sea would glisten like a sheet of tinfoil, but the sky did not remain that way for long, and clouds, filled with the heaviness of approaching snow, closed in and hid the sun. And so it was with Erin's emotions. She vacillated between a desperate hope of finding some other alternative and the utter desolation of knowing that there was none.

Finally she took refuge in action; she would go to the post office, maybe the fresh air would relieve her mind of some of its intolerable burden. A letter was waiting for her from Peter, a letter that had been posted in Vancouver and had taken over a week to arrive. She tore it open and unbelievingly absorbed its contents; he was coming to Abbotsford and would arrive on New Year's Eve unless he heard from her to the contrary. Dumbfounded, she stared at his precise handwriting. Today was New Year's Eve, so she should have phoned him last night at the latest, but it was too late now. She went home, knowing that a visit from Peter today would be the last straw.

'Hi——' Simon's low drawl surprised her; she hadn't heard him come in. 'Are you feeling better today?' He smiled at her as he bent down, his lips brushing her lightly. 'I waited, then I decided to come and roust you out of bed, lazybones.'

She looked at him quizzically. 'You waited? What do you mean?'

'Wow, my girl, you really are in bad shape this morning—don't you remember? We're driving up to Halifax this morning.'

'Oh, my, I . . . I forgot all about it. I don't think I can.'

Simon's eyes darkened. 'What's wrong, Erin? You were upset last night and you still seem jumpy. Tell me what's happened to you.'

She pulled herself away from him, 'No. I mean, nothing's the matter. I just . . .' uttering an exclamation of frustration, she strode to the window, realising that the time had come to tell him, she couldn't avoid it any longer. 'I just have to speak to you, that's all.'

'Well, I'd say it's about time. Come on, we can talk on the way.'

'No!' She swung round angrily to face him. 'Will you please stop making things so impossible and so difficult . . . more difficult than they already are!'

He shrugged, puzzled by her outburst. 'God knows, I'm trying to understand what's wrong, but how can I if you won't tell me?'

'I can't marry you, Simon,' she blurted, avoiding his eyes.

The words hung heavily in the air, silence like a shroud wrapped itself around them. She was startled by Simon's unexpected laughter. 'Come on, Erin, stop the teasing, it's not a good joke.'

'I'm not teasing you, Simon, and I'm not joking. For God's sake, listen to me—I mean what I'm saying. I'm not going to marry you. I can't.' She wanted nothing more than to throw herself in the warmth and security of Simon's arms, wanting to end the absurdity of it all, but she held herself in check.

He walked over to her. 'No, you're not joking, are you?' His body tensed, his eyes became unfathomable dark pools as he questioned her. 'What in hell is going on?' He gripped her shoulders roughly, till she winced in pain.

'Stop it, Simon, you're hurting me!'

He released her but remained dangerously close. 'I want to know what this is all about and I want to know now. It's time for some straight answers, Erin.'

Grasping at straws, frantically searching for some explanation other than the truth she could never reveal, she saw Peter's letter lying on the table. She bent down, picked it up and held it out to Simon. He read it quickly, his face stern, and then threw it to the floor. 'So your Peter's coming back for you, is that it?'

'Yes, yes, that's it. He'll be here today probably. And I owe it ... owe it to Peter to ...'

Simon muttered a harsh oath, his voice strained and controlled, but anger bubbling dangerously near the surface, 'You owe Peter! God, what foolishness! You owe him nothing, absolutely nothing, and you know it. So let's get real, Erin, I want the truth.'

'I am telling you the truth,' pleaded Erin, misery filling her voice. 'I am. When I got his letter this morning and realised that he was coming here, I realised too that ... I couldn't marry you, or anyone else, not while there's still Peter and I.'

Simon stared stonily at her. 'While there's still you and Peter,' he muttered. 'I don't believe a word of it, Erin. I know what we share and it's worth one hell of a lot more than you're indicating to me now.' He reached out for her, his voice demanding and challenging. 'Now come here and tell me the truth of what's going on in that head of yours.'

Frantic now, and fearful that all her resolve would melt swiftly away at the slightest touch, Erin violently shook her head and backed away. 'No, I don't want you to touch me. I ... I want you to leave. It would be best right now.'

The sharp ringing of the doorbell halted Simon's response of angry disbelief. Erin moved hastily to the door, opened it and there, bag in hand, stood Peter. Without waiting for an invitation, he strode into the room, bending and kissing Erin casually as he entered. She recoiled from his touch, but fought with herself to conceal any evidence of this. She smiled, her face and voice strained and not really concealing her consternation at his arrival.

'You look surprised, my dear. Didn't you get my letter telling you I'd be here for the New Year, if I didn't hear from you to the contrary?'

Erin stared glassily. 'Oh yes, I was expecting you, Peter. It's just that—well, you're earlier than I'd thought you'd be.

I thought you'd be here tonight some time.' She hesitated, then added, 'It's good to see you, Peter, it's been a long time. Too long.' The words rang hollow in her ears. But Peter wasn't listening. He stood facing Simon, and holding out his hand in greeting.

'Hi. I'm Peter Hall.'

Simon made no move to either acknowledge Peter's presence or his greeting. He looked straight past him to Erin. 'I want to talk to you now, Erin, alone and outside,' he said roughly.

Erin's heart was pounding painfully, but she did not go with him. 'No, Simon, I'd prefer it if you'd leave.'

Simon's face paled. 'Yes, Erin, I'll leave, but by God I'll be back. I mean to have the truth from you ...'

'I've told you, Simon, it's finished, and that's the truth, as much as you need know.'

At this point Peter intruded. 'What's going on here, Erin? Who is this, anyway?' He turned belligerently to Simon. 'She told you to leave and I think that you'd better do just that.'

For a single frightening moment, Erin thought that Simon would violently remove Peter from his path, but slowly he moved his tense frame to the door and opened it. He stood there for a moment, his back to them, an icy blast of air rushing past him and into the living room. 'I'm coming back, Erin. I just don't believe you.' Erin braced herself for the explosion of a slamming door, but he closed it quietly and left.

'Well, dear Erin, and who might that be?' queried Peter silkily.

'That was Simon Grayson, a friend of mine from the college,' she responded quietly, not looking at him. She felt torn between her desire to run to Simon and her desire not to be with Peter. How her perceptions of Peter had changed in the last few months! She had come to see him as she never had before, and she did not really like what she saw.

'Are you going to keep me standing here, Erin, or are you going to welcome me properly?'

He did not wait for her to answer but walked over to her

and took her in his arms and kissed her firmly on the mouth. She struggled to free herself from his grasp and, succeeding, tried to hide the revulsion that welled within her at his kiss.

'Come and sit down, Peter, I'll make you something hot to drink. A coffee? Hot chocolate, perhaps?' Her voice was shaky and sounded thin and false.

'No, thanks, Erin. Come and sit with me and tell me what's been happening all these months.' His eyes glinted strangely and Erin feared that he would discover her secret. Foolish woman, she admonished herself inwardly, everyone must see, all who have any insight can surely tell. Peter could not be so blind as not to see what had passed between her and Simon in those few minutes before Simon's departure.

She pulled herself together and told him tonelessly about her work at the department, told him about the town and the people she had met and made friends with. She carefully avoided all mention of Simon, and prayed that he too would steer clear of speaking of him. Finally, she could think of nothing more to say to him. A heavy silence fell between them and she thought angrily, what a fool you were to think you could have married this man and thought to spend a lifetime with him, when after twenty minutes you have nothing more to say to him.

But Peter seemed not to notice, or more likely he chose not to notice how strained she was with him. 'Tell me, Erin, what do the natives do here to welcome in the New Year? What celebrations can we attach ourselves to tonight?'

Startled, she looked wide-eyed at him. 'I . . . I forgot it was New Year's Eve. Well, there's a party at the university for the faculty, and there's a local dance and . . .'

'Good,' he interrupted her further explanations. 'We'll go to the faculty party, I think.'

'Really, Peter, I don't feel like partying tonight. I have a bit of a headache. I think I'd rather just spend a quiet night at home.' Her heart pounded at the thought of going to the party and seeing Simon there. She couldn't face him, not again, and maintain the enormous and painful deceit she had woven to save him from the wrath of Francine. No, she couldn't go. But she did not reckon on Peter's insistence.

'I didn't come all the way from Montreal to this tiny dot on the map, Erin, to spend what you call a quiet night at home. Get ready—we're going to the party and afterwards we can talk about our future.'

'Our future? What are you talking about, Peter?' she asked, surprised.

He came over to her, pulling her close to him, and kissed her again with a plastic fervour. 'I want you to come back to Montreal with me—tomorrow.' He raised a hand to stem her protest, 'No, I'm not asking you to marry me, I understand and accept your feelings about that, but we know each other so well, Erin, and I think that we—well, we could have an understanding. We could share an apartment—it's cheaper in the end, you know.'

What Erin felt now for him was utter and total revulsion. She drew herself out of his arms and stared unbelievingly, her voice a mere whisper when she finally spoke. 'You think I would live with you, knowing that you don't love me and knowing that I don't love you, for convenience? Because it would be "cheaper in the end"? My God, Peter, you don't know me at all, do you?'

'Come on, love, take a tablet to get rid of that headache and get dressed for the party. You need to relax.'

She continued to stare at him in disbelief. He hadn't heard a word she had said; her protest had fallen on deaf ears. His voice called to her from the bathroom, 'If you like we could make a little announcement at the party, tell everyone of our plans.'

Erin rubbed her aching head with cold and shaking hands. No, no, no—this couldn't be happening! Somehow she had become trapped in a long and unending nightmare, and please God she would awaken soon and find that she had been dreaming. But she did not awaken and she knew that now she had no choice but to go to the party with Peter and face what had to be faced. Perhaps too her appearance at the gathering with Peter would make Simon believe her decision not to marry him, would make him stop his pursuit of the truth of what had happened—the truth that could destroy him.

*

The strains of music reached them as they walked from the car to the faculty club. Peter talked incessantly, apparently taking no notice of Erin's absence of response. His hand held her elbow possessively, but she did not bother to remove it; it would all be part of the image that she would present to people at the party and to Simon in particular.

The party was well under way when they arrived, but she could see Simon nowhere in the crowd. Strange how breathlessly her heart waited for the mere glimpse of him; strange how empty this crowded room seemed without him. She and Peter spent the evening chatting with people; she introduced him as a special friend from Montreal, and strove to look happy and relaxed, while all the time she walked the tightrope of her feelings. She had introduced Peter to Nadine and Allen, uncomfortable and guilty at the look of hurt and amazement that filled Nadine's face; they talked briefly and then melted into the maze of faces and voices.

'Did you say her name was Grayson?' Peter asked, a strange note evident in his voice.

'Yes, yes, I did. She's Simon Grayson's sister. We work together, as I already told you.'

'You and Nadine, or you and Simon?' he asked sarcastically.

'Oh, Peter, stop it! You know full well what I mean.' She was too tired to argue or explain any more and did not fight him when he suddenly led her to the dance floor.

'Come, my Erin, time to thrill the crowd and charm the masses with your skills as a dancer. You've been avoiding it all night. Time for a nice slow waltz, a waltz meant for lovers.' He smiled smoothly down at her and drew her close. It was useless to struggle and she knew it; Peter would have his way, and she allowed herself to be led.

'Mind if I cut in?' Erin held her breath at the sound of Simon's voice, low and resonant, his hand resting firmly on her shoulder.

Peter smiled charmingly. 'Not at all, old man, I was just telling Erin that this was a dance for lovers ... and there you are, like a little touch of magic. Help yourself, Dr Grayson, I'm a generous man.'

Peter's voice, despite its veneer of charm and friendliness, held a tone of spite. Simon's face darkened.

'Simon, please ...' Erin pleaded quietly, not wanting them to make a scene.

Simon pulled her easily into his arms and her whole body responded to the feel and the masculine smell of this man as he pressed her closer. 'What in hell is this all about?'

'Nothing, Simon, really, that's just Peter's way, he ...'

'Don't try to explain him to me, and I want to know why you're here—with him!' He spoke these two words as if he were spitting something repulsive from his mouth.

'He flew in from Montreal, I had no choice. Besides, you know what we once meant to one another—I can't forget that. I told you he was coming. Please, Simon, let me go. This is useless.'

But he did not release her, instead he stopped dancing and firmly guided her into the library adjoining the dance floor. He closed the door behind them.

'No, Simon, let me go. Please!'

His only response was his mouth seeking hers, pursuing her with a fierce determination. She fought his assault on her senses, but her body betrayed her and responded to the hardness of his body against hers. 'Oh, Erin,' he moaned, 'I don't believe you love Peter, not after the way we've been together.' The muscular length of his body held her firmly against the wall.

'Please, Simon, I ...' She tried to push him from her, her hands pressed against his chest, but he would not be moved.

'Don't, Erin, don't fight me,' he whispered. His mouth plundered once again the sweetness of hers, seeking the very depths of her, and she could fight him no longer. Her hands slid from his chest and wrapped themselves in his thick brown hair. Her whole being cried out for completeness with this man, a completeness that could only be found in union. He felt her surrender and she felt his desire. 'You're mine, Erin, you're mine,' he groaned.

Erin suddenly came to her senses and realised the danger of what was happening. 'No, Simon, I'm not yours. I don't belong to you ... and I never will.'

He stepped back as if she had struck her. She could see

the frustration and the pain in him. 'Damn it, Erin, I want the truth from you and I want it now,' he demanded angrily.

'What does it take to make you see the truth, Simon? I'm not going to marry you, I've already told you that. No matter what! Can't you understand? What more do I have to do to make you understand?' Her voice broke in a sob, 'So leave me alone ... just leave me alone!' She turned from him quickly, pulled open the door and ran from the room, tears streaming down her cheeks.

She and Peter stayed for a few more dances, Erin not wanting to arouse Peter's suspicions of what had happened between her and Simon. She watched stonily as Simon and Francine danced; Francine was happily oblivious of everyone except the man who held her in his arms. At midnight, she bravely bore Peter's possessive kiss and felt her heart would break at the sight of Francine in Simon's arms, and at the sight of Simon and Francine leaving the dance together. She had done it, she had driven him into Francine's arms.

The drive back to her house was a silent one, for she could not bring herself to speak, least of all to Peter. She had come to despise his smooth good looks and his phoney façade of friendliness. Charming he was not, as far as she was concerned. He held the door for her as she got out of the car and then quickly opened the boot and pulled out a small suitcase. He walked up the steps and entered the house before her. Suddenly it dawned on her that he intended to spend the night with her.

'I'm sorry, Peter, but you can't stay here.'

'Oh—what's this? Don't tell me you're the same old prudish Erin I used to know,' replied Peter sarcastically. 'I thought that after tonight and since you didn't try to call me, we'd come to something of an understanding, Erin.'

She turned on him angrily. 'You assume too much about me, Peter, and you always did!'

He moved closer to her. 'Now, Erin, don't get that temper of yours flaring. This is to be a friendly little visit, nothing more. The engagement is off, I accept that. That doesn't mean that we can't be *good* friends. Come on, Erin, it's the twentieth century—get real, girl.' His hands touched her face, and moved to caress the back of her neck, but she pulled away from him.

'Don't touch me, Peter. I don't want you to touch me ever again. I want you to leave, now!' Her voice rose emphatically.

'Well, well, well,' he smiled tauntingly. 'My little Erin's grown claws to match her temper these past months. Tell me, the great Simon Grayson must really be something, he must really be good, if you'd turn me down now. What's the matter, Erin, were you too inexperienced to satisfy him?'

Erin's anger exploded as her hand struck him across the face. 'Get out! I want you out of my house, right now. He's a good man and I won't discuss him with you.'

'Be careful, sweet and innocent Erin, you can't send us all away.' He moved closer. 'You should have let me teach you a few things, experience is a definite asset, believe me, my dear.'

Erin walked to the door, shakily afraid that he would not leave and knowing full well that on this lonely stretch of beach, isolated from everyone, there was really nothing that she could do to make him leave.

Peter shrugged angrily and grabbed his coat from the chair. 'This is really too bad, Erin. We could have made a good team, and I wouldn't have insisted on marriage.' He glared at her with undisguised hatred. 'Don't be expecting me to come again, I'm not willing to play your little games. This is your last chance—come back to Montreal with me tomorrow and forget about this half-baked town and its local hero that you seem to be so taken with. Be sensible for once in your life.'

Erin spoke with steely control, 'Go away, Peter . . . Just go away!' pronouncing each word succinctly. She closed the door firmly behind him, breathing a sigh of relief at his departure. She locked and bolted the door, then turned out the lights and went to bed, her heart bruised and aching for the touch and closeness of Simon.

The grey light of dawn came early, and finally Erin gave up her struggle for sleep. It was hopeless—she had tossed and turned all night, seeking relief and escape in the un-

consciousness of sleep, but to no avail. But throughout the
long night she had come to understand that she could no
longer remain in Abbotsford. She did not have the strength
to stay and see Simon married to another woman—to Francine Haley. She must leave, and she rose early to begin her
task of packing.

She wandered around the rooms, feeling as she never
had before the terrible constrictions of space. The house
had become a prison, and now all she could await was her
escape; but something within her told her that the prison
she had so carefully constructed was one which she would
carry with her wherever she went, one from which she
would probably never free herself. She began systematic-
ally taking down the pictures from the walls of her studio,
packing and repacking things in boxes, unable to think and
decide which item should go where. Finally, in angry frustration, she flung a photograph of Peter across the room
and sank into a chair. 'I can't do it. I just can't do it. It's not
fair to either of us. I can't leave him'—the words and feelings pursued each other in an unhappy whirl in her troubled
mind, but she knew she would make herself stand firm.
They must not touch Simon, he must be kept safe from
Bendix. She would fight to preserve his career at the college,
no matter the personal cost to her.

She looked up suddenly to see Simon standing in the
doorway looking down at her, his eyes searching the depths
of her for the answer he sought.

He walked over to her and sat down on the floor by her
feet. Immediately, sensing the danger inherent in this closeness, Erin started to get up, but Simon's warm, steady hand
stayed her flight.

'Stay where you are, Erin. We have to talk.'

She shook her head, unable to meet his troubled eyes.
'No, Simon, there's nothing more to say. I've already told
you, I can't marry you, and that's all I have to say.'

'Damn it, Erin, you're not making any sense! I don't
even know what started this. I've racked my brains trying
to figure out what's happened and I don't even know where
to begin because you won't tell me.' He reached out and
took her small hand in his. 'I love you, Erin, and if we're

going to deal with whatever's bothering you, then you have to trust me and talk to me about it.'

Almost Erin was persuaded, so strong was her desire to throw herself into the arms of this man who loved her so simply and honestly. But she would not let them take everything he had worked so hard and long for, and she firmly withdrew her hand from his.

He sighed, shaking his head sadly. 'Is it that you're just nervous about the idea of marriage, Erin? Is that it? We don't have to marry right away; it can be a longer engagement if you like. I won't rush you.' He gently touched her face. 'I'll wait until you feel easier about it. I'll wait as long as you want.'

'No, Simon,' she murmured, her voice almost failing her, 'I just can't marry you—not now and not ever.'

'Tell me why, Erin—that's what I want. I want some answers. I know what we share, and there's not too many people who have the kind of relationship we do. We love each other, Erin, that's enough for me. I can't understand why all of a sudden, in one single day, it doesn't seem adequate for you.'

She could not argue any more, but sat and stared at the floor, wanting him to go and leave her to the misery of the awful decision she had made. His being there, so close and so vulnerable to what she was doing, only made it more difficult for her.

Simon was standing, staring out at the water and at two lonely figures who walked along the beach. 'I've been offered the chairmanship of the English Department, Erin,' he said tonelessly. 'I told Kevin I'd let him know one way or the other this morning. I think it depends a lot on us and what we decide to do.' Erin gasped inwardly at the ironical closeness to the truth his unconscious statement had been, but her face revealed none of her surprise. She responded quietly, her voice revealing very little interest in this turn of events.

'Fine, I'm happy for you.'

Simon turned suddenly from the window, his face pleading for some kind of explanation for what was happening. 'Please, Erin, I know this thing with the department hasn't been easy for you, but it hasn't been smooth sailing for me either. I've been trying to keep my head above water with it. I need your help, Erin. Can't you understand that I love you and I need you with me?'

'What help could I give you, Simon? I'm not the person to assist you with your career, believe me.' Her words were cold, her tone bitter and cutting, and Simon flinched visibly as if she had struck him. But he continued.

'Is that it? Is it my work at the college? Do you resent that? If so, let's talk about it and try to work it out. We don't have to stay here, we can live somewhere else if you want. I can find work somewhere else, but in the name of God, Erin, tell me why all this is happening.'

Her heart was breaking at the sight of the pain she was causing him. It was then that he noticed the partially packed suitcase on the floor by her bedroom. 'What's that? Where are you going?' he asked accusingly, pointing at the suitcase.

Erin drew a deep breath. 'I'm leaving Abbotsford, Simon. I'm going back to Montreal and I'm going to open a studio of my own. Teaching and living in a small town just isn't for me, I've discovered.' And she added quietly, 'And I'm going to marry Peter.'

He swung round, the impact of her last statement evident on his pale face. 'Look at me, Erin!' he demanded. She felt the fierce grip of his hand on her arm as he whirled her roughly round to face him. 'I said look at me, damn you! Look me in the face, in my eyes, and tell me you don't love me. Tell me it's Peter Hall you want to live with. Tell me —and make me believe you!'

She saw beneath his fierce anger, the look of pained desperation, and she knew the truth of his love for her. In a brief blinding second she tottered on the edge of telling him the truth, of stopping this damning charade and telling him of Francine's threats and intentions. But quickly she called on all her reserves of strength and forced back her terrible confession. She looked him full in the face, her eyes unblinking, her mouth firm.

'I don't love you. I love Peter. I'm not going to marry you, I'm going to marry him. I'm packing now to go with him to Halifax this afternoon and catch the early evening flight to Montreal. And there, within the next few days, we shall be married. It's all decided, Simon. I'm sorry if this whole thing hasn't turned out the way you'd hoped, but I can't marry a man I don't love and it would be no bargain for you if I did.' Inside she was crying out for the pain she was carving into Simon's face. He stood staring down at her for a long lonely moment, staring and saying nothing, until Erin felt she would be choked by the stricken silence.

Simon drew himself up to his full height and looked for a moment as if he might strike her, as if he wanted to reach out and destroy the very breath she drew. 'Yes,' she thought, 'hit me—do something, do anything, but don't look like that, don't stand there and look like that.' Unable to stand the silence a moment longer, she spoke again, her voice a hoarse whisper. 'I think you'd better leave now, Simon, I have to finish packing. Peter will be here within the hour.'

He turned abruptly and strode to the door, flinging it open with such force that it struck the wall, his voice filled with a hatred that she had never before witnessed. 'God, what a fool I've been, what an absolute and total fool! You really have been a deceptive bitch, and I curse the day I met you.' He stepped out on the porch and their eyes met, for one last time, and he cursed the love he had for her. 'Damn you, Erin, damn you to hell for what you've done!'

She stood there for a long time, the sting of the cold air whipping around her from the open door. She no longer had a sense of her own reality. She had done it. She had been able to convince him that she didn't love him, but there was no sense of victory in the accomplishment. Instead she had the terrible feeling that she had foully and foolishly murdered them both, murdered the beautiful and rare thing that they had shared. His final words, 'Damn you ... damn you ... to hell ...' echoed in her ears, whirled in her tortured mind, and she was all of a sudden sure that his curse would come to fruition. She was damned to a living hell without this man; her life would be a dark and endless night without the light of the love they had shared.

She had saved his career and the work he loved so much, but at what a terrible cost to them both.

Overcome by the desolation of his departure and the destruction and pain that she had slashed into the fabric of their lives together, she collapsed in a storm of weeping on the floor, unaware of the cold wind that blew and curled wisps of fine powdered snow around her. 'Oh, Simon, oh, my precious Simon, what have I done to you? ... what have I done to us both?'

CHAPTER TEN

'STOP avoiding me, Erin! I want the truth, and not the truth you seem to have given Simon. I want to know what you said to him.'

Nadine had arrived late that same afternoon, bursting in on Erin as she had just finished her packing. The house was barren and their voices echoed in the gloomy emptiness. Nadine was angry and bewildered, not understanding what had happened between Erin and Simon. In her usual direct way she demanded an explanation, which Erin awkwardly eluded giving.

Erin shook her head. 'Leave it alone, Nadine. It's finished, and Simon and I are finished. Just let it be.'

Fury rose in Nadine's face and in her voice. 'Damn it, Erin, I won't let it alone! I'm no innocent fool. Give me credit for having a few clues, will you? A blind person can tell from the look on your face that you're not happy, and you're on the verge of collapse. So what in hell is going on, and I want to know *now*.'

'Nothing. Nothing. Nothing!' Erin's voice rose in desperation as Nadine's attack threatened to breach the barrier she had erected to protect the secret of what she had done. 'Now please leave. You're as hard to convince as your brother,' she added cruelly.

Nadine flinched at this remark but pushed the advantage she sensed she had gained. 'Oh yes, and you managed to convince him quite tidily, didn't you? Yes, indeed, you did an excellent job in that quarter. I just came from his place and I've seen the fruits of your labour and your convincing words.' She moved closer to Erin. 'Tell me what you told him. I want to hear what a woman could say to my brother that could do what I've just witnessed.'

Still Erin fought to retain her secret. 'Nadine, I want you to go. I want you to leave me alone. I'm leaving in a few hours and I need time to finish things up here. Please, I'm sorry it all ended like this. Really I am.'

'Really you are! My God, am I supposed to stand here and accept that paltry excuse? That you're sorry—"really you are". And you think that's enough. Have you seen him? Have you heard what happened this morning at the staff meeting? Have you? Maybe not, or you wouldn't be standing there speaking such empty useless things to me! Well, I'll tell you what happened. He was attacked and belittled and brought to his knees by our crusading Professor Bendix!'

Erin, shock evident in her face, gasped her surprise. 'No —no—he couldn't have! He wasn't supposed to, not if I . . .'

Unaware of Erin's words, Nadine rushed on. 'Simon was offered the position yesterday, or maybe you already know that. Maybe he had a chance to tell you before you so kindly struck the fatal blow. Did you know that much?'

'Yes, he told me,' whispered Erin.

'And I can see from what happened you obviously were very happy with his success—you rushed to his side to offer him congratulations and support.' Nadine's fist struck the table with a thundering force; Erin had never seen her this angry or overwrought. 'Damn it, Erin, I want to know what you said to him to make him go into that meeting this morning and take it all without raising his voice to defend himself, not even once. Not a single word did he say! And believe me, Bendix wasn't kind. Bendix's time had come at last and his prey had been more than softened up for the kill.'

Nadine's voice broke as she clasped her hand over her mouth, her eyes wide with despair. But she kept on, through tears mingled with choking sobs. 'Bendix has killed him, Erin, he has nothing left to fight him with, nothing.' The fear in Nadine's eyes flooded her voice as she sank on to the couch. 'At least before, when he lost Elice, he struggled to survive, he wanted to live and go on and find something worthwhile. At least he fought it. But you've taken it all from him this time. He's not had an easy life, Erin, not a happy one, but still he tried and still he hoped. And he wasn't a mean man. He was good and kind and loving. He was the best family anyone could have had and I'm lucky to have been his family. But now, this time, I just know it, he's not going to make it.'

She paused, fighting for control. 'He was drinking when they met this morning and he said nothing to defend himself against Bendix's accusations. And now the college has deferred its final decision. Bendix is going to win, Erin. I've just come from Simon's place and he's written his letter of resignation. He's leaving town this afternoon, he's just walking out and leaving everything and everyone that meant anything to him, that gave him the will to survive.'

Nadine's tone changed now, filled with a bitterness that Erin had never before heard in the girl. 'But you know, he's not going somewhere to start again, Erin—oh no, he has nothing so constructive in mind, I'm sure, but I can't get him to admit it.'

She straightened and flung the final accusation at Erin. 'He's leaving this afternoon on *Early Summer*. Did you know that? Tell me you know that, and tell me he means so little to you that you could have driven him to that.' She grabbed Erin roughly by the arm and pushed her to the window. 'Look at it out there! Look long and well and remember it for ever. If you let him leave, if you drive him to that, knowing he has no intention of ever coming home, of ever reaching land again ... and it's you ... you're the one who's sending him! And to think you were my best friend and I loved you ... now you're killing him and I hate you for it ... I hate you ... if you let his happen to him!'

The girl flung herself away from Erin, her body racked with unleashed sobbing. 'Dear God, what can I do, what can I say to make you understand? To make you help him?'

Erin stood staring out at the leaden sea, the grey breaking white against the snow-crusted shore. Ice cold and demanding, ice cold and threatening, calling for the life of the one man she had ever loved. And for an instant she remembered that day, long ago in September, remembered the trip back from Halifax and the time when the sea had sought to claim him, and together they had fought and defeated it. But now it would have its own. As Nadine had said, now Simon intended to go to the edge and beyond.

And she did not cry, but stood erect and staring silently at the sea as it moved in its eternal rhythm, constant and for ever, no matter what happened in the lives of the people around her. Slow and for ever, grey breaking white, and she felt the tears slide down her cheeks but felt nothing within her, no feeling but a tragic inevitability. 'I can't, Nadine,' she heard herself say. 'I can't stop him.'

Nadine leapt to her feet, her eyes red and swollen. 'And why can't you? Tell me you don't love him—convince me as you did him and tell me how you made him believe it.'

Erin absently wiped at the tears on her face, her skin pale and drawn. 'He'd never believe me, Nadine. He'd never believe that I still love him, that I've never stopped loving him. I've done a good job in convincing him, he'll never trust me again. I can't save him.'

'Why, Erin? Why did you do it?' Nadine shook her head, pleading for an explanation of the motivation of this girl who so obviously loved her brother. 'Tell me why, because I know you love him. I know it.'

'Yes, I do love Simon. I loved him as I've loved no man before, as I'll love no man ever again. And I did it to save what I thought was important to him. Francine said ...'

'Francine? What's she got to do with this?'

'Everything. That night at the reception, when Simon announced our engagement, she came to me and threatened to destroy his career if we married. She said if I married him at the expense of his career he would never forgive me and that ... in the end we would have no marriage anyway. He would come to hate me for it. I ... I couldn't take it away from him ... I love him too much.'

Nadine paced the floor, vacillating between disbelief and wild anger. 'I don't believe it! It's too ridiculous. It's so damn stupid . . .'

'It's true,' Erin said lifelessly. 'Francine intends to marry Simon herself, once I've left.'

'Francine doesn't love Simon,' Nadine interjected hotly. 'She never has and never will. Francine only loves Francine, and Simon knows that.'

'I know she doesn't love him, but that wasn't her purpose in wanting to marry him. She wanted position and status in Abbotsford and felt Simon's career was so promising he would be able to give her what she wanted.'

Nadine turned to her. 'And you made that decision for him?' she said sharply. 'You decided for Simon what he should do with his life?'

'It wasn't like that. I thought it was the only thing to do, I did it for him because I loved him. Can't you understand that?'

'Oh, I don't doubt that, but don't you think you owed him a little more respect than to make a decision like that for him, without even talking to him and telling him what happened between you and Francine? I just don't understand that kind of thinking, Erin. You know him—you got closer to him than anyone ever has. You know the kind of man he is, and yet you would walk out and leave him, and to what kind of a life? A life totally devoid of love and affection? A life with Francine?' Nadine paused before adding, 'And what possessed you to believe he would have chosen to marry Francine Haley? He wouldn't have, Erin. He doesn't love her and he never has; he would never have married her.'

The floodgates of Erin's emotions burst open and she fell into the other girl's arms, tears streaming down her pale face. 'Oh God, Nadine, what can I do? How can I possibly undo all the damage I've done? I've hurt him so terribly. He must hate me, he must!'

Nadine held her gently away from her. 'Go to him, Erin. Go and tell him truthfully what you've told me. Make him believe in you again. Make him believe in living again. You've got to try, there's no other way.' Nadine opened the door. 'He deserves to know the truth, he deserves that much.'

After Nadine had left Erin stood motionless, still stunned and shattered by the impact of what she had done to Simon, staring unseeingly out at the snow-covered beach. She walked with the unknowing intentions of a robot into her bedroom and picked up her jacket from the bed, where she had flung it last. She buttoned it as she made her way down the steps and along the beach in the direction of Simon's house.

His car was alongside the house where it usually was, parked at its same careless angle, but the house gave no hint or clue of being inhabited. Although the day was grey and dark with clouds which threatened more snow, no light shone anywhere within the house. For a moment Erin hesitated, thinking that perhaps he had already left, that the house was empty; but *Early Summer* was still tied up at the dock and there was the car. So Simon must still be inside. She walked tentatively up the steps and approached the front door, knocking once, twice, and then after a few moments, a third time. But there was no answer, no responding footsteps from within to indicate an inhabitant. Almost she was persuaded to walk away, so as not to cause any more pain for either of them, but something within her stopped her from abandoning this man who had loved her so well and so completely. She tried the latch of the door, but it was locked, so she moved slowly around to the side of the house and peered in through the glass doors of the patio. She gave the handle a slight tug and the doors slid noiselessly open. She entered and closed them behind her.

The scene that greeted her was one that in the immediacy of the first impact, made her think Simon's house had been vandalised. But on looking more closely she could see there was a pile of clothing and gear strewn messily on the floor; Simon was preparing to leave, as Nadine had said. Over by the fireplace, papers had been tossed carelessly—some partially burned by the smouldering embers, others scattered on the rug. She knelt to pick them up, only to discover that they were part of Simon's manuscript. She rose and called out his name, but the answering silence seemed only to attest to the house's emptiness. Dropping the papers on the rug, she walked through to the library. There, slouched over his desk, was Simon's inert body, an empty bottle lying on its side next to his arm.

'Simon ... oh, Simon ...' Erin's voice almost failed her at the sight of him. He stirred, lifted his head and looked at her, but his expressionless face showed no indication of recognition. He was unshaven, his thick dark hair unkempt. She repeated his name, pleading for a sign that he knew her and that she had returned to him.

'Simon, please!'

Still he continued to stare through glazed and glassy eyes. She moved slowly towards him, her hand reaching out unconsciously to touch him and soothe away some of the pain she had caused. He stood suddenly, swaying unsteadily, grasping at the edge of his desk for support. 'Get out of my home,' he growled, as he pushed past her, going down the hallway to his bedroom. She followed him, now desperate to make him understand what had happened.

'Simon, please ... listen to me ...'

He whirled on her, coming so close that she could feel the squeezing strength of his punishing hands on her skin, but he didn't touch her, his steely control stopping him inches from her body. 'What more do you want from me, Erin? There's nothing for you here, nothing, so I want you away from me now.' This time he did grab her and his fingers bit into the soft flesh of her thin arm as he pushed her roughly from the room. 'Now get out!'

Erin could control her emotions no longer and all the pain and hurt of the last days welled up inside and exploded in a wash of tears and racking sobs. 'Please, Simon, don't send me away before you listen to me. Please!' His back was to her and he seemed unmoved by her sobbing plea. But she could not leave until she had said what she had come to tell him; perhaps it was possible to repair a small part of the horrible damage she had wrought. She drew on all the strength she could gather. 'I'm not going until you hear what I've come to tell you. I'm going to say it, no matter ... no matter what you do ... I ...'

He pushed past her, flung open the front door and began throwing his gear out on to the porch. Then sudden realisation of what he was doing struck her and she moved towards him, her voice shrill with fear. 'No, Simon. *No!* You can't go like this, you can't! You'd never make it in weather like this!'

She grasped his arm and tried feebly to stop his preparations, but he flung her easily from him. 'I told you, Erin, get away from me! Go home and leave me alone.' He slung a duffle bag over his shoulder and walked down the steps, heading for the dock and *Early Summer*. Still Erin pursued him, desperate to make him listen to her, to hear her explanation. 'Simon, you can't! It would be suicide and you know it.'

'It's my life, Erin, and it has nothing to do with you or anyone else. I'll do with it what I want.' He began piling his gear in the boat.

The surface of the wharf was slippery, covered with frozen spray. Erin heard her voice, made thin by the shrill wind that lashed her face with stinging salt spray, pleading with Simon. 'Oh God, Simon, please listen to me. It wasn't like I said before.' But he would not listen and pushed her roughly away from him as he leaned down to pick up the last of his gear. Neither of them reckoned on the fact that the wharf was so slippery; as he pushed her, Erin lost her balance, struggled to find a footing on the edge of the ice-covered boards, but slid off the side into the icy waters of the harbour.

The sudden impact of the sea made her gasp and water filled her nostrils and her mouth as she felt herself sinking below the surface of the grey waters. She could not fight or struggle, for the devastating coldness had stilled any resistance, and she closed her eyes against the terrifying darkness. A hand from somewhere grabbed for her, missed, and once again she drifted downward, the coldness now not a noticeable thing, the darkness no longer terrifying but pleasant and almost inviting; somehow in her mind she equated the darkness which engulfed her as a kind of sanctuary, a place of promised peace.

But something, some force was struggling to bring her

back from it, to take this newly found peace from her and she struck out blindly, helpless against it. 'Leave me ... leave me alone ... let me go ... I ... don't ... want ...' Words slurred with a fatigue that was sudden and all-engulfing; she could no longer struggle and gave herself up to the force that fought to reclaim her.

Somewhere in the distance, a long distance away, a voice demanded her response, demanded that she give up her place in the velvet darkness. 'Breathe ... dear God ... breathe!' Over and over again, the words in rhythm with the pressure against her back, like an ancient chant to fight and destroy the evils of darkness, demanding her return, pulling her back to the agony of the cold and of pained lungs. Suddenly her thin body was racked with convulsive spasms. She was choking, her lungs gasping for breath, her body overruling her mind and fighting to live.

A voice filled with a kind of rough tenderness pulled her from the floor. She was standing, swaying weakly in the middle of Simon's living room, and he was standing there before her, pulling the sea-drenched clothes from her. Her jacket lay in a sodden heap on the floor by the fireplace. 'Here, take off those wet clothes, I'll get some towels and a bathrobe.' He disappeared into his bedroom, returning with the robe he had promised. Erin had not moved, nor had she removed her sodden clothes. She stood there fighting against the rising nausea in her stomach, her fingers numb and trembling as they tried to undo the buttons of her blouse, which clung to her thin frame like a wet outer skin. 'I told you to get those clothes off immediately. Do you want to catch pneumonia?' Simon's voice was clinical and cold.

'I don't care. I don't care about anything any more,' she muttered.

'That makes two of us, then, wee Erin,' he responded almost sadly, as he stripped the blouse from her quivering shoulders. He roughly towelled dry her naked body, wrapping her tightly in his robe, and bound her wet hair in a towel. 'Sit over here and I'll light a fire to take the chill off.'

Gradually warmth seeped back into her shivering body and a lazy drowsiness claimed her as she sat curled up in the chair. They sat for a long time by the fire, not speaking, not looking at each other. Finally in a small tentative voice, Erin tried once more to make him hear what she had come to say. 'Will you listen to me now? Hear me out, that's all I ask of you. I'll leave then. I won't stay when you don't want me. Just listen, that's all I ask.'

Simon turned to her, his eyes threatening a dangerous violence that she had never before seen in them. 'Perhaps I shall throw you out now. I've heard all I want to from you, Erin. I'll listen to no more.' He stepped towards her, his large frame looming dangerously over hers. Then suddenly he stopped. She shuddered at the unmasked hatred in his eyes. 'On second thoughts, maybe now I should take what I deluded myself into believing was mine.' Without another word he reached out and seized her, pulling her roughly to him, his mouth seeking hers with a brutal force.

Her eyes wide with fear, Erin struggled futilely, managing to pull herself away long enough to gasp, 'No, Simon, please ... don't do this, listen to me, you can't ... not this way ...'

'Can't I, Erin? We'll see what I can do.' He lifted her easily into his arms and moved back into his bedroom, kicking the door shut behind him and throwing her roughly on to the bed. 'Take off your robe. I'm going to give you something with which to compare your precious Peter Hall!'

Erin scrambled quickly off the bed but was nevertheless trapped; she could never make it past him to the door, nor could she reach the balcony before he intercepted her. But she had to try something, to make some move, so she ran to the balcony, only to find the glass doors locked and immediately she felt Simon's iron grip on her arm. 'There was a time when you pretended my touch was not so repulsive to you. Can't you manage one final act before the curtain falls and the play closes for the season, Erin?'

'I wasn't pretending, Simon, I wasn't. I loved you ... and I love you now. If only you'd listen to me! What I said to you was because Fran——'

But before she could continue his mouth claimed hers and he drew her close, his body moulding itself to hers, close and demanding and challenging her to respond. He lifted her once more and carried her to the bed, this time lowering his own body down next to hers. But the anger and bitterness seemed to have melted away and a gentleness and tenderness surfaced instead. He drew the robe from her shoulders, his hands seeking and finding the soft flesh of her breasts.

Time hung motionless between them as his body sought to claim hers, as he kindled the fire of desire within her. He rained kisses on her mouth, on the warm softness of the valley between her breasts. 'Oh, Erin, Erin ...' he moaned as his body shuddered violently. He tore himself away from her. 'God knows how much I want you. I can barely stand the thought of another man touching you in the way I never can.' He rolled away from her, his voice muffled by the pillow into which he turned his face. 'I want to hate you, but I love you, Erin, and I can't stop loving you. Go before I do something that I'll regret for the rest of my life. Go before I take what belongs to Peter.'

Erin could neither speak nor move. Finally she was able to say, in a voice that was barely audible, 'There's nothing I have that belongs to Peter, Simon. I sent him away yesterday morning. We aren't going to Montreal to be married. I told you before that I couldn't marry a man I don't love; even when I said that to you he'd already left. I have no intention of marrying him, not for a long time, not since we ended our engagement last year—and definitely not yesterday.'

Simon had turned to look at her, but she could not meet his questioning gaze. 'I want to stay with you, Simon, if you'll let me stay.' The words came with a flood of fresh tears as her last reserve collapsed. 'I said those things to you yesterday because I had to make you believe I didn't love you, to make you leave me. Francine ... the night we became engaged ... she threatened to destroy you if I didn't break the engagement immediately ... and she and Bendix ... they said they'd bring you to your knees and that if I loved you I couldn't do anything else but let you go. And I did love you and I do ... love you. So I did what she said, I broke our engagement. And now Francine's going to marry you, not me ... and she'll help you with your career and some day you'll be president of the college and ...' she gulped, 'I just don't want you to hate me, Simon ... I couldn't stand it if you hated me ...'

So swift was his movement that Erin had no realisation of what had happened, but the next moment she was firmly held in Simon's arms, his voice soothing and tender and touched with a new hope. 'Hush, my love, quiet your fears. I won't be marrying Francine—not when in a few days I shall have you as my wife.' Erin struggled to look at him, but he held her firmly, his face pressed against her hair. 'Now listen to me and know the truth of how I feel about you. I can't live without you, wee Erin. It's not my teaching at this college and it's not my writing that mean the most to me—it's you. It's the loss of you that would destroy me, Erin, not the Bendixes and the Francines of this world. Them I can fight and will fight, and I'll survive them too, as long as I have you with me. Tell me, Erin,' he whispered, 'tell me that you'll never leave me again.'

'I've never really left you, Simon, my heart and soul were always yours.'

They lay together on the bed listening to the crash of the waves on the shore until the shadows of the late afternoon darkened into night. The darkness was but another blanket to cover and comfort them in their rediscovery of the love they shared. Erin snuggled and burrowed deeper against Simon as she said quietly, 'Please don't make me go home tonight, Simon. Let me stay here with you. Please!'

'I'll never let you leave me, Erin, not tonight and not ever. You are home,' he said huskily. 'Besides, I feel certain that this year there's going to be an early summer, and I've waited for one of those all my life, as long as I've waited for you. I love you, Erin Grayson, and the early summer you've brought to me.'

And there's still *more* love in

Harlequin Presents...

Yes!

Six more spellbinding romantic stories every month by your favorite authors. Elegant and sophisticated tales of love and love's conflicts.

Let your imagination be swept away to exotic places in search of adventure, intrigue and romance. Get to know the warm, true-to-life characters. Share the special kind of miracle that love can be.

Don't miss out. Buy now and discover the world of HARLEQUIN PRESENTS...